A Drama of the Caribbean
Copyright ©2006
Singing River Publications, Inc.

No portion of this book may be repro-
duced, stored in or introduced into a
retrieval system, or transmitted, in any
form or by any means – including photo-
copying – without prior written permission
of Singing River Publications, Inc., except
in the case of brief quotations embodied
in critical articles and reviews. For information, address inquiries to Singing River
Publications.

ISBN: 0-9774831-0-X

Published by
Singing River Publications, Inc.
PO Box 72
Ely, MN 55731-0072
www.singingriverpublications.com

Author: William Brennan
Illustrations: Celine Farrell

Editors: Isla Hejny, Jeff Stanko
Design & Layout: Michael Wood
Computer Entry: Frances Silverberg

Printed and bound in Canada.

The story of Antoine Lavalette and the Jesuits in France is historical fiction based on the account of Lavalette's adventures found in a book by the prominent French historian, P. Camille Rochmonteix. The full title of the book is: *Le Père Antoine Lavalette al la Marinique, d'apres Beaucoup de Documents Inedits par Le P. Camille de Rochmontiex de la Compagnie de Jesus* (Paris: Libraire Picard et Fils, 1907).

This book was brought to my attention by Bishop William Rice, S.J.

— William Brennan, S.J.

100-YEAR CHRONOLOGY

1715: Pope Clement XI issues a Decree *"Ex Illa Die"* ruling against the Jesuits and forbidding various Confucian, Buddhist and Taoist rites and customs for Christian converts in China.

1742: Pope Benedict XIV's Bull *"Ex quo singulari"* is signed condemning the Chinese Rites. Catholic missionaries are expelled from China by the Emporer Kangxi.

1755: English privateers capture valuable goods in transit from Jesuit enterprises in Martinique, forcing the Jesuits in Martinique to bankruptcy and considerable debt. Civil lawsuits ensue to attempt to recover the losses from the Society.

1759: Portugal expels the Jesuits. 133 members of the Society, put ashore at Civita Vecchia, are kindly received by Clement XIII and by the religious communities, especially the Dominicans.

1762-1764: The Jesuits are made illegal in France and all its dominions; and their institutions and schools are shut down.

1763: In a pastoral letter read in all his churches, the Archbishop of Paris expresses his bitter regret at the suppression of the Society in France. He describes it as a veritable calamity for his country.

1767-1768: The Jesuits are expelled from Naples, Parma, Spain and the Spanish dominions.

1769: Cardinal Lorenzo Ganganelli is elected as Pope Clement XIV.

1772: At Rome, Cardinal Marefoschi holds a visitation of the Irish College and accuses the Jesuits of mismanagement. They are removed by him from the direction of that establishment.

1773: Pope Clement XIV publishes the Brief *"Gravissimis ex causis"* which established a special congregation of five cardinals to superintend the Suppression of the Society of Jesus, the appropriation of its houses and goods.

1774: Christopher de Beaumont, Archibishop of Paris, writes to Pope Clement XIV, regretting the Brief of Suppression. Frederick II of Prussia and Empress Catherine II of Russia refuse to promulgate the order to suppress the Jesuits.

1814: Pope Pius VII restores the Society to full legal validity.

A DRAMA OF THE CARIBBEAN

CHAPTER I

A twenty-four-foot sailboat glided around the northwest tip of Martinique heading for the port of St. Pierre. It had traveled seven hours from Dominique in the hot sun and dead wind on the open strip of the Caribbean that lies between the two islands. Gracefully moving over the blue water, the boat slowly approached the shallower water along the coast where the marine life tinted the water green. Standing in the open space left by the billowing jib and clad in black cassock and broad-brimmed hat, Père Antoine Lavalette, tall and prematurely gray, steadied himself with a hand on the mast. He looked down the coast where he could see a three-masted schooner at anchor in the distance.

Guiding the boat was a black man, a Carib, Bratel Ivar. He slouched comfortably with his shoulder against the tiller and one big bare foot on the boom rope. He piloted by leaning to left or right, putting pressure on his foot or releasing according to the feel of the wind. Bratel was born to the sea; that was why Antoine chose him. He was a descendant of the bold seafarers who left the northeast shore of South America in huge dugouts to explore and conquer. They married among the indigenous tribes and also with the African slaves who came later. It was obvious in his face; the full lips, flat nose and dark skin; that these were features he and his kinsmen inherited from the Africans who predominated in the islands. They remained a group apart, maintaining their own language which became known as Carib. Many of them became teachers in the village schools throughout the islands.

Bratel was an important partner for Père Antoine, priest of the Company of Jesus and Superior of the Jesuit Mission of Martinique since 1748. Twice a month Bratel was at the helm of the small sailboat that plied the route to Dominique. Once there, he was head sacristan for the Masses that were said.

He hired the mules, packed the saddle bags, and contacted the homes where Père Antoine would say Mass. He went ahead to see that there were meals prepared, a clean straw mat for the priest to sleep on, and provisions for a convenient corner with a potty.

There were thirty villages on Dominique. Antoine tried to say Mass in at least three villages per month. His goal was to cover all of them at least once each year; it was no easy task. He had responsibility for twenty-seven main villages back in Martinique. When first appointed Superior of the Mission, he was a one-man missionary. Unlike his few Jesuit companions, he was blessed with a strong constitution. Moreover, he loved the climate and the open sea. The salt air was a stimulus to his soul, something he could not find in France. Unlike many of the French colonists, who had left under Louis XIV, Antoine loved his new home.

He had found the ideal partner in Bratel, but, particularly on this last trip, he especially wondered whether Bratel was going to keep up the pace. It had been easier for Bratel to watch over the distilling of rum in the factory back in Martinique. On this trip to Dominique they had visited four villages, spending four days in the last one alone. Bratel had to make all the arrangements, including helping dig the grave for the funeral of Antoine's old friend, René Comte, long time colonist who, like the priest, had found a new home in the islands. Even though funerals were not to Bratel's taste, Antoine found them an occasion for a couple of days of rest. The sea breeze with its salty tang was always refreshing and lying on the sand looking out on the green and blue water was a delightful respite.

Bringing himself back to reality, he realized he must do something to keep Bratel happy. The man loved to sail their little boat. He was not enamored of mule trips to the villages. He had to be the taskmaster while Antoine did the teaching; when they arrived it was his task to round up the children for catechism. There were times when Antoine was called to leave to check on the cane fields, or the lime orchard, or the plantain, or the cocoa beans drying in the patio. Then Bratel had to handle the catechism classes alone. Another one of his tasks was to go around from house to house to find out who was willing to let the priest use the cleanest straw mat in the home for the next visit. Also, there was the question of which families would bring in the rice and beans, the coconut milk, and with luck, one egg when the pair came again. This was a side of his loving flock that Antoine never saw. Bratel saw the impatience and unwillingness of these people when he arranged the details of the visits. Antoine began to see that they put on a different face as Bratel complained more and more. He had said, angrily, that he would prefer going to the market back in Martinique where he had to haggle and dicker with the sellers. It became clear that Antoine would have to give Bratel some kind of break.

It would be hard to replace him. During the evening services, he led the songs and kept the children from running all over the place while Antoine heard confessions. He lit the candles and rustled up a table and a table cloth. However, morning was Bratel's moment of glory. Antoine never heard a complaint about that. Bratel sweated over the Latin prayers for Mass, learning to pronounce and articulate to perfection. And the people sitting on the grass strewn dirt floor listened in awe as he pronounced the strange sounding language.

Antoine needed him for baptisms. There were always baptisms, at least one in every village. Once in a while there was a marriage. Bratel kept the record books. One of his major duties was keeping the books from getting wet, and keeping the ink from spilling on the vellum.[1] This was no small task, especially in the rainy season when the squalls hit with little warning.

However, as he thought about it, Antoine realized, yes, Bratel had a lot to do but he also had a lot of variety to his day — much more than he did in the rum factory where he had been a good overseer. He had the joy of sailing between the islands and he came home well paid for his troubles. Bratel was paid in gold and silver. None of the workers in Dominique, Martinique or St. Eustache was paid in gold or silver coin. Even the ships from the English colonies had to come down to St. Pierre and the French islands to be paid in coin and not in paper.

As he looked back on his devoted pilot, Père Antoine decided that before the next trip he must have a good talk with him to be sure that the man knew how valuable he was in the care of souls. But he would have to think about that later because right now, they were coming slowly into St. Pierre. In a few moments, they would reach the pier where small sailing boats tied up. Both men now looked anxiously to see who was waiting on the wharf, but for different reasons. Bratel had his eye on his two little girls who were waiting for their daddy. They had been watching for some time. As usual, once small sailboats rounded Point Du Bourg, the wind was not strong enough to push them very fast. Sharp eyes spotted familiar sails and neighbors spread the word, so the little girls were ready.

Antoine espied his partner, Isaac Judah, short in stature, swarthy of face, who rarely came to greet him on his return. When he did show up, there was always a new and interesting reason for his appearance. Surprisingly, Isaac moved faster than the young boys around him to catch the rope that Bratel threw to him and quickly wound it around the post.

---

1 *Vellum: fine parchment made of calfskin, lambskin, or kid leather, used for binding or as a writing or printing material.*

"A new priest has arrived; he wants to see you immediately," Isaac cried, before Antoine had time to jump off the boat onto the wharf. "He says he's come from Rome. He acts so officious; I don't like him. I don't like the way he treats me. Besides he asked to see the books — and I refused!"

The two began walking together along the wharf; Antoine had a couple of rough woven sacks with his belongings over his shoulder. Bratel walked behind them with the saddle bags.

"Isaac, we have a problem which I haven't told you about," Antoine said, after a long pause.

"Yes, I know," said Isaac. "After I refused this priest the books, we had a long conversation. His name is Père de la Marche, by the way. It took me a while to understand why he's here. He acted like we were committing some kind of crime, buying and selling at a profit. I said to him, 'I don't know much about this Catholic Church, but is there some other way of doing business besides buying and selling at a profit?' He said that it's forbidden for priests to be involved in business. I asked him how Père Antoine and I would get out of debt that if we don't engage in some kind of business?"

"And then?" asked Antoine.

"He just shrugged his shoulders as if our debt were of no importance. Frankly, I don't understand the man. I tried to explain to him that we had been working together for almost fifteen years, you and I. We've been absolutely honest, never cheated a customer, paid our debts. If it hadn't been for those Englishmen, we would not only be free of debt, we would have a surplus of half a million French francs. And now we're struggling to pay off what we owe. I told him to just let us alone."

"And how did he react to that?"

Isaac raised his eyebrows, sighed and then frowned. "Père de la Marche said, 'You Jews are only concerned with money.'"

"He said that?" said Antoine, shocked; he reached over to put his arm around Isaac's shoulder. "Some Christians — even priests — don't act like Christians, Isaac." They had been walking very slowly along the wharf. They had reached the shore. Both looked southward toward the schooner that lay at anchor.

"I see that Jacob is here," said Antoine, changing the subject. "What did he bring us this time?"

"Seven thousand board feet of pine! That's the way he deals with us. It's not fair! We pay him in gold, cash. He can't get that from the English in

Jamaica. He feels free to dump anything he pleases on us."

"Well, Isaac, those Yanquis are hard bargainers. We can sell most of the load in Trinidad, and we've found some customers in Venezuela. Besides, you know how we need him, if ever we're going to get out of debt."

"In all my years here, I've never met a harder bargainer than that Jacob Byrne. He makes a good living off us."

"But don't forget he has to pass the vigilantes on watch around Jamaica. We can't forget what happened to us there, and besides, he risks his ship every time he goes back to Boston."

"I don't know about that. I've said before that if he were Spanish, or French, or from the islands, his route might be risky, but being Yanqui, he can talk his way by the English. And, as for Boston, he's well known, and the customs agents know how well he pays."

"But still, running the coast and finding his way through the islands down here has to be a hard life, Isaac."

"How many of those other Yanquis captains have a priest friend who knows the coral reefs like you, who has taught him the patterns of how to escape the privateers who rove these parts? What a bargain he has with our milled sugar. The English settlers have to send their sugar to England and then buy it back."

"Come, now, Isaac, I have heard this a few times before. Spare me. I'm tired from two weeks in Dominique. But, you're right, he is a hard bargainer. Go down to the ship and tell him I will see him tomorrow. I'm going up to the house now."

By this time, Bratel had caught up with them, one daughter on his shoulder, the other clutching his hand. His smiling wife was beside him. Antoine stooped down to hug the oldest, Marlene, and kissed the younger one, who was riding high, on the cheek.

"Eloise," Antoine said to her, "glad to see your Daddy back?" And then to Bratel, "I'll see you at the office tomorrow."

Then as he and Isaac prepared to part, a woman with a basket of mangoes on her head and a child in her arms called out.

"Père Antoine, welcome back! How was your trip? We had a squall this morning."

Antoine touched the baby on the forehead in blessing.

"Thank you, Margola. We had no rain. As a matter of fact, we were becalmed a few times. When we rounded Point Du Bourg, it got worse. But we made it. What is the price of your mangoes today?"

"Three for an ecu. But for you I will put in an extra." Deftly she swung the basket off her head without dropping the child. Antoine reached into his purse.

"And Tarvis — is he well? He had some fever when I left."

"Yes, mon Père, father is well enough by the grace of God and the Virgin. You know how it is with the fever; it comes and goes."

"I was able to buy some quinine from a visitor who came from Guadeloupe. I will have a good supply. Our malaria patients will have some relief for a while."

"Thank you, Père. It's always good to have you back,"

With that, Margola lifted her basket back onto her head and moved off.

"I'm amazed at the way you can handle their language," said Isaac, who had not been a party to the conversation.

"There's a smattering of French in the Carib dialect. Not that difficult. After all, we had to study Latin and Greek and a little Hebrew in the seminary. And don't forget I was in Point Carbet the first few years I was on the island. Two Masses each Sunday, one in French for the colonists, the other in Carib for the Blacks."

"Just let me bring up one more thing about Jacob," Isaac began, as they prepared to part. "The way he talks about the Catholics and the Pope of Rome behind your back — he calls you people 'Papists.' I think that's the word. You never heard me talk like that."

"He blows hard, like the wind, but, still he is our friend, Isaac," responded Antoine. "We need him; we avoid talking about religion."

By this time they had reached the little slope that led up to the Jesuit residence.

"Oh! Oh!" said Isaac. "Look who I see up there on the front porch!"

Antoine could easily recognize one blackrobe, Père Beauharnais. The other was obviously the stranger that Isaac was talking about.

"Should I come with you?" he asked.

"I don't see why not," responded Antoine.

Slowly they approached the frame building, upraised on posts and stuck into trench type holes that were kept filled with water to block the termites.

The front porch offered a fine view of the bay of St. Pierre. It was a favorite evening spot for the priests. Above the house and to the left, the slope ran up to the sleeping crater of the fire god who, according to the elders, had in previous times spouted flames and burned the faces of the people who live in the islands. The French settlers had given it a new name: Mt. Pelée.

As the pair approached the front steps, the two cassocked figures stopped chatting. Heavy set and very grey, Père Beauharnais stood up to greet his long time friend, Antoine. Long the pastor of the Church of St. Pierre, Beauharnais was gradually losing his vigor, but not anxious to return to France where he would be retired. As always, he was happy to greet Antoine on his return from mission trips. The man next to him was the newcomer whom Isaac mentioned. He was a smallish man with a mustache, gaunt face, and piercing eyes. . .

"This is Père de la Marche," Beauharnais began as gently as he could. "He has come to us from Rome."

Antoine climbed the porch steps, motioning Isaac to accompany him. He bowed to the guest and said, "This is my friend and aide, Isaac Judah."

De la Marche nodded stiffly.

"I have been anxious for some time to meet you, Père Lavalette. I have already had to deal with Judah here, and found him uncooperative. Hopefully, you will assist me on the task I have been assigned to do. And I trust Monsieur Judah you will be more open with me in the future."

"If Père Antoine is in agreement," replied Isaac.

"Père Antoine will be in total agreement. I come with full authorization from Rome to investigate what you two have been up to these past years."

Isaac looked to Antoine for a sign. Antoine merely shrugged his shoulders.

"I guess I can take my leave now," said Isaac. He turned to go down the stairs.

"I want to see you tomorrow in the office with the books," de la Marche called after him.

Isaac looked to Antoine for approval; he nodded. With that Isaac went on his way down the slope. Then Père Beauharnais got up to leave the two alone.

"You are aware," began de la Marche, "that I come with full authorization from our Father General[2] in Rome and with the formal approval of His Holiness[3]."

"It sounds rather formidable," said Antoine. "Going to such lengths to deal with a simple missionary thousands of miles away from Rome."

"I don't consider you a simple missionary, and there are many people in France who don't think you are very simple either. By the way, I suggest that you get rid of that Jew who works for you. He was very rude and uncooperative."

"You have no idea how important he is to me," countered Antoine. "He is no mere employee. He doesn't work for me; he is my partner. He is the brains of the business."

"You chose the right word, 'business.' That is precisely what the Jesuit order and the Pope are concerned about, you being in business like a common merchant. It's no wonder that you work with a Jew. That must be how you became contaminated with and entangled in this commercial enterprise."

"Look, Père de la Marche," Antoine was a bit riled, "I have just returned from seven hours on the open water in a sail boat. I am weary after two weeks in Dominique. I promise to hide nothing from you, but couldn't we wait until tomorrow? In the morning I will take you down to the office where we can examine the books with Isaac, and then we can go down to the Wellstone and talk with Captain Byrne."

Reluctantly, de la Marche was forced to admit and recognize that his companion was indeed weary, and nothing could really be accomplished without looking at the books and investigating the whole operation. After all, that was what he had come for. He had not come to argue. The two parted. Antoine headed for the hammock which hung in his small room. De le Marche had a bed in the guest room.

The following morning was a delightful day in April; it was still the dry season. The pungent salty sea breeze blew gently. Antoine was in a deep sleep, the kind only a veteran accustomed to a hammock could enjoy. It was approaching eight o'clock. His visitor had long since finished his morning Mass, wolfed down his breakfast of tea and papaya, and was standing impatiently waiting for Antoine to wake. Finally, he could stand it no longer and began shaking the hammock. It was a while before Antoine came to. Sitting up on the edge of the hammock, Antoine was holding his head in his hands.

---

2 *Father General is the title of the General Superior of the Society of Jesus.*

3 *Pope Clement XIII*

"Père, this is my day of rest. I sleep a bit later, then go down to the parish to say a late Mass. I'm not ready to talk to you about our books. Isaac will show you everything you want to know. You won't need me."

"I do not want to be left alone with that Jew," said de la Marche impatiently.

"I am not ready for a fight, Père, certainly not at this time in the morning. Besides, there are a couple of things that are very irritating to me. First, your attitude towards Isaac. You forget that the reason he is here in the islands is that his grandparents were driven out of Brazil in the last century. They had to accept baptism or abandon their livelihood and leave. Many could not afford that; they had to accept baptism against their wills, and when they did the Catholics called them 'maranas,' which means 'swine.' Isaac's family chose to leave rather than submit. Second, you know perfectly well that our own Jesuit theologians have condemned forced baptisms in New Spain and New France. He is my friend; he stood by me when we lost our cargo. He could set up his own business any time. Besides, we need his knowledge and experience if we are ever to get out of debt."

"If you had followed Church Law, you never would have incurred any debt," said de la Marche. Then after a pause, he added, "Well, all right, I will leave you alone for now, but tell me how do I find the Jew?"

"This is not Paris, you know. Just go down to the wharf where the big ship is and ask for Rachon, Cartier et Compagnie. Everyone knows where our little office is."

With that, de la Marche left Antoine in peace and started down the slope for the waterfront. As Antoine had said, it really wasn't that difficult to find Isaac. There were mules being loaded with cargo from the Wellstone; many of the slaves were carrying heavy loads on their heads and shoulders. De le Marche had to weave his way through the crowd. He found what looked like an abandoned shop opposite the ship landing where the sign said Rachon, Cartier et Compagnie.

Isaac welcomed him in and invited him to sit down near the desk on top of which were a half dozen large-size ledgers. One of them was open. Isaac had been writing down some figures with his large pen. He shook the nib into the ink well, and laid it down for a moment.

"Where would you like to begin, Père?" he asked his visitor.

"I guess we could begin with what you have just been putting into the ledger. Tell me what you have there."

"I have just entered seven thousand board feet of lumber, fifty bales of cloth, forty hogsheads of fish and seventy hogsheads of flour for which we owe Captain Byrne 90,000 *livres*."

"And what do you propose to do with this shipment?"

"We can't sell the lumber here, so we will ship it to Barbados. A merchant there by the name of Trelawny handles our trade."

"And the flour?" asked the priest.

"The flour we can sell here, a good part of it. The rest we send to Guadeloupe and to St. Lucia," explained Isaac.

"The fish and the cloth?" queried de la Marche.

"There is a lot of demand here among the Catholics for the fish. The fishing around here isn't too good. I'm sure you know we have a large Catholic population in the islands. We don't have to look for customers; they come to us in small boats, mostly little merchants. The cloth we send on to the English islands. It brings a good price."

"And the profit from all these sales?" asked the priest.

"We use part of it to pay off the Captain, another part to pay for expenses in shipping; another part has to pay for food and clothing for the slaves. What's left we send to the Rothschilds' house in Amsterdam to be sent on to Leoncy Freres in Marseilles."

"Quite a business you have going for you," commented the priest dryly. "But what about the sugar? What I learned in France was that Père Antoine had plantations for sugarcane."

"Of course," said Isaac. "But we handle the sugar differently. When Captain Byrne returns from Africa with wine and slaves, he loads up with our sugar and molasses. The sugar goes north to New York and the molasses goes to Boston for the rum trade."

"So, you are involved in the slave trade! Hasn't Père Antoine ever said anything to you about the cruelty and immorality of buying and selling people?"

"We did talk about it once, before we lost our ships. Antoine felt bad that we used slave labor. He has always given them money when they needed it, treated them well, and repaired their houses. Now that we have this heavy debt to pay, he says we really can't worry about where the workers come from. We can't do anything about it anyway."

"But you do buy slaves for the plantations." His visitor stated with emphasis.

"Yes," admitted Isaac. He shrugged his shoulders helplessly.

"There's something I don't understand," said de la Marche, changing the subject. "You talk about shipping north to Boston, but earlier you also mentioned Amsterdam. I'm confused. Amsterdam is in Holland!"

"New Amsterdam," corrected Isaac. "In the 1660s, the name was changed to New York. That's a Dutch settlement up there, somewhere near Boston. We ship our white sugar that way and the Dutch crews take it to Holland."

"That seems like a long, tedious and round about way of shipping to Europe. You must spend several months in the process."

"You're right. But, it's only during the last two years that we have used this route. Perhaps you don't know that we lost two shiploads of sugar worth 600,000 *livres* to the English privateers around Jamaica, so we can't risk that route to France anymore. This way is safer, and given time we will pay off our debt."

All the while, Père de la Marche was taking notes without comment. He just continued to ask questions as Isaac took him on a tour of the warehouse where the products of Rachon, Cartier et Compagnie were stored. Isaac left him alone for several hours to go through the books by himself so that by the time the shadows began to lengthen, the priest had a fair comprehension of the entire enterprise.

That evening by candle light, de la Marche confronted Antoine with all that he had learned.

"There really is no need for me to emphasize the fact that you are engaged in what Church law calls commerce. You and that partner of yours are clearly buying and selling at a profit like any common merchant."

"You don't really see our problem, Père," began Antoine.

"I certainly do," interrupted de la Marche. "You are violating Church law plain and simple."

"But it is not that simple," countered Antoine. "We owe Leoncy Freres more than a million francs. We have to pay that debt."

"You shouldn't have run up the debt in the first place."

"We didn't run up that debt. We sent 450,000 *livres* of sugar and 150,000 *livres* worth of indigo in payment of half of what we borrowed. We would have cancelled everything in two years. We split the shipment in two parts.

That cost us extra money, but we did it because we thought it would be safer. If the pirates caught one, there was always the chance that the other would get through. But, English privateers captured our shipment. We were robbed by legalized thieves. They have writs of authorization from the Governors of the English islands, writs to steal and rob and kill, if they think it necessary."

"But, what I am saying, and what the Church is saying, is that you embarked on a scandalous course forbidden to clerics by getting into business in the first place."

In exasperation, Antoine stood up and began to walk back and forth.

"Does the name M. de Cresols mean anything to you?" he asked de la Marche.

"No, why should it, and what difference does it make?"

"Fourteen years ago M. de Cresols came to me to hand over his sugar plantation to the Church. He was weary of life in the islands, and wanted to go back to France. He didn't want to sell his land here because he would have been paid in colonial francs which lose fifteen percent of their value back in France. He came looking for advice. And what you don't know, and what you have not asked about," stressed Antoine, "was that in 1745, our mission was 90,000 *livres* in debt. I was both Vicar Apostolic and Jesuit Superior. My responsibility was to raise money each year to maintain the works of the Church in two islands. About a third of what we needed came by delayed ship from France, and I say delayed because sometimes support never did arrive. Minimum expenses, clothing, feeding the men and the slaves came to at least 100,000. To keep the roofs from leaking in these tropical rains, which you have never experienced in France, you have to be constantly vigilant. Have you ever heard of heavy pouring rain that lasts for twenty-four hours straight, sometimes for two full days? Remember, we had makeshift chapels and little churches in two islands. Our men were constantly sick, unable to visit the villages and minister to the people. It took me five years to discover that thin cotton cloth could protect them from mosquitoes. Try sleeping on a beastly hot night under a cloth tent which you don't dare remove for fear of malaria. Père Gatin's health was ruined here.

"Père Fourier died because we had no medicine, nothing to remedy his illness. Père le Grange, I sent back to France. The diet and the rigors of this kind of life were too much for him. He needed a cook and a decent house to live in which I, as representative of the Church and the Company of Jesus, could not provide. The African slaves and the Caribs, the people who could help us get out of this debt, were living in squalor."

"No one is denying that you found the mission impoverished and in need of financial help. But nothing could justify your buying and selling at a profit, like a common merchant. This has been an affront to God's church, to the priesthood and to the Jesuits."

"How does one bring a mission out of poverty into some kind of self-support? You borrow money and you make improvements, then you try to pay back what you owe. And that is precisely what I have been trying to do. My credit was perfect. And I would have paid off all of my creditors if the English pirates had not come on the scene."

"I am not here to contemplate what could have happened or should have happened. I have my orders to find out what actually did happen. Did you or didn't you engage in commerce?" asked de la Marche.

"And that is the only question! The benefices that support the churches in France, from where do they get their money?" Antoine was deliberately nasty. "Doesn't the merchant world have something to do with building our churches and keeping them open? And who feeds the bishops? Or does the manna come down from heaven?"

"Now you *are* being disrespectful. The Church depends on good will offerings; it does not enter the business world as you have done."

"Yes," said Antoine dryly. "The Church does not enter into the business world. It merely goes to the poor and the lowly, like Jesus, to build its cathedrals and establish benefices for its humble bishops."

"I do not appreciate your sarcasm. You forget you are the defendant here. It behooves you to be more respectful of Holy Mother the Church."

"I am not trying to defend myself. I am trying to make clear that regulations from Rome have nothing to say about a complicated situation thousands of miles away."

"You are missing the point. Nothing you have said in any way justifies getting involved in buying and selling, like a common storekeeper. The priest should live a life that is above such earthly concerns."

"Basically, what you are saying is that I wanted to be a merchant, and I regretted being a priest and I got into business with no regard for the gospel call or my people."

"I am not saying that. I am just saying that *however* you became involved in buying is of no concern to me. I *am* saying that it was wrong — beneath the dignity of a priest and forbidden by the Church. It must stop, and I am here to stop it."

"I tried to make clear that the initiative was not mine. M. de Cresols came to me to negotiate the sale of his plantation."

"There is no sense continuing this discussion."

"True. Because you want to stop listening. In 1747 a Royal decree forbade the colonists to sell coarse sugar. This was a serious problem. Some of my Mass-goers in all three islands shared their anger with me. That's when I went to Isaac Judah who was in the sugar business. I asked his advice and he found a solution. By extending the refining process, adding the juice from the papaya, one could produce a stage that was a step up from coarse. You could call it semi-refined, which we did. The Marine Office wanted to do to us just what England was doing to Jamaica and her other colonies, that is, force them to ship coarse sugar to the mother country for refining, and then buy it back. It was foolishness, especially since we had a thriving market to the north of us."

"I do not want to hear a lecture on the history of your business operations."

"But, what you are refusing to listen to is why the planters like de Cresols started to come to me. He was not alone. Jean Bouf and his brother-in-law and others started coming for advice. It was then that Isaac Judah came to help me and we formed a company."

"Exactly. A company," put in de la Marche, "which is absolutely unlawful for priests."

"A company exists for profit, personal profit. I did not use a *centime* for personal gain. I established the mission on a sound financial basis. I repaired the huts we used for chapels and built new little churches. I rebuilt the residences for the priests and for the slaves. I improved the food supply, as never before and medicines, too. Not only that, I purchased tin plates for the corners of the thatched roofs so that the heavy rains could drain into barrels. These served like cisterns, so that the women and the slaves didn't have to go down to the rivers or springs and bring back heavy wooden buckets on their heads."

"I am sure that there are many who are impressed with your accomplishments. I am not one of them," injected de la Marche. "Nor are the Jesuit superiors, nor the Vatican."

"It was not my intention to glorify my deeds. I am trying to make you see that I found myself in a difficult set of circumstances and I tried to find a solution."

"Granted, but it is your solution that I am authorized to investigate and correct if possible and necessary."

"I realize that, but I also feel that you are not giving me the sympathetic understanding that I deserve."

"In turn you must understand my position. Take, for example, the name you mentioned, Jean Bouf. My information is that the Bouf family lived in Dominique, not Martinique. You were summoned before the Minister of Marine Affairs to defend yourself for investing in a foreign island. What Church authorities are duly disturbed about is that you are not only carrying on commerce forbidden to clerics, but causing international problems for the government of France."

"There is much more to that story. M. de Rouille summoned me to France on the grounds of a complaint, of an accusation. He was given false information about my actions. Once he heard the basis of the complaint, he exonerated me completely. He issued a letter of exoneration which I have in my file."

"But our Catholic faithful do not understand a priest being involved in a legal dispute of any kind. It is a cause of scandal."

"There is what we used to call in the seminary 'Pharasaic scandal.' Criticizing Jesus for working a miracle on the Sabbath. This is the kind of scandal involved here. The truth is that M. St. Etienne, the complainant, was furious with Isaac and me over our refusal to handle the sale of his plantation. We told him we simply couldn't handle his estate at the time. We told him to wait. He was insulted. He knows the law. He's the one who went to the governor, M. de Bompar, who didn't know how to deal with the accusation of trading with a foreign country. That's why he referred it to the Minister of Marine Affairs in Paris, Comte de Rouille."

Père de la Marche did not respond; he tried to walk away.

"You can't just turn your back on me. You have to listen. I was called back to France on the basis of an erroneous charge. And you can find it in the correspondence with our superior, Père de Larousse. Governor Bompar believed that collecting rent from the houses I built was commerce forbidden to priests and religious. He also believed that when we sold manioc plantains and pineapple over and above what we needed for the slaves, that, too, was commerce. I lost almost a year over this before I could return to Martinique."

"I find it hard to believe that a governor would be that ignorant," de la Marche responded.

"All I can say is that you have to consult Larousse when you get back to Paris. And you can also talk to Père de Sacy who knows me well, better than anyone in Paris. He will verify that Bompar hadn't the slightest idea of what he was talking about. My interpretation of why I was delayed is that the Minister of Marine Affairs didn't want the governor to look like a fool, so he pretended to be thinking over the matter and consulting with Church authorities. If you will come down to the office, you will see the copy of the letter in which he completely exonerates me. He doesn't apologize as he should. The delay was extremely costly to the mission, and was the beginning of the indebtedness that Isaac and I are struggling with now."

CHAPTER II

A ntoine was depressed. It was futile to make de la Marche understand what he had been through. What did a priest from Rome know of the high seas! He left the house to walk alone. Above him was the barren cone of Mt. Pelée, the fire god; below was the sea and the open water. He looked out. It reminded him of *that fateful day*. He had been so happy and proud, relieved after three years of poor sugar harvests caused by a fever among the workers, a fever which reached epidemic proportions, and a hurricane which leveled most of the following year's crop and made the cutting next to impossible in the mud and water.

Now he began to walk along the sandy beach. He walked and walked. And as he did he began to reminisce further. How could he forget what had brought all this about! The scene was before him. The day had begun. The flashback was complete. He was again standing on deck, listening to the crew talk about what a great day it was for sailing. He felt secure in the French merchantman as it rolled in the lofty waves. He prided himself that he was not affected by the rolling of the ship, as even some of the sailors were. There had been a time when this was not so. He had gone through the agony of leaning over the rail. But no longer. This was no doubt a reward for the many trips he took to Guadeloupe for Mass and confessions and visiting villages. There was a stretch of blue between the islands — deep water, which meant big waves. He had acquired what Captain Byrne would later tell him in English was called "sea legs."

He recalled how he had looked back at the schooner that was behind them. It was obviously a faster ship, but it had to hit a slower pace to follow the merchantman which contained the major portion of their sugar, molasses and indigo.

They had set out in bad weather from St. Pierre, leaving a gloomy Mt. Pelée behind. Passing Guadeloupe and St. Eustache, they had soon moved beyond the islands and were heading for Jamaica and the Europe sea lane. It was pleasant and uneventful sailing because the sea was relatively calm. As he recalled, it was the second day out of Jamaica that the drama began. The crewman on watch called to the priest. Tucking his cassock under his belt, he had managed to make it up the rope ladder to the crow's nest. The crewmen who gathered below were impressed by the agility of the black-robed figure going up the ladder. Once in the crow's nest he learned how to use the telescope to scan the horizon. Jamaica was still barely visible from the height. There was also a small boat, on the northern horizon. Antoine climbed down to the cheers of the crew.

The next morning, however, the crewman on watch called to him again, only this time it was not for diversion. The little ship on the horizon was quite a bit bigger than he had thought. It was a great deal closer, and appeared to be following them. It was too soon to be sure, thought Antoine lightly. The watch had another idea he didn't want to share with the priest. By the afternoon the watch identified the ship as a three-master with a gun mount. The captain began to show concern.

"It's faster than we are," he blurted out to the priest. "We could keep out of range if we didn't have so much cargo."

"I don't understand why you are worried, captain," Antoine remembered saying.

"Mon Père," the captain had replied. "Your business doesn't teach you about privateers."

"Privateers?" he had asked innocently.

Yes, it only been a few hours later that he learned in reality the word meant legalized pirates. They had letters of authorization from island governors to inspect shipping that might be contraband. Contraband was cargo from an alien nation that could be sold in the English ports, provided a generous share went to the governor.

Antoine missed the irony, still focusing on the idea of contraband. He continued innocently to ask why they should be concerned, since they were not carrying anything but products of human toil, certainly nothing against the law.

It was only later that he understood the captain was trying to be patient with him.

"Père, gold, especially in Spanish ships," the captain said, "is considered illegal by certain English ships. Coffee, sugar, indigo particularly, anything that can be sold in   Jamaica is also highly illegal for them."

"But, that's stealing." Antoine had been so innocent.

"Yes, Père, to you, perhaps," the captain explained gently, "but not to privateers, who have letters which make it legal for them to raid ships provided they bring the loot back to Jamaica where profits are divided up between the governor and his cronies."

Antoine thought of his cargo — four hundred hogsheads of sugar and molasses, thirty bales of indigo. His chance to pay off his indebtedness! The look on the captain's face was not reassuring.

Antoine spoke, "What can we do? What must we do?" Reality had struck home.

The captain shrugged his shoulders.

That night, all on board did not sleep well. All were along the rail at dawn to see whether the ship was companion or pursuer. In the early light, it was only twenty lengths behind them. All its sails were rigged. It was coming as fast as it could.

Antoine was the first to recognize the flag.

In a shout of joyous relief, he cried out, "It's French. Thanks be to God!" But the look on the faces about him subdued enthusiasm.

"It has to be a friendly ship," he tried to insist to his onlookers.

For a person in such dire circumstances, the captain showed remarkable patience with the clerical mind. He wanted to spare him as long as possible. He could not bring himself to tell him that one of the commonest tricks of pirates was to carry flags of all their would-be victims. It was only when they were closing in on their prey, that they hoisted the black flag of doom. It was a clever device because it usually terrified the crew of the target ship.

So the captain said nothing; the silence on the ship needed was enough. It wasn't until the next morning, after the sun was well up that the French flag was replaced by the black. The pursuer passed the sloop. It was bent on bigger game. It was now only a few hundred yards away.

Antoine remembered how he had grabbed the captain's arm.

"You've got to do something! You've got to do something! You can't just let them steal all that we have worked so hard for."

"I can't risk the life of all on board," said the captain. "These people are ruthless."

"But we have a cannon at the back. We have a right to defend ourselves."

The timing was perfect. At the very moment Antoine spoke, a flash of flame came from the pirate ship and a cannon ball hurtled past the bow. All were terrified except Antoine, who for the rest of his days would never be able to explain his reaction.

Isaac had suddenly appeared at his side; he had spent a day and a half below checking a leak that threatened the sugar. He had been concentrating on moving hogsheads and was caulking. He missed the suspense of the day before. He had just learned of their peril. He grabbed Antoine's arm. Unlike Antoine, he had taken in the situation immediately, and had sensed the mood which later would haunt Antoine's memory.

"Père, be calm. There's nothing we can do to defend ourselves. These are professional criminals."

"But the cargo, our debts, all our work," had been his frantic reply. Unbelievably, he had said, "There's a cannon at the back. We can fire back. They won't dare hit us and sink us. They will lose their loot."

Isaac had tried his best. He pleaded with him not to do anything foolish. But for some inexplicable reason, he was beyond logic at the moment. Antoine rushed to the back of the ship. On the way there he found Noel Marcel, whom he had known as his altar boy in Guadeloupe, now a crewman.

"Help me, Noel. We have to defend our cargo. Show me how to load this cannon."

Noel tried to get through to him that a crewman did not do anything on his own. His explanation meant nothing to Antoine at the time. During an attack, the quartermaster had powers of life and death over the crew.

Till his dying day, he would not forget how he had recalled their time together at the altar and the catechism class, in which Noel had been a docile pupil. He had emphasized his role as the priest, sermonizing about the right of private property and the commandment forbidding thievery. God's law entitled them to defend themselves.

Poor Noel! He was terrified by the pirate ship, terrified by his priest, befuddled by the dilemma of whom to obey. Antoine would never be able to explain to himself or others how he had succeeded in persuading Noel to go against all he had learned as a seaman and showed his priest where the powder was, how to load the cannon, take the flint from under the canvas, light the fuse and fire.

Despite his agitated state, Antoine managed to load the cannon ball, stoke the barrel, aim, strike several sparks for the wick, and unbelievably, fire the cannon at the approaching ship. And what was more unbelievable, the cannon ball crashed into the side of the enemy at deck level, felling three men who were preparing hooks and rope for the assault.

That scene would haunt him forever.

Moments later the captain and the quartermaster came running with swords and pistols in their hands. They started for Noel, crying, "This is mutiny. You imbecile!"

"You'll die for this," screamed the captain. "You've gotten us all killed."

It was then that Antoine had stepped forward, taking the blame.

"You crazy priest! I was out of my mind to let you aboard. I have a wife and family. I will lose it all, my ship, everything," he had wailed.

It was then that there had been another roar, this time from the pirates. Three guns fired. One destroyed the rudder; the other two raked the center deck, destroying the tiller ropes and the steering tackle. The merchantman was now unmanageable.

All the crew stood helpless. Grappling hooks were soon hurled from the enemy sloop. A four by twelve frame thundered down on the deck, locking the marauders to their victim. A dozen screaming men with faces painted red and black came rushing over the rail. Swinging their cutlasses, they cut down the four first men they encountered and ran them through for good measure, leaving them bleeding, to die on the deck.

"So," the pirate leader shouted, approaching the captain with sword up high, "you chose to fire on us instead of surrendering. You know what that means, captain."

He started to swing his sword.

Antoine stepped in front of the captain. If it had not been such a mortally dangerous scene he might have been tempted to laugh at the look of astonishment on the face of Captain Bart Rhone, the pirate leader. Taken by surprise, his mouth fell open, and he actually dropped his sword. Apparently, nothing in his brutal career had ever prepared him for this. Antoine had not meant to be heroic. Slightly deranged as he was, he felt it his duty to declare his guilt in front of the pirate chief.

"It was I who fired the cannon. I did not ask the captain. I did it on my own."

Bart still had not moved. Completely stunned, he could not reply. He had backed off and turned to his cohort. It was only when he was facing his men that he was able to collect himself sufficiently to deal with the strange enemy before him in black cassock. It was a wordless appeal for what to do.

"He's a papist," offered the first in command, thus relieving the non-plussed Bart Rhone for a moment. "It might be bad luck to kill a vicar. And we've had plenty of that for the past six months."

"Why don't you tell him we'll spare his life if he joins us," said another member of the crew. "I think a parson aboard might just change our luck."

By this time, the attackers had lowered their swords. They were all equally befuddled. Bart finally regained his composure. "We have to do something," he had said.

Antoine sensed rather than understood what the man was saying. Perhaps this was his time to die. He bowed his head and prayed, fully aware that Bart took a menacing step toward him, sword up high, ready to swing.

"Who helped you? You couldn't have done it on your own." His words were lost on Antoine.

Before Antoine could even attempt a reply, the captain jumped forward.

"He helped him," shouting and pointing towards Noel.

"Tie him up," shouted Captain Bart Rhone. He had regained his voice.

Before the men could move, Antoine quickly ran over to stand in front of Noel. This time, Bart was ready for anything Antoine would do.

"Get out of the way, priest," he commanded in loud tones. Antoine nearly fell as he was pushed aside. Rhone then signaled to his men to grab Noel.

"But he is innocent; I am the one who is guilty," Antoine had pleaded.

"All hands, follow me! Get this vicar out of the way."

How could he forget the silent procession to the stern where the cannon still stood uncovered, still hot from the recent blast.

"You know what to do," the leader said. Roughly they tied Noel to the cannon with his head in front of the barrel. They took their time so their audience could easily figure out what they were about.

Antoine was the last to grasp what was about to happen.

"No, no, he is innocent! I'm the one who should die," he ran forward shouting.

But Bart was fully in command now.

"Take that lunatic parson below," had been his reaction.

Antoine had resisted as best he could. But two of the biggest seamen took their post in front of him, and began hauling him toward the hold.

"Don't you want him to see the show, Bart?" one of them had asked.

"All right," said Rhone slowly. "But keep him away from me till it's over."

Antoine struggled futilely, doing all he could to resist, pleading, and beginning to cry heavy tears for what he had brought upon Noel, a memory that would haunt him for the rest of his life. His near hysterical pleas had been drowned out by the roar of the cannon, as the head of Noel disappeared with the cannon ball out to sea.

The pirates untied the body and left it on the deck so that all could see the headless corpse lying in a pool of blood. They left it there for twenty-four hours until the stench was so great that no one could stand it. Finally, they forced the captain and the first mate at the point of the sword to throw the rotting body into the sea.

The pirates had taken over the ship and repaired it for sailing. Then they took everyone back to Jamaica.

CHAPTER III

"Good morning, Père." Antoine was suddenly jolted out of his reverie. He had walked several miles along the beach, aware only of his thoughts.

"Are you well, Père Antoine? You seem to be lost." Lorraine Cherage, an old parishioner, had come down to the shore after noticing the priest strolling aimlessly along the sand, staring out to sea from time to time.

"No, no, yes, I am fine, thank you, Lorraine. I went for a stroll along the beach."

"Quite a stroll! I'm here at my mother's house. You're ten miles away from town. Come up for a cup of tea before you start back."

"Thank you, no. I will just head home. I am fine, Lorraine."

"Are you sure, Père? We have all heard that there is a priest here who seems to be some kind of an investigator from Rome. We love you, Père. We don't want any foreigner to be harsh with you."

"Thank you, Lorraine. Thank you." He was touched. "Thank you for your kind offer. I must hurry back. Bye bye."

As he turned and began the trek back to the St. Pierre residence, he realized as he had never done before, that this was his home. So many of the people — colonists, slaves, Caribs — were like Lorraine. He loved it here. They loved him; he felt he could say that with all humility. He was different. Too many of his colleagues stayed in the islands only out of a sense of sacrifice for God and for the salvation of souls. He wasn't staying here just to advance the Kingdom. He did indeed love it here. The climate was marvelous, and so were his people. He was always at home in a small sail boat between here and Guadeloupe and St. Lucia and Dominique.

The pirate incident had changed everything. Why did God do this to me? This was his first thought and then he caught himself. How many times had he preached not to blame God in adversity!

He so wanted to put his Roman visitor out of his mind. Where would it end? There was no point in trying to tell de la Marche about the piracy. The laws of the Church and the jurisdiction of Rome were the only items on that man's horizon. He didn't seem to care about what really happened or why. What if he learned that a Catholic priest had fired a cannon that killed three buccaneers! What if that story ever got to Rome? Perhaps it had. How could he ever make de la Marche understand what had happened in Hispaniola? Where and how could he begin to make a Roman mind understand a deal made in a tavern filled with pipe smoke and the smell of rum? A priest in a cassock amid that atmosphere should be excommunicated without trial.

And yet, it had been in Hispaniola that the gloom and depression over his losses and the specter of Noel had been dispelled. Not totally, of course, but at least cast into the background for the first time. After the pirate attack, he and Isaac had come into the biggest port they had ever seen, Montecristo. At anchor were ships from Spain, France, Portugal and the English colonies. After begging passage here and there, and hopping from ship to ship in their circuitous journey from Jamaica back to Martinique after the pirate attack, he and Isaac had the good fortune to meet Captain Jacob Byrne of Boston. He was a portly man, nearly six feet with a complexion, partly due to the exposure of the sea winds, and partly due to his taste for rum. He had a beard with a touch of gray.

It was really Isaac who opened up a whole new avenue of hope. Without his English there would have been an impossible language barrier. Sometimes from the way the Captain howled while Isaac was speaking, it was obvious that his command of the language lacked finesse. Nevertheless, thanks to contacts with relatives in New York, Isaac was able to make himself understood, and make friends as well. It was entirely because of Isaac that he roused himself from his depression, and got up enough nerve to leave the lodging from which he had not strayed even to walk along the waterfront. He had sought out the residence of a local curé, staying out of sight. Still brooding over his misfortune, he was waiting for a ship, any ship to go their way. In the meantime, Isaac was hobnobbing with the sailors along the wharf of Montecristo.

One day, Isaac convinced him that it was vital to come along. It was in possibly the biggest and noisiest tavern along the wharf that the strange interview took place. Silence reigned. All the seamen put down their pints at the sight of a black cassock coming in to sit at a table. The sight of a Yanqui ship's captain pulling up a chair, sitting down with a priest, a jug of rum between them, and engaging in a three-way conversation, punctuated by shouting, laughing, and arm waving was a scene to be recorded for naval history.

Isaac was in the middle. Each time Captain Byrne roared with laughter after something Isaac had said, more and more seamen left the bar and crowded around the strange trio, drinks in hand. At first, Antoine felt self-conscious and embarrassed because he was so out of place and understood little of what was being said. There was loud chatter in three languages. Soon he sensed the rough-looking crowd was becoming friendly.

After the novelty began to wear off and the sailors went back to the bar, Antoine really focused on Isaac who was translating what Byrne was saying. This was the Yanqui's first trip to the Caribbean. Montecristo was a place where French and English shippers, and Spaniards too, found common ground to meet and make deals, far from their colonial masters.

Listening to the noisy conversations in the taverns, Byrne had picked up the story of Isaac and his misfortune with the privateers. Moreover, he had learned that Isaac was a manager of two sugar plantations which had produced a cargo of almost a million *livres*. Byrne needed all the molasses he could get his hands on for his Boston market. Besides, because of the Molasses Act, like his Yanqui ship-owning companions, he was not disposed to have his sugar sent to England to be milled, as his English overlords demanded.

Antoine tried to absorb all this amid the smoke and noise and smell of rum. It took several hours of painstaking exchange, but finally, an agreement began to take shape. It felt like hope for the future. One thing he never thought of as important was that the Yanquis had to deal with paper currency, whereas the transactions in the islands were in gold and silver coin.

The biggest relief of all for Antoine was that he and Isaac would never have to fear Jamaica or the pirates again. Byrne and his Dutch crew were formidable. No ordinary buccaneers would dare to approach them. True, there would be a tedious delay in a roundabout journey that would take the route up the coast of New England, and then they would have to transship to Holland. But the way was safe, not absolutely safe, of course, but infinitely more secure than the European course. Actually, the details of a new contract were a tremendous boon to Byrne with one exception, which took Antoine some time to grasp. It was not easy for Byrne to swallow the fact that he had to include a priest in the bargain. It was bad enough that Antoine was a papist, but a priest to boot! Isaac had to be at his diplomatic best.

"So," said Byrne to Isaac, "this is the papist who fired on the pirates. Well, I'm pleased to meet him, even though he is a Roman. He's famous in these parts."

After a brief exchange with Antoine, Isaac said, "Captain, Père Antoine says he needs safe passage for his sugar and molasses. We've just suffered a terrible loss. Can you help us?"

With a glance at Antoine, "He says he thinks he can, but he's not so much afraid of pirates, as he is of the preachers back home," Isaac quoted, "especially when they hear he's working with a Catholic priest." There had been a loud roar of laughter in the background from the audience, who understood English.

Antoine smiled when he learned what Byrne had said. He went on to say to Isaac, "Please tell the captain that we're coming to him because we have learned that the pirates fear Dutch-manned crews more than they fear God. It is common knowledge," he added, "that the Dutch are ready to put up a fierce fight for their cargo, while the Catholic crews from Spain and France were not. We are in dire need of help, and we promise to cooperate with him in every way we can."

Isaac struggled for a long time, but finally, Antoine was pleased with the reply in which Byrne explained that it was never safe to ship sugar and molasses to Europe, and that the real market was Boston, a lot closer. The only danger was the English brigs which patrolled the east coast of the colonies.

After that Antoine sat silently, unable to follow the conversation, as Isaac answered the burning question of how a priest became involved in the sugar business by recounting for Byrne how the French colonists had become dissatisfied with life in the Caribbean, and found themselves unable to sell their property at full value until Antoine showed them the way. This made sense to Byrne, although he wasn't very critical. Still he didn't want it known too widely that he was trading with a Jew and a Catholic. Any misgivings he had, however, were easily resolved as he realized that he had a market that would be reliable. There was no way he could resist the alluring trade with the French and Spanish islands where they paid in coin, not paper, and silver and gold at that.

From this point on a great friendship was born, the trio of Jacob, Isaac and Antoine. After a modest beginning, they began to realize profits of sixty, seventy and even a hundred thousand francs. It was tedious and time consuming. They did not realize their profits until after Jacob had sold their sugar crop in Boston. The next step was that Jacob bought furniture, tools, lumber and with the help of Rachon-Cartier sold the merchandise in the islands. It was only this final sale which provided Antoine with letters of credit that he could send to Père de Sacy in Paris for the cancellation of his debts to his investors. Most of the year went by before he could do anything about reducing this debt. Only once were Isaac and Antoine able to make a direct shipment to Holland. This involved a complicated process of shipping to Boston with Jacob, transshipping to New York and then to Holland under the safe care of a Dutch crew. Nevertheless, this resulted in a 300,000 franc payment on their debt.

The time-consuming aspect of this venture, unfortunately, allowed more and more opportunity for rumors to spread across the waters and eventually reach Paris and then Rome, where eyebrows were raised in horror at reports that a priest was doing business in the Caribbean, shipping and trading like a common merchant. And what really caused the gossip was that this priest was a follower of St. Ignatius of Loyola, a Jesus-ite, or, as the English said it, a "Jesuit."

· · · · · · · · · ·

Antoine came back to reality. Going and coming along the beach had been an escape into the past. He was still searching for words with which to convey to de la Marche what he had suffered and why he had been forced to seek some kind of profitable venture.

One cannot live in the past. He was the first to admit that. He was quite tired from his walking. There was emotional exhaustion, too, from the memories he had conjured. Now that he was once again in the shadow of Mt. Pelée, he decided it was time to rest. He sat down on the beach, not worrying about how much sand would get into his clothes. He had to face the present. That meant answering to an investigator from Rome about what he was doing. Isaac had said on their way back from Montecristo, that the name Lavalette was already becoming a legend. He didn't want to be anybody's legend. He wanted to stay here in the Caribbean. He wanted to give Blacks and Caribs decent employment — especially the Blacks. He had never really felt comfortable about owning people. But St. Paul had urged slaves to obey their masters. He was an apostle, but he never condemned slavery. Maybe he was a coward, after all, like Antoine, who didn't know how to deal with a difficult moral problem. But, if he provided simple housing, and some money to buy food and clothes, surely the Lord would forgive him. He wanted his sugar plantations to flourish too. Above all, he wanted to be free of debt, to pay back those who had invested in his enterprise, to help settle the accounts with the banking house of Leoncy Freres et Gouffre. And at last he was on the road to completing his dream. But, how did one deal with authority from Rome when you had taken a vow of obedience?

How could he make real to the closed mind of de la Marche the reception he received when he and Isaac finally put in at the wharf in St. Pierre! When Byrne's Wellstone docked, the whole island knew what had happened. By the first Sunday after their arrival, both the Caribs and the slaves had come to greet Antoine and express their condolences for his losses. At the same time, they expressed joy and relief that he and Isaac were back safely. Few people returned from an encounter with pirates. Eggs and chickens, casava , papaya, coconut milk and a special drink called coquette were the signs of welcome. Several of the merchants forgot their jealousy long enough to stop Antoine and Isaac to express their regrets. For the first time in two months, Antoine was a different man. He was touched to the heart by this display of affection and sympathy. It was an immense reward, an unexpected tribute for his dedication to his home away from home. He had cried and laughed at the same time. But, he was truly consoled.

The event changed his attitude completely. He was deeply grateful that, unlike some of his ordained comrades, he had not found the missionary work too grueling or threatening to his health. He was grateful that he was able to take the heat of calamity and the humidity of the tropics in stride. Many of his companions had been unable to take the heavy rains, the diet, mosquitoes, fever, all the handicaps that undermined missionary zeal in the Caribbean. How consoled he felt for his struggle to say Mass in Carib, his efforts to remember difficult first names, and to visit homes. This had been something of a new experience because the Caribs preferred isolated dwellings to small villages. After Antoine had ministered among them for fifteen years, many had changed their ways and began to live in bigger clusters.

In all humility, he had to admit that he did have an impact on the material side of the islanders lives. In the seminary he was taught that humility was the prize. A priest was always to call himself an unworthy servant, no matter what. Moreover, his vision should always be on the spiritual apostolate, never on the material. Never take your eyes off Jesus crucified was the exhortation from Jesuit formation directors. Did all this mean that he had to pass up the opportunity Jacob Byrne presented, and humbly obey Père de la Marche? What about their ties with Isaac? The combination had brought quality lumber from the north, unavailable here in the islands. The result was miraculous! Replacing bamboo frames and thatched palm leaf roofs that leaked in the thunderous tropical downpour with frame dwellings contributed to both the physical and spiritual well-being of the island. For the first time in both slave and Carib houses, the rain didn't just drain off. It was caught by the folded tin they had imported, and filled wooden barrels which stored the water far into the dry season.

But reminiscing didn't accomplish anything. By this time, he had no idea what the hour might be. He was stiff now from sitting on the sandy beach. But he felt a lot better.

Still, he had to face the present in the person of a man who was a greater threat than the pirates. How to deal with him? He reviewed his options. Should he make a special point about the material benefits he had brought to the people? Would that impress a man coming from Europe? Well, maybe the difference he had made in the local housing wouldn't mean much to de la Marche, but what about the malaria medicine? Because Captain Byrne had gone on to Barbados and Venezuela, he was able to bring back a supply of chinchona bark which jungle tribes had been using for centuries. European settlers in Venezuela called this malaria medicine "Jesuit bark" Captain Byrne had said. Perhaps de la Marche would be mollified by learning that Jesuit missionaries in South America had done something besides preach the gospel.

Or maybe he should stress how much he had suffered from being misunderstood, unjustly recalled to France to explain himself, and even threatened with death at the hands of pirates. The main thing was that he had to face the present. He jumped up, shook the sand from his cassock, and began to walk back toward the Jesuit residence. He must not show anger. He must pray to the Holy Spirit for intercession. He must rely on persuasion to win over de la Marche so that he would have time to stay and settle all debts.

CHAPTER IV

"Where have you been?" demanded Père de la Marche from the porch of the residence, as Antoine slowly approached. "We've been looking for you all over town. No one has seen you since eight o'clock this morning?"

"What time is it?" asked Antoine.

"I am sure you are concerned about the hour. We were supposed to meet at nine."

"I am truly sorry. I forgot about our appointment entirely," said Antoine.

"I doubt whether it makes any difference to you, but the time is actually four in the afternoon."

"I just lost track of time," observed Antoine.

"You most certainly did," said de la Marche stiffly. "I must say I thought you were trying deliberately to avoid me."

"Why would I do that?" asked Antoine.

"You and that associate of yours have been anything but cooperative. I wouldn't be surprised if you sailed off to Dominique. As a matter of fact, your boat was gone, and a man named Bratel, your pilot, told me he thought you had left."

Antoine walked up the steps of the porch to take a chair opposite his visitor.

"What is it that you have to tell me, Père?" There was a note of weariness in his voice. He had journeyed far on the ship of nostalgia.

De la Marche took a letter from his packet of papers.

"As I am sure you are aware, I have finished two weeks of carefully examining the books, the receipts, the bills of lading, the security deposits, customs payments, everything. I shall carry to Rome all the notes I have taken here.

"Before I continue, I feel it is my obligation to read to you the letter of authorization which I bring from our Father General."

As Antoine patiently listened, he looked up beyond his visitor at the cone of Mt. Pelée. How many centuries ago had it erupted in fury? When would it do so again?

"What did I read to you?" suddenly barked de la Marche.

"Excuse me?" responded Antoine.

"I'll read the first sentence again. Please pay attention this time. It is very important, supremely important."

Antoine had heard nothing.

> "In my role as General Superior of the Company of Jesus, I hereby appoint Francois de la Marche of the Society of Jesus, from Poitier as my deputy to investigate charges brought to my attention against Père Antoine Lavalette, Superior of our Mission in the Antilles. The charges claim that he has been and is still engaged in commerce which is forbidden to clerics by the law of the Church. Said Père de la Marche has full authority to act in my name on behalf of our Company and in accord with the instructions received from the Sacred Congregation for Religious, which instructions have been reviewed by His Holiness, Clement XIII, happily reigning."

De la Marche paused, allowing Antoine to fully grasp the import of the letter. It was a rhetorical pause, making Antoine feel like a child, an effect which seemed to be clearly intended.

"Did you understand fully what I have just read to you?"

"Of course," replied Antoine. "You have forgotten that you read this message to me shortly after you arrived."

"And now for my final evaluation and message," he continued reading, but in a more solemn tone.

> "And I, in my capacity as representative of the Company of Jesus, and confiding in the authority that has been conferred on me by Holy Mother Church, do hereby deprive you, Antoine Lavalette, of your posi-

tion as Vicar Apostolic of the Church's Mission to the Antilles. Furthermore, I do also remove you as Superior of members of the Company of Jesus, who serve in Martinique and Dominique and Guadeloupe. And, I further command you to relinquish these offices immediately and return with me to France for subsequent review and judgment on charges of violations of the Canon Law of Holy Mother the Church, charges to be brought before the Provincial Superior of the Society of Jesus in Paris."

De la Marche paused. Even he was a bit overwhelmed by the ponderous language he had delivered in solemn tones.

Since there was no obvious reaction from Antoine, de la Marche continued.

"In addition, I also command you to observe silence about this judgment and removal from office until such time as formal letters arrive from Rome."

"You're insane!" Antoine exploded. Then, after a lengthy pause, "I have spent more than sixteen years here and you come in two weeks and condemn everything I have done."

"Not true," de la Marche defended himself. "My orders were to investigate the charge of commerce, forbidden by the Church. I am not condemning your work as a missionary here, only your deviation from your priestly duties by engaging with the Jew in buying and selling."

"And that's all that is at stake — whether or not I have offended Holy Mother the Church?" asked Antoine incredulously.

"That is why they sent me here. My task was to verify or reject the charge against you."

"And that is all that is at stake here?" Antoine said sarcastically. "Was the law broken or not? Which one of your lofty advisers in Rome or Paris has so much as thought of the burden of supporting this extensive mission? Buying food, providing shelter, building places of worship, instructing catechists to assist in the work of teaching which the priests cannot possibly carry on without help! Any alms that come from France take two to three months, at the minimum, to arrive here. And when and if they do arrive, they provide revenue for a third of our costs at best."

De la Marche stirred uncomfortably because he could not refute Antoine's statement.

"I cannot enter into any more debate. That is not why they sent me here."

"What about the debt which the pirates caused me? I wasn't responsible for that!"

"As I have said many times already, you shouldn't have been engaged in shipping in the first place."

"That is an intelligent reply," said Antoine, getting up from his chair and beginning to walk back and forth in an effort to control his fury. "The reality is that I owe close to a million *livres*. I can't just turn my back on that debt. No one can. And I am a priest. You can complain; every one in Rome can complain about me, what I should or should not have done. I have an obligation to my creditors. That is an obligation in justice. There's a law about justice, paying off your fair debts. It goes back to Moses, there was no Church law then."

"That is not my problem. My mandate is to find out if you have been engaged in a commercial operation or not, and if so to apply Church law at once."

In a fit of frustration, Antoine struggled to come up with a reply, but found it useless. Perhaps the best reply was silence. In the interlude, he stopped walking back and forth and just stood for a moment looking down at his seated companion.

Now de la Marche stood up, too, breaking the impasse, as they eyed one another. With finality he said, "I am really at the end of my patience; I cannot continue this back and forth argument. My decision is final. Yesterday, I visited with Isaac, who informed me that he expects your friend, the Protestant from Boston, within a week or so"

De la Marche continued, "I have made arrangements with Isaac to book two passages. I did not indicate who was to be my fellow passenger. You and I will sail together up to Jamaica, transfer ships, head for Marseilles, and then back to Paris where we are to meet with your Superior and his consultants. I am obliging you not to mention my decisions to anyone until the day of our departure."

Antoine turned his back on the man. Without a word he started down the steps heading for his refuge, the sea shore. His mind was in turmoil. On the one hand there was the doctrine so often repeated in the seminary: There is an intelligent, sympathetic Being who revealed himself in the plan and order of the universe. He does not create chaos, He eliminates it. Could He not eliminate the chaos in Antoine's brain, a simple priest who had promised to trust that this God would guide him through obedience to all Superiors in the Jesuit Order? And now a group of these same Superiors with the help of Rome, had put their heads together to say that all he had done during these years in the Caribbean counted for nothing. It was all a big mistake, a deviation from what God wanted of His priests.

Was it wrong of him to rebuild the dilapidated houses where no one lived? Was it wrong to collect a modest rent from those houses once they became habitable again? How could he forget his first rainy season in St. Pierre? He had to pick his way through a bash of buckets in the priests' house because the roof leaked. Several of his priests actually caught colds in the chilly rooms during the heavy rains. Begging was useless in an area of little revenue. He had to borrow.

He had left the path from the priests' residence by this time and come to the dirt road that ran parallel to the shore. There were clusters of houses left and right. The thatched palm leaf roofs caught his eye particularly because they stood in contrast to the frame houses. Fifteen years ago, they were all thatched roofs.

But, that was not a happy line of thought. He had been brooding too much. What did you do when all was gloom and doom? You had to find some one to talk to about it. Then, the thought came to him. If he kept on his course, he would come to the Ursuline Convent. Mère Sophia! It was getting dark. The nuns were either at supper or getting ready for vespers in the chapel. Possibly there was time. She was so bright and pleasant. She always greeted him far more warmly than the others when he came for Mass in their chapel. She had sought him out for counseling. The more staid nuns found her a bit too outgoing. But what really upset them were her two German Shepherds which she kept as pets. It was completely against the Holy Rule to be walking along the shore alone. That one of the dogs was a female companion, named Luli, was a flippant and disrespectful way to refer to the Rule of always walking with a female companion.

She had sought him out for counseling; now it was his turn. Men shouldn't be asking advice of women, but right now he didn't feel like a very strong man. Nor did he feel that he could share his burden with his fellow Jesuits, not even with Père Beauharnais. He had the sense to ask for religious perspective from a quasi-neutral person, Mère Sophia. By this time he was within sight of the modest chateau-like convent. Nuns were always so much better at building than priests, even in the tropics. They let the builder alone, not pretending to identify problems or produce solutions, not interfering. Suddenly, the back door opened. Out came Mère Sophia with her two dogs on leash. She called to him.

"Good evening, Père. What a happy coincidence! I was too busy to walk my dogs in the morning. Don't tell anybody. I overslept besides! Can you believe it, a superior coming late for morning prayer!" She paused, "You look so depressed."

She caught up with him. "Come, let us walk together for a bit."

"Good to see you, Mère Sophia. It'll soon be dark. I did so want to see you. I thought it might be too late, but here you are. Perhaps we can share a few minutes before nightfall."

He was stymied for a moment because he looked over her head to see a couple of curtains moving at a second floor convent window behind them.

"I think we're being watched," he managed.

"Get away, Luli, and you too, Tiri," she scolded. "Let Père Antoine alone." She didn't turn her head.

"Oh, don't worry about them," she took him by the arm. "It takes twelve to sixteen weeks at least for a reply to their complaints about me, twelve at least to get there and just as much, maybe more, to get back."

"I can fend for myself," she added. "Sometime, I will tell you more about me than my prayer life. It's you I'm worried about. I have never seen you look so distressed. Has that visitor caused you some problems?"

He nodded.

"He's commanded me to leave the mission and return to France."

"Where does he get that kind of authority?" she challenged. "You're so important to this mission!"

"He comes loaded with documents from my superiors in France, my Father General in Rome, and the Congregation for Religious, which means the Pope."

"They're all pretty far away. Why don't you do like I do? Just ignore them. My Mother Superior doesn't want me back there. I'm too frivolous; I'm too familiar with the priests and with men in general."

"What about obedience? I'm supposed to obey the slightest indication of my Superior's. This comes from St. Ignatius."

Mère Sophia bent down to unleash the dogs. Luli and Tiri went scrambling down to the water and began leaping into the breakers, nipping at one another. A large palm tree had been uprooted in the fierce winds of the previous October. It had fallen onto the beach from the small ridge where a line of palm trees stood. Its roots were still covered with earth, so it was still alive. It provided a perfect resting spot from their stroll. She motioned Antoine to follow her up the slight incline to where the trunk lay.

"That is the best example I have seen here of the force of the tropical winds," she said. "Look at the thousands of tiny roots, and then at the resilient trunk. You'd think those trees could bend and bob so no wind could ever bring them down."

"The natives say their word '*huracán*' means some kind of fearful god with extraordinary power," added Antoine. "They weren't far from the truth." By this time they reached the tree trunk and were able to rest against it, half-sitting, half-standing. They continued to watch the dogs at play. The sun was dipping below the horizon.

"We both share the same religious formation," she began thoughtfully. "We believe that by submission to the cross, Jesus brought the way of salvation to the world. Virtue resides in humility. God guides us through our superiors. Wasn't it your holy founder that told the story about the monk who watered the dry stick because his superior had told him to? That's what my novice mistress told us. 'Blind obedience' was what she called it."

"Once a month," added Antoine, "we heard that story as we ate in silence in the dining room."

"I got in trouble with the superior who sent me here." Sophia went on. "One of your own Jesuits gave us a retreat in Soisson. He said that there was no such thing as 'blind obedience.' My superior was shocked when I quoted his exact words: If it were blind, then it couldn't be obedience; and if it were some one actually obeying, it couldn't possibly be blind." She paused.

"I remember vividly her saying, 'Oh! Those lax Jesuits. They are sophists who will try to get around any rule they can.'"

"That's where I am now," said Antoine as he reached for a handful of sand, and began pouring it out. "Where does reason come into play?"

There was a lull in which they both watched Luli and Tiri running up and down the beach. The German Shepherds were tired of gamboling in the waves; after shaking off the water, they started to chase one another. She would soon have to call them back, but as long as there were no other dogs around or people to bother, she let them play.

"I've only been here a short time, but all I have heard about your shipping sugar and molasses and other products, has been complimentary. No one I know thinks you're making money for yourself or the order. My sisters have high praise for the way you have brought the mission out of poverty, built houses and chapels, but then suffered incredible losses, through no fault of your own."

He was grateful for the kind words. He desperately needed someone to listen. She had not been on the scene when it all began. He didn't want to overwhelm her, but she had been such a good listener so far, surely she would hear him out.

He started by recalling how M. de Cresols had come to him. Weary of the tropical isle, not willing to take a loss for the devaluation of his investments, he had come almost at the beginning when the mission was at its poorest. His half-hearted cultivation of his land left three-fourths of it to be developed. It had been a godsend for Antoine. It established his reputation as an employer who paid well. When Cresols got back to France, especially Marseilles where his family had been well known, the name Antoine Lavalette came to be mentioned for the first time.

Antoine had not been too long in his narrative. Sophia had never heard anything about Cresols, but as she listened, she had called Luli and Tiri to her side, put them once again on a leash. They were tired now, and eager to lie at her feet and sleep.

So Antoine went on to explain the first critical event that made him a public figure back in France. Jean Bouf, in Guadeloupe, heard of the successful trade off for the Cresols plantation and wanted the same for himself. Everything went well. All involved were satisfied. It was St. Etienne in Martinique who caused the trouble. He, too, wanted out of his commitment of growing sugar in Martinique for retirement without losing any money exchanging colonial francs in France for national currency. For Antoine, the problem had been that St. Etienne wanted attention immediately. There was no way Antoine could handle Bouf, attend to the extensive Cresols plantation, and at the same time work out an arrangement with St. Etienne. Although he thought he had made clear to the man that he couldn't handle three plantations at once and although he had told him to wait, it was not enough. St. Etienne was offended and surprisingly vindictive. He was also clever enough to make his animosity highly damaging to Antoine's career. It was he who dug up the facts of the territorial dispute between English and French claims to Guadeloupe. He made his righteous appeal to Governor Bompar, that the priest was guilty of treason to the State by carrying on illicit business operations with England. Thus was Antoine thrown, for the first time, onto the French stage.

This meant a summons to appear before the King's Council in Paris, where he successfully defended himself. Not only that, members of the King's inner circle were highly supportive of the priest's challenge to England's jurisdictional claims to Guadeloupe. So once clearly exonerated, he had the good fortune of being something of a popular social figure. He was invited into nice homes. There he courted investments for his plantations, which needed francs because they had been hit by two catastrophes in his absence. A hurricane and a flu epidemic among his workers caused the loss of two successive harvests in a row. Antoine not only won sympathy for his unjust recall to France, and also for harvest losses, he won more than 500,000 francs in credit deposits in Leoncy Freres and Gouffre in Marseilles.

All this history was entirely new to Mère Sophia. She listened without interrupting. Her dogs slept on. She was fascinated with the story. What he didn't tell her was that his Jesuit Superior, Père Larousse, in France, was not all that thrilled with Antoine's becoming a national figure. There were rumblings in Rome about the kind of publicity a priest, above all a Jesuit, was getting.

"Père Antoine," Mère Sophia said after her long silence, "I think you're going to have to enlist all the people here, not only in St. Pierre, but all over the island and in Guadeloupe, to help you deal with this Père de la Marche."

"No, no, I can't do that," he replied. "De la Marche has forbidden me in obedience to talk about the command to leave."

She did not reply.

"Please, Mère Sophia. Perhaps another time you can talk about this. I'm so confused. I really do not know what to do. You are the only person in whom I felt I could confide. I don't want to get into trouble with my superiors or with Rome, either."

"You can trust me, Père," she said as she roused Luli and Tiri. "I will guard your confidence. As we said, it is a matter of obedience."

It was dark. What a scandal it would be for her back at the convent and possibly in the town! A nun and a priest out together after dark!

CHAPTER V

The following day was quiet and uneventful. It was a Wednesday in late July, a time of unruly winds and sudden squalls that drench the unwary before they can run to shelter. Captain Jacob Byrne was delayed in coming back from Barbados. The hurricane season was upon them; it was time to leave the Caribbean behind.

Two days passed. Antoine was depressed and frustrated. He wandered about the town, stopping at random to call on parishioners and engage in taking tea and chatting. The people loved his visits; they always had. Despite his inability to tell them what was really on his mind, he found it a pleasant diversion to make small talk and give them his blessings as he left. Between visits, he walked down to the harbor to look southward for any sign of the Wellstone. He avoided calling on Isaac which left the man puzzled and apprehensive. Isaac was kind enough not to press his friend, or follow him through the streets. He would have been quite naive not to suspect the cause of the priest's unusual behavior.

Friday afternoon at dusk, the word came that Jacob had put in to shore, and was anxious to move out in the morning. Isaac delivered the message personally to Antoine. De la Marche was on hand to overhear what they were saying. Allowing sufficient time for Isaac to leave, he approached Antoine.

"I am going down to the pier. I will give the message to your friend, late though it be. Remember, you are under orders to speak to no one about this."

Antoine merely nodded and went to his room. He did not feel like eating supper. He climbed into his hammock with the half-hearted hope that sleep might deliver him from his heavy thoughts. Mercifully, after breathing rhythmically for what seemed a long, long time, he dropped off.

Shortly after dawn, he could not possibly sleep any longer. He got up, poured water in a basin and began to wash up. He felt uncomfortable in the clothes he had slept in and busied himself making a change. Then he started out on his morning routine, heading for the beach north of the residence. He had a couple of hours to himself. When he reached the end of the property, he started to go straight, instead of turning to the right heading for the beach. Habit! It was automatic to walk to the church downtown where he usually said the morning Mass. He would never say Mass there again. So he turned to the right, walking as he watched the sun climb above the horizon. Maybe there would be another day when he would be eager to greet the rising sun.

By this time he had reached the cove where his sailboat was docked. He tucked up his cassock and began dragging the boat to the water.

"Père, where are you going at this early hour?" It was Mère Sophia with Luli and Tiri again.

Startled by her sudden presence, he was still able to counter her question.

"I should ask the same of you."

"I saw you go by the convent and immediately began to worry."

He sat down on the boat and began taking off his shoes and stockings. Next he reached under the seat for the sail and began to pull it up, still without replying. He began wading out into the water pushing the stern.

"Surely, you're not taking a long sail, are you, Père?"

He could detect a note of anxiety.

"No, I just have to do something physical and mechanical. I feel as though I haven't slept all night. Don't worry. I'm not doing anything foolish."

She watched in silence as he jumped into the boat, waited for the jib to catch the morning breeze, and started moving slowly out into the blue, and after a bit sat down at the tiller.

He turned to wave to Mère Sophia as she stood there watching with her dogs.

After watching the sun come up and breathing in the fresh salt air, preoccupied with the sail and the tiller, enjoying the rolling rise and fall of his vessel, with his back to the land, it was as though he had left the world behind for a better one where the colors were blue, dark blue beneath and light blue above, sprinkled with white. It was illusory, pleasant though it was. He had to return. Reluctantly, he recalled that he had agreed with de la Marche that the three of them would celebrate Mass together.

It would be some comfort that Beauharnais, his long time companion, would be at his side as they invoked the presence of the Lord upon the altar in what was to be his last Mass on Martinique. He reflected that it had also been a sad scene when Jesus first offered the bread and wine with His companions, fearful of what lay before Him on that First Good Friday.

He had to swing around and leave the tranquility of the open sea behind him and head for shore. It was always a bit of drudgery to put in, unfurl the sails and haul the boat to the cove — particularly oppressive this morning. But, duty was duty. In a short time he was trudging up the slope to the residence with the unpleasant prospect of standing like a little altar boy beside de la Marche as chief celebrant. Coming into the tiny chapel to vest for the ritual, he was greeted with a severe look.

"We have been waiting almost a half hour for you" was de la Marche's morning greeting.

In a moment all three priests bowed before the altar and the ceremony began. Just after the communion, when Antoine tried to pray, he did his best to stave off a rush of tears. In an effort to hide his feelings, he left for the sacristy where he hung up his chasuble.

"You cannot leave the altar before the final blessing," de la Marche called after him sharply.

Before Antoine reached his room to weep alone, the quiet of the priests' residence was suddenly disturbed by heavy steps on the porch and pounding at the front door. The disturbance was soon accompanied by a chorus of shouting voices, demanding the priests' attention.

"De la Marche, we want to speak to you," came a loud shout. Terrified, by hearing his name, the visitor went to the window of the chapel. Among the group of men on the porch was the sea captain with the Jew at his side. Behind them, a large noisy group, perhaps sixty or more. What astonished de la Marche was seeing four nuns in the front row, one holding two dogs on a leash. Later he would learn that the Superior of the Ursulines had brought her companions to the protest. Before the day was out, Antoine would learn that their encounter on the beach had aroused Mère Sophia's suspicions. There had been an early breakfast in the convent, and with permission of Mother Superior, two by two, the nuns had begun to call on the populace, so that by Mass time the townsfolk were wide awake.

De la Marche turned from the veranda, fear in his eyes. His voice trembled as he spoke to the gathered crowd. "You have roused the townspeople against me. I have committed no crime. It is you who are the criminal." His voice was shrill and piercing. Antoine heard him clearly through the walls of his room.

De la Marche continued, "I only came to do my duty." He shouted so the whole house could hear. "I came here under holy obedience. This Lavalette is a criminal. I commanded him to tell no one, and he has roused the town."

The shouting outside continued unabated. De la Marche fearfully went down to the vestibule. Before he could summon enough courage to open the door, however, Antoine came down to pacify the crowd. They were respectful now, but not before giving Antoine a big cheer. Mère Sophia let go of her leash. Luli and Tiri leaped up the steps to be petted.

"We're here to see that Marche fellow." Unbelievably, it was Captain Byrne speaking for all.

"We want to invite him to Jamaica for a free trip."

Antoine was speechless. He raised his arms helplessly.

"We're not here to talk to you, Père Laval." It was the first time he had used the word "Père" in addressing him, and he never had gotten his name straight.

"No, we want to escort this Marche to my ship." This was Isaac butting in.

"We all want to talk to him," echoed Jacob. This was followed by a shout of approval from the crowd.

Antoine went back into the vestibule. It took a while to convince de la Marche that he wouldn't be hurt. After a bit of persuasion, punctuated by a few curses shouted from the crowd, the fearful priest came out behind Antoine.

"You want to take Père Antoine from us!" More than one voice raised the challenge to the cowering priest. Poor man, he had never experienced anything like this in his life. People always obeyed their priest.

"I am only carrying out orders. You must send your complaints to Rome. It's not me who is responsible for recalling Père Lavalette."

This met with a derisive howl.

"There's your answer, priest," said Captain Byrne. "Get your stuff ready. Come with me. You have passage on my ship. I am setting out this morning in a couple of hours. You go, Père Antoine stays."

De la Marche was too frightened to reply, much less assert his authority again.

There was a short delay while Antoine escorted de la Marche to his room to pick up his valise. He had been ready to travel, but not alone.

Then began the strangest procession ever witnessed on Martinique. Merchants, slaves, ordinary parishioners, sailors, Caribs, nuns, three priests, and two dogs, all wound their way noisily down to the wharf where the sails of the Wellstone were unfurled and ready to propel Captain Byrne and his men north to the Atlantic.

It was awhile before the crew assembled on the deck with de la Marche meekly in their midst. Only when the sails began to fill with the meager wind and the ship began moving slowly away from the dock, did de la Marche regain his courage.

Shaking his finger at Antoine, he shouted, "You'll regret this Lavalette. I'll see that you are punished for defying Church authority. Yes, you'll regret this all right."

He went on shouting at the top of his voice, but the rest of his words were drowned out by the loud cheer celebrating the fact that Antoine was staying while his critic from Rome was heading for the open sea.

As the crowd dispersed, Antoine did his best to thank as many as possible for the affection and support they had shown him. It took a while, but finally he was free to set out alone. He sought out his favorite retreat, the sandy seashore.

He was not happy about embarrassing his papal visitor. He felt guilty about defying an order from Rome. He knew Church Law as well as anyone. He didn't need anyone to tell him that priests were forbidden to buy and sell at a profit. He had also done his best to convince de la Marche that he was not responsible for the debt, but that it was a matter of justice to try and pay back what was owed. And it was within his means to clear his debts. Captain Jacob was his intermediary. Together with Isaac, the three of them could get his coffee, sugar, molasses, and manioc to New York for shipping to Holland. It was more costly and more time consuming; but the main thing was that it was safe with the Dutch crews.

There was turmoil in his brain, nonetheless. He was secretly thrilled at the way the people solved his problem for him, touched to the heart by the way Jacob acted, and Isaac, too. He wanted so much to rejoice that the obnoxious visitor was sailing north, without him. But, still his conscience vacillated between what he and Isaac and Jacob could do about paying back what they owed, and the obedience that he had promised long ago, and what would happen in Rome when de la Marche gave his report. Would it be uncharitable to pray for a pirate attack, or possibly a storm at sea that might keep his nemesis from reaching Italy? There was always hope.

The September planting was six weeks away. Lots of work lay ahead of them. Harrowing good ditches for the water to run off, breaking up the sod where the stalks were to be planted, cutting and inserting the joints, all this both here in Martinique and in Guadeloupe. He would have a lot to oversee between now and September. The harvest would be in the spring at the height of the dry season. Give de la Marche six to eight weeks to get to Europe, two weeks more to get to Rome, another three weeks to a month to complain and prepare some punishment. It would be March or April before any letters arrived. Surely, they might have a shipment of anywhere from 200,000 to 400,000 *livres* worth of sugar and cocoa, packed and ready for the roundabout trip to the north.

He decided to promise both Caribs and slaves a premium of foodstuffs and clothes over and above their wage as a bonus for a successful harvest. He would have to tell them that this would be the most important harvest of his life. That meant constant vigilance and heavy hoeing to keep the weeds from winning the battle. Only much later would he learn why weeds were so anxious to flourish with the sugar cane. Mt. Pelée, with its gloomy cone, was not alone in the islands. Together with its ancestors, Mt. Pelée had risen from the sea to pour forth the lava that became the volcanic rock and then the rich basaltic soil which was home to the sugar cane, but alas, also to the weeds.

He forgot about de la Marche completely during the next weeks, commuting between the islands, concentrating on a successful planting.

The months went by slowly. The rainy reason brought plenty of water, but thankfully, no hurricanes, big or small. His voyages in a small sailboat were rockier than ever between Martinique, Dominique, and Guadeloupe. At last, January came and the beginning of the dry season, still with no reports or letters from France or Rome. He was able to say Mass in forty villages. There were First Communions and baptisms, and this time even a few marriages, which seemed to say that the Lord was blessing him and might continue to bless him. He was able to put all gloomy thoughts from his mind as he concentrated on his ministry.

Somehow the weeks went by and it was cutting time. Now the Caribs were in the fields as usual. But this time they were not alone. Antoine came in on horseback every few days, sometimes at the former Cresols ranch near Point Carbet, and then to the Bouf hacienda over at Guadeloupe. He couldn't wield the machete, but he did his part with the hauling. He became a familiar figure walking alongside the ox carts. He even helped in the standing of the cane stalks to prevent fermentation. He kept a heavy cloth upon his shoulder. Every time he did so, his cassock was soon dirty. So dirty in fact, that at the end of the day, the women insisted that he take it off for them to wash. What everyone enjoyed was the following morning, seeing his cassock swinging from a tree like a ghost, their priest in shirt sleeves walking through the mud to the grinding mill where the wash tubs were.

The cutting season was almost over when another black cassock appeared in the field near the sugar mill. He came riding in on horseback, pulling a second horse that was saddled but without a rider. All the nearby workers stopped as the newcomer approached the mill. It was Père Beauharnais, who had come from St. Pierre. It was extraordinary for one his age to travel up the coast on horseback. Not too many remembered the elderly priest. But the word soon passed that Antoine had a visitor. Both men and women took advantage of the moment, happy to take a break, but also curious. A couple men hurried into the mill to call Antoine, who soon came out to greet his old friend warmly. He was filled with misgivings, hesitating to ask him why he had come, although he was perfectly aware of what the message would be. And he knew the kind of person Beauharnais was, one who would go out of his way to soften a blow of bad news because he was a man of compassion. They went together into the cane shelter where the stalks were stashed for grinding.

"We have received some letters from Rome, Antoine."

"Yes, I can imagine. I was hoping to be spared, but one can dream only so long."

Without a word, Beauharnais handed Antoine a packet with a message in careful Ciceronian Latin. There was really nothing more to talk about; both men were fully aware of the contents even without reading them.

"It was very thoughtful of you to come all this way to bring the news. I thank you."

"I am so sorry," said Beauharnais.

When the two blackrobes emerged from the cane shelter, a small group of men and women had gathered. One woman took the bundle of stalks off her head and came closer.

"Is it bad news, mon Père?"

Antoine nodded. He could not speak.

"Is it so hard to tell us?" another woman asked.

Beauharnais spoke for him.

"I am afraid it is very bad news. Père Antoine has been called back to France. He will have to leave us."

"Surely, you will you be coming back to us?" offered one of the men.

Antoine was still not able to speak. Standing forlornly, he was looking at the ground. One by one the workers approached in silence and touched his shoulder. One look at his face made them afraid to speak — even words of consolation.

All the work stopped, even in the mill, though it was only two in the afternoon. The news spread quickly. Soon the sixty-odd workers assembled as Antoine prepared to mount the spare horse. It was a solemn and silent assembly. The whole island knew that there had been a visitor whom no one liked, and that this stranger was trying to get rid of Père Antoine. Words were useless.

Antoine turned in his saddle and waved to the crowd who waved back.

A man, Cesar, manager of the mill for many years, broke from the crowd and came up beside Antoine.

"Couldn't we go to the Governor to petition him to use his authority to keep you here with us? We can't manage without you."

"I will send Isaac here to finish the milling," said Antoine shaking his head. He and Père Beuharnais then rode off slowly.

This was no place to try and explain the kind of message that had reached Martinique from Rome. He was suspended from saying Mass or hearing confessions, or carrying on in any way the administration of the Mission of the Antilles. Père Beauharnais was to be acting superior until such time as a successor could be sent. This kind of order was not like getting rid of de la Marche. He could always plead that his people had sent de la Marche home, and this was true. But now, this kind of new mandate from the Vatican and his superior in Rome left no room to plead for delay. Lavalette had promised obedience. He could not in conscience defy the order to leave.

It would have created chaos in the people's minds if he tried to stay and challenge Rome. Moreover, the priests in the islands would raise a storm, as well as bishops in the surrounding region. Obedience was the way. It would allow him to go back and argue before an audience more sympathetic than de la Marche. He would also have Père de Sacy at his side whose job in the Mission Development Office kept him better than anyone else as to what the difficulties were in financing a ministry far from France.

Antoine had a lot to think about as he and his fellow priest moved at a slow trot back towards St. Pierre. He had time to read the details of the document that Beauharnais had handed him. He read again "Suspensus a Sacris." That was the most painful! To be forbidden to say Mass until he reached Paris was a heavy burden. It had been so much a part of his life ever since he was an altar boy, to believe that each day you received Jesus into your heart with the sacred host. The other terms, like "Cessatio autoritatis Ecclesiae" didn't hang so heavy upon him. He had never really looked upon himself as a major Church authority in the Antilles. The title of "Vicar Apostolic" always reminded him of wearers of the purple in Rome. He rarely thought of himself like that here in the Caribbean.

Jogging along, he forwent the Latin text to focus on the French commentary. He was blamed for starting an insurrection against the legitimate ecclesiastical representative, Père René de la Marche, placing him in life threatening circumstances. This meant that in addition to flagrant disobedience, he was charged with criminal assault against a cleric. The punishment had not as yet been defined by the Holy Office. However, if he did not leave Martinique at the first opportunity to appear in Paris at an Ecclesiastical Court, he would be dismissed from the priesthood, with recommendation to the Society of Jesus that he also be dismissed from any type of affiliation with the Order. The final barb was that he was a disgrace to a religious order which vaunted its obedience to the Church as one of its most prestigious claims to honor.

It was mid-afternoon when the pair arrived on horseback from the sugar field. They tied up their horses, calling one of the slaves to take them to the small shed behind the residence.

"It will be a few hours before the news is all over town," Beauharnais said. "I will see to it that you are not called to the parlor."

Antoine went to his room without replying. He needed a lot of time to reflect.

The following morning Antoine went walking towards the shore. Surprisingly, the news had not spread as they expected, so people greeted him in the usual fashion. At first, he tried to get up the courage to go down to the office and inform Isaac. Then he changed his mind.

When he didn't return that afternoon, there was some apprehension on Beauharnais's part, but nothing like his reaction the next morning when he found Antoine's room empty, and learned from Bratel that the small sailboat was no longer tied to the pier. No one had had seen him sail out. Beauharnais had a moment of panic, but then remembered that Antoine was in the habit of taking a short sail by himself south to Pointe Sables, a small village where he had friends he had met when he first came to the island. This was a bit out of the way, and was actually one of his favorite places to hide for a quick rest. It was only a couple hours down the coast, a lovely sail on a nice day. Actually, Antoine had set out the previous afternoon, deciding that seclusion was the best medicine for the moment.

There was a tiny cluster of houses on Pointe Sables. This was where his old friends, Marie Celeste, Aunt Hessie and Uncle Loize lived. They were some of the first people he had come to know on the island. Shortly, after his arrival in 1745 he had been invited to say Mass in their house because Uncle Loize was down with fever, and Aunt Hessie was very worried. Many a time during the three years he had been in St. Pierre, he regularly dropped in at Pointe Sables. Then later, when he had become head administrator — he never liked to call himself "Vicar Apostolic" in the presence of Aunt Hessie and Uncle Loize — he could not visit them as he liked. Whenever he had a chance, this was the spot he sought to get away from the burden of affairs. When the cane cutting, the milling, the shipping worries became too heavy and his clerical duties pressed upon him, this was his haven.

Celeste and Hessie were not so taken aback by his sudden arrival. They had become used to his unexpected arrivals. But his sad demeanor was surprising and sobering. It was so unlike him. After welcoming him warmly, they asked no questions, but set up his hammock in the usual spot between two palm trees behind their house, a shelter protecting him from the sea breeze and the sunlight.

Marie Celeste and Aunt Hessie brought him some casava and rice as the sun was going down. They prepared black coffee whose beans had been roasted with brown sugar.

"Why you so sad, Père?" asked Hessie finally.

"I have to leave you and the island, too. I must go back to France."

"Oh, no, Père. Why you do that? We need you here. You friends with everybody," chimed in Marie Celeste.

"Some other time I will tell you," said Antoine. "Not now."

Around the fire when it was dark, he warmed up, and they began talking about old times. Uncle Loize recalled the priest's first visit, the time Aunt Hessie had asked him to bless her little portable shrine with the tin roof. It enclosed a statue of the Virgin Mary. While Antoine was going to his saddle bags for the prayer book, Loize and Celeste did some loud whispering in Carib to Hessie. Even though he didn't quite catch what they were saying, he had guessed. So, when he came with the holy water and prayer book, pretending to start the ceremony, he suddenly knocked the miniature house shrine from her hands. The back part broke open on hitting the ground. Out fell the image of Mama Chacla, the patron of the islands, which had been concealed behind the Virgin Mary.

"She like the old ways," Uncle Loize had said, chiding his wife.

But the incident was soon forgotten, and as the years went by they became closer and closer. As a matter of fact, they became used to finding him in the hammock when they got up in the morning. Often on a calm night, he would set out from St. Pierre. Hessie or Marie Celeste would come upon him in the morning. He knew how to find his hammock without disturbing them. He would go down to the shore during the day, do a bit of fishing, and then spend a good portion of the afternoon resting. This had been his routine when the work became too heavy.

This time it was different. He barely greeted them, just broke the sad news and that was all. He went to his hammock shortly after their meager supper. It wasn't more than an hour later, however, that he began waving his arms and shouting in his sleep. The two women came running to his side. Hessie held one of his hands. Amazingly he didn't wake up. Celeste took hold of the top of the hammock and began swinging it gently. She began to hum a tune. Then both of them began to sing a lullaby softly:

> *Rock, a rock, a rock, Boysie. Boysie can't sleep.*
>
> *Rock, a rock, a rock, Boysie. Boysie can't sleep.*
>
> *Look up town, look down town, find Boysie there.*
>
> *Look up hill, look down hill, find Boysie there.*

The arm-waving stopped; his voice was quiet. Soon they left him.

The following morning after a complete rest, Antoine was able to unburden his soul to his three friends. He told them about being summoned to France. He had to obey. There was some slim hope he might return. He didn't go into the details, just that there were problems with the Dominique plantation that he had to explain to his superiors in Paris.

There were hugging and tears. Then they all walked down to the shore where he had tied up his boat. As usual, he took off his shoes and stockings, tucked up his cassock and, with the help of Uncle Loize, he began pushing the boat until he could jump in and catch the morning breeze. His three old friends stood there on the sand until he was a small figure in the distance.

CHAPTER VI

It was only an hour or two before he was bringing his little boat to the small pier that was easily visible from the porch of the Jesuit residence. Really, it didn't matter now what time it was, or how long it took. Coming from the south he had to swing around the harbor. There were always a half dozen sailboats at least of different sizes at anchor fronting St. Pierre. Jacob's Wellstone was the most prominent. But today, it didn't hold his gaze for very long. It would be a long time, perhaps never, before he and Jacob would once again be bending over bills of lading and cargo lists. He turned away to focus on steering past the small cluster of rolling craft with their furled sails.

Once he circled past the harbor boats, he turned his attention to the little pier from which he had set out so many times over the past fifteen years on cruises, big and small. He hadn't told anyone where he was going, nor even that he was hiding out for a short time. So he didn't expect to see anyone waiting for him, but to his surprise, a small crowd had gathered. They must have spotted him as he was swinging around the harbor. Beyond them, he could see another group, much farther away, clearly visible on the porch of the residence.

The shallow water came up fast. He jumped into the water, unmindful of cassock and trousers. With one hand he towed the boat, in the other he carried his shoes and stockings.

"Don't. We'll take care of it." Isaac came running to the end of the pier to catch the rope and tie it to the post. His shout was late because Antoine was already wading barefoot to the shore. There was Captain Byrne followed by Isaac, and behind him were Bratel and several others.

"We were worried about you, Père," Isaac said as Antoine hopped up on the edge of the pier and started to wipe off his bare feet and put his shoes on.

"You didn't tell anybody and your boat was gone. We wondered if you went out to sea." Isaac caught himself. "I'm sorry, Père, I didn't mean that." He turned to Byrne for help. "We were worried, weren't we?"

Jacob had come in the previous evening, and heard the bad news for the first time. He was truly upset; he had sought out Isaac the first thing in the morning. And when the word came that the people had spotted Antoine's boat coming around the harbor, he hurried down with Isaac to the small pier.

"Look, Laval," Jacob was very emphatic, "there's no need to leave us." He stretched out his hand. "You have a place on my ship always. I need a parson aboard. I've always said that. Besides, there are Romans up there in Boston. I've told them about you. They want to meet you."

"Thank you, thank you," Antoine said. He put his hand on the Captain's shoulder. "You know how much I want to keep working with you and Isaac."

"Why do you have to pay attention to anyone as far away as Rome?" insisted the Captain. "We'll pay off that debt, me and Isaac. Tell them to leave us alone."

Antoine finished lacing his shoes and stood up.

"Can't we talk about this some more?" queried Isaac as he and Jacob fell in behind Antoine who didn't appear to hear what was said. Antoine began greeting all who came to meet him. Their faces showed that they were worried about him. Now that they had found him, they wanted him to stay. Politely and gently, Antoine told them it was no longer within his power to stay. He slowly broke away from the little crowd and began walking with Isaac and Jacob toward the Rachon Cartier office.

As they drew near, Jacob suggested they drop in at the tavern across the street from the office. Antoine declined, but Jacob went in and ordered three pints which he brought over and set on Isaac's desk. The three sat down together, well aware that this might just be the last time.

It soon became obvious to his two friends that there was no turning back, no point in bewailing the turn of events. Their previous relationship had established a bond that would not ever be forgotten. The two would never understand the ways of the Catholic Church, so there was no use trying to explain. As a result, they did their best to put departure out of their minds for the time being. They began to reminisce. They recalled the unforgettable scene in the tavern in Hispaniola where they first met.

What a stir they had caused! The seamen, the officers, the crews and captains could not take their eyes off the trio. The Jew from Brazil, the Yanqui from Boston, the priest in the black cassock. It had really been a godsend for Jacob and Isaac, but mainly for Antoine. It had been a hopeful sign just after the terrible loss of his cargo, and the indebtedness it forebode. And the strange threesome proved an extraordinary boon to one another. They turned their backs on what had been for the most part an unexciting past to begin a joint effort that was totally new and rewarding. The sugar problem that had crippled the shippers out of Boston had been relieved. Markets were opened in the Caribbean for products in exchange for white sugar and molasses and payment in coin. Isaac's life had been drab and routine, with little expectation beyond the horizon. He had lived under the shadow of the cruel ostracism of Brazil, but he found a Christian who trusted him — absolutely. Further, this Christian was willing to share an adventure on the high seas, in marketing and finance, in what became a struggle for debt reduction.

But soon the nostalgia faded away. Any further effort at conversation proved difficult. The three stood up, finished their ale and without a word they shook hands, Yanqui fashion, and parted.

The farewell at the church was far more difficult. Fortunately, the day was Thursday. Only a few days remained before Sunday services. Antoine had forty-eight hours to compose himself for this good-bye. Jacob would leave that afternoon, and what was more, he planned to return to attend the Roman Mass of farewell, provided his crew promised not to tell anyone when they got back to Boston.

Sunday's Mass was a trial. Mère Sophia enlisted her nuns to practice with the children. It was hard to hold back the tears while the little ones struggled with the Greek Kyrie, asking God's pardon for all. They rose to the occasion almost like adults as they chanted the Latin words of the Gloria in Excelsis.

Antoine made it through the sermon because it was short. But distributing the hosts to the people, especially the children devoutly kneeling at the altar rail, was beyond what any human could take without breaking down. He wept unashamedly.

After Communion he sat at the presider's chair in long silence. He then rose to offer the final prayers and blessing. At the door, somehow, he found the strength to hug his people without crying again.

At the dock, he was able to get into a rowboat before a large crowd gathered. He didn't have to go through the ordeal of hugging and embracing again. Seated with two seamen rowing toward the Wellstone, he turned and waved adieu to his people.

Once aboard, he quickly went below to tiny quarters with just enough room to string up his hammock. He could not bring himself to go back up on deck to stand at the rail while Captain Byrne took the wheel of the ship as it moved slowly in the light afternoon breeze on its way north to Jamaica.

There was one more farewell when Byrne's ship reached Kingston. It was genuine. Jacob grabbed his hand warmly; Yanquis didn't like embraces among males. There were too many crewmen around for them to show any signs of real affection, but their eyes met in a language all their own.

With Byrne as his emissary, who was well known around the pubs, it was not a serious problem to locate passage for Antoine. A captain, Thaddeus McElwane, commanded an English frigate bound for London. It was leaving in three days. It was lucky for Antoine that Jacob could bridge the language gap, so the cassocked figure would not have to deal with English in London. McElwane was acquainted with people who knew Byrne, so for a few extra gold coins, he was willing to make a short stop at Punta Delgada in the Azores, which was not far off his route. There Antoine could find easy passage to Le Havre or Bordeaux.

After an eternity, the frigate came into Punta Delgada, Azores. The first thing that struck Antoine was that they were not too far from Portugal and the continent. The second, that there was still another language to contend with. But with signs and grunts and gestures, he was able to make clear to the Flemish and Portuguese speakers that he was on his way to France, not England. It was a struggle because there was more traffic on its way to Marseilles rather than Bordeaux or Le Havre. Since the banking house of Leoncy Freres at Gouffre was in Marseilles, Antoine did not want to appear on its streets for fear of being identified.

Finally passage was arranged, and after two more days at sea, Antoine arrived in Le Havre. Home at last, speaking his language, he was able to bargain along the waterfront and in the public market which was within easy walking distance of the harbor. He found passage on a carriage drawn by four horses. Several chickens and turkeys heads hung down on the sides. There were four people on the roof, traveling for half fare, who enjoyed the company of two cages of pigeons. Alongside, there were seven people waiting. They greeted Antoine warmly, as if they had known him for years. The reality, he soon learned, was that the driver was stopping all passersby trying to get one more passenger for the trip to Paris. He needed eight inside and four on the roof. Antoine's appearance brought relief to all. What had seemed to Antoine a burst of Catholic piety at the presence of a priest companion, now appeared for what it was, the "carriage is ready to leave at last!"

The trip was long and dusty. Added hardships were the stops on their journey. Although the majority of the travelers were headed for Paris, there were several who got off along the way. Each time they stopped, Antoine walked like a cripple for several minutes because of being so cramped. But once free to stretch his legs, he and the rest of the passengers could wander around the shops and cafés while waiting patiently for their driver, who drove the nearby streets shouting for passengers. Eventually, they were on their way again.

Outside of Paris, they stopped at an inn. It was mid-afternoon. They would be taken to the central marketplace that was not far from the Church of Notre Dame and the Isle de la Cité. Antoine was anxious to find another carriage. Several of his companions on the journey pleaded with him to stay. The driver would not leave until he had found another traveler. By this time, Antoine had made friends with everyone. The cassock he wore made people feel free to approach him. It was hard to turn them down. He agreed to wait, although he wanted very much to see Père de Sacy to learn how the Jesuits of Paris looked upon his status.

He had confided his last name to no one, nor did he mention the order to which he belonged. All he had said was that he was destined to go to *L'Hôtel Dieu*, the hospital run by the Sisters of St. Augustine. Before he left Martinique, he had found a seaman bound for the Azores, and Le Havre to whom he entrusted a letter of introduction from Mère Sophía to Mère Elisette, the hospital administrator. In it he begged for a room in exchange for chaplain services to the sick. He was apprehensive about going to the Jesuit residence where his friend, Père de Sacy lived. He was leery about the reception he might receive from his brother Jesuits. Their residence was not far from the hospital. He would be able to visit them by night.

But all thought of the hospital was driven from his mind as he journeyed through the streets of Paris. He was jostled, thrown and cramped all at the same time as he and his companions tried to stay upright on the planks that served as seats. He felt he was doing penance for his sins as the coach bounced over cobblestone passageways and through the mud puddles. He was soon to learn why coachmen had to be fierce tyrants. The way they raced through intersections enraged all pedestrians. For the sake of their passengers, they didn't dare stop. Never in his life had he heard such foul language from those scurrying for their lives and the driver as well. Curses were hurled back and forth. He could not stop his ears because he had to hold on desperately to the plank to keep from being dashed against the side of the carriage, or landing in the laps of his fellow passengers. At the same time he couldn't let go of his knapsack which he held in front of his face to ward off the slop water and other refuse that accompanied the curses of the angry pedestrians. A chorus of ribaldry came as well from the vegetable sellers, rag merchants, vendors of hot breads, soup oysters and porridge, but especially from the water carriers, who were trying to balance their buckets, dodge out of the way and curse at the same time.

Nothing like this had happened on the tranquil island of Martinique. Begrudgingly, he had to admire the driver, who not only bore the brunt of the foul language, but the lumps and slop that came his way, while keeping the four wheels astride the smelly ditch that ran down the center. Careening to either side would mire the carriage, or pitch it on its side.

At one point, bloodshed or injury was imminent. The driver had to swerve suddenly to avoid a collision with a man on horseback who came galloping around a corner. For a few scary moments the driver had to whip his horses mercilessly because the right wheels were plowing through the mud and rubbish. By the slimmest margin, the carriage avoided getting stuck, righted itself and then charged on. But in the process, it knocked down the poles of a broom seller's tent. All the passengers held their breath. If they had to stop at the next intersection, the furious broom seller would catch up to them; they might never reach the center of the city. But their driver had learned the skill of his trade. He rushed on and through the intersection with such speed that he intimidated all challengers.

By late afternoon, Antoine's frantic ride through the streets was behind him. He could now see the spires of the Cathedral of Notre Dame. He ignored the ancient residence of the French kings on his left, and was relieved to look out upon the Seine to his right. Two bridges separated him from his goal, the Pont Neuf where he could look upon the statue of Henry IV, and the Pont au Change where one could cross to the church. In front of the entrance to the bridges was the public square, where carriages were hired out. Here he debarked with his knapsack, bidding farewell to all.

"You are going to the cathedral, mon Père," said a woman companion, as they were picking up their things. Antoine nodded, and pretended to be a pilgrim like many around him. But, he succeeded in falling behind a bit by luring a street urchin to carry his knapsack with a flash of a coin. He walked on to the Petite Pont where one could cross to the front of the cathedral. As he reached the front steps, he looked around to see if any of his travel companions was watching. Seeing no one, he started down the path that led to the rear of the church building. Admiring the imposing Gothic structure was not on his mind.

"Oh, mon Père," a woman with a young daughter called to him before he could head for the hospital.

"We have just arrived from Provence. We would like to receive the Holy Communion tomorrow at the morning Mass. Would you by any chance be hearing confessions?"

Instinctively, he started for the church door. Then he caught himself. He had been forbidden to hear confessions or preach until he had been given permission by Church authorities.

"Many pardons, Madame. I, too, am a pilgrim recently arrived." He hesitated for words. "I do not, I cannot...I am not an authorized priest here in Paris just yet. Perhaps you could find a confessor inside the church."

Once the woman and daughter disappeared into the cathedral, Antoine took another path. Notre Dame was not his goal. L'Hôtel Dieu lay behind the church. Antoine hurried on. A queue of poorly dressed and ailing people sought to be admitted to the hospital. He took his place on a bench at the rear, even though many of the sickly motioned him to go before them. He could not do that. There were bandaged hands and heads; two men leaned on crutches. A mother held a crying baby.

"Mon Père," a weary nun sought him out. "You must pardon. I have been so busy. I did not notice you in the line."

"No need of pardon, Sister. I have a letter here of introduction to Mère Elisette. Would you be so kind as to present it to her?"

"There is no need, Père, come. You present it to her personally. I will take you to her at once." The nun escorted him to a tiny office where they found Mère Elisette, head down, with a large pen in her hand, filling out several death certificates.

"The priest wishes to speak with you, Mère," said the nun, who then bowed and left.

"Thank you, Sister Therese," said Mère Elisette as she put down her pen. "There are many deaths here in L'Hôtel Dieu, mon Père," she sighed. "And how may I be of service?"

"I have here a letter of introduction from Mère Sophia of St. Pierre, Martinique. It is she who suggested that I seek lodging with you here."

"You need no introduction, Père. She wrote to me some time ago. She speaks highly of you."

"And by the way, how is she? It has been some years since we saw one another. She was Marguerite Navire in our village. We grew up together."

"She is well, by the Grace of God, Mère Elisette. She is not all that happy to be a prioress. But she is very dedicated, and brings a youthful dynamic to all that she does, especially to the elementary school. She has done marvels with the children's choir.

"She is a dear friend of mine, and she has explained somewhat the problems you face there in the islands."

"I need a place to stay, and freedom to move about and contact as many people as possible to help me. You see, there are many people who don't know what has happened on Martinique. I am sure there are reports spreading about me that are in need of correction. If you have the time, I would like to explain to you some of the difficulties I faced in Martinique."

It had been an awfully long day for Mère Elisette. She was doing her charitable best to listen to what Antoine had to say.

"I don't wish to overwhelm you with my troubles, Mère." He saw the weariness in her eyes. "Perhaps I could explain tomorrow when you are more rested. But as for now, is there any chance that I can be of service to you here in the hospital. All I would ask in exchange is a small space with a bed and simple fare."

He paused a moment. "I imagine you have a resident chaplain, but I could be his helper."

Mère Elisette smiled. It was her first smile that day.

"You think there are priests in the city that would be willing to live with us here? We have never had that luxury. We would be delighted to have a resident priest. But even if one would volunteer, we don't have a room for him right now, nor can we pay him very much. We are always overcrowded. In fact, the people accuse us of laying the dying patients on the floor to make room for those who can be cured."

"I have slept on the floor in the villages where I have said Mass," Antoine said. "I am ready to do that again. You will see that I will attend your sick."

Mère Elisette was touched. She was trying to understand what Antoine had said. It was a plea for help. Never had she been in such a position. Priests were usually so self-possessed. She studied his face carefully. It was hard at the end of a day to be faced with a puzzling encounter like this. But, there was something that Mère Sophia had written that she struggled to recall. It had to do with this priest's critics, and his unflinching spirit in the face of opposition. . .

"I would take you in a minute, Père. Believe me, we need you. The only thing that gives me pause is where I can put you. We don't have a decent room. What once was supposed to be chaplain's quarters has six cots."

"But, I tell you I am used to cramped quarters on Martinique and the other islands, especially in the rainy season. Nothing could be worse. I don't need a cot. All I need is a space to hang a hammock, and I wouldn't need the space during the day, only at night, I could hang it up in the evening and take it down in the morning."

Mère Elisette was deeply impressed. This man was willing to sleep like the poor.

This was something she had never seen in the priests she had known.

"We could slip a cot into the chapel!" she mused after reflecting a bit. "Perhaps only a mattress."

"That would be perfect. I would be close to the Lord. After all, He had to sleep in an animal food trough the very day he was born."

Mère Elisette smiled again, her second smile of the day.

"Come with me." She picked up Antoine's knapsack. "I know where there is a spare mattress. But, have you eaten? I will take you to the kitchen first. Not fancy, but solid and nourishing."

The pair began to walk through the high-ceilinged open ward which was the hospital. They had to pick their way delicately. There was almost no space for them to walk among the more than one hundred cots and mattresses.

Antoine had only gone a few feet, before several patients raised themselves up as best they could, seeing the cassock and then waving to the priest; they called for a blessing. He stopped to make the Sign of the Cross over them. Most of the others were either too sick or sleepy to notice him.

"The priest will come back tomorrow, my friends." Mère Elisette steered him to the end of the long hall where the small chapel was. Some eight cots had replaced a number of pews. There was coughing and wiping of spittle on dirty rags.

Mère Elisette looked at Antoine for his reaction. She was wondering whether he would be up to the task he was setting for himself. She waited.

"Nearby parishes are pretty good about sending priests for the last rites. But it is next to impossible to get them to visit our patients. We desperately need visits to the women who are pregnant. They wait with a lot of fear."

She continued. "The only space I can offer you, Père Antoine," this was the first time she used his name, "is behind the altar there, as you suggested."

He surveyed the scene. If this was the price he had to pay for what he was after, he would pay it. He could string up a hammock. He was used to that. He never did need a lot of space for sleeping.

"You can leave your things right here, mon Père. We will see to it that a mattress is brought. See that door over there to the right. It leads to the quay. It's the best we can do for a bathroom. You will find your way when you get used to the darkness. We don't want you to fall into the Seine. Oh, by the way, you can come and go that way. You won't have to come through the ward. And in the evenings, you may want some fresh air. You might find some corpses on the quay from time to time at night, but we try to move them to the barges as soon as possible. You know there's the twenty-four hour rule."

Antoine completely forgot the problems that were on his mind. He was in a new world.

"And how long have you been here serving the sick, Mère Elisette?" he asked in quiet admiration.

"I'm going on my seventh year, come November. Oh, one more thing, I will have to talk to the archbishop in the morning, mon Père."

"Please, Mère Elisette," pleaded Antoine, "trust me in this also. Yes, eventually we must get the permission of the archbishop, but for a few days, please allow me to stay and work with you."

"All right, Père, but you know all to well that this arrangement will need higher approval. Unfortunately," she added, "that's the way it is."

"I am truly grateful to you, Mère." Antoine took her hand in gratitude.

"But, don't worry about the archbishop. I have been after him for help. I don't expect too many questions," she concluded as she was leaving.

"Your house is well named Hotel Dieu; it is truly the House of God," he said gratefully.

She paused a moment, then turned back to say: "…and large crowds came to him, bringing the lame, the crippled, the blind and the dumb, and many others; these they laid down at his feet and he cured them."

The words of Mère Elisette came to him later as he lay on his flimsy mattress, trying to adjust to the sounds and smells of human misery. But her words did not bring him peace. It was certainly not the mattress that kept him awake. It was more comfortable than the criss-crossed leather strips and the straw mat popular in the villages of Martinique.

Here in what was France's oldest shrine to the alleviation of human misery created by the noble Order of St. Augustine, he wondered about his own service to God. He had become one of the companions of St. Ignatius, promising to seek the glory of God at all times, ever ready to help others to live holier lives. And what had he done? Had he brought relief to the sick like Mère Elisette, or the teachings of Jesus to little children as Mère Gervase and Mère Sophia did in the villages around the island? What was he now? A rejected priest, exiled from the place and the people he had come to love. The Order that had received him to work under the banner of Christ was embarrassed on account of him. Rome itself had sent a visitor to investigate him, and now they had recalled him from his work.

This would be the first of many nights he would spend on the floor of *L'Hôtel Dieu*, waking and falling asleep again as he struggled to find a way to convince his fellow Jesuits that they should let him go back to Martinique.

CHAPTER VII

After a series of sleepless nights he made up his mind to call on the only Jesuit who was really familiar with the whole financial situation in Martinique. Père de Sacy was a friend on whom he could absolutely rely. He had to find out just what de la Marche had said, and to whom he must go to tell his side of the story. Antoine had paid little attention to his adversary back on the island. But he did remember him mentioning some financial troubles of the Marseilles banking house. Antoine would have to find out about that. It would be awkward because no one knew that he had returned from Martinique. He didn't want it known that he had been removed from office and summoned back to France. He was hesitant about calling on the only friend who could help him; but he had to know what de la Marche had said and how many people knew about it.

He thought about this for several days. In the meantime he followed a simple routine. He went from cot to cot, down on one knee for the most part, listening. This, he realized immediately, was the most important aspect of his presence. He blessed with Holy Water, prayed prayers of the sick and anointed with Holy Oil. He preferred that phrase to the proper title: "Extreme Unction," because that expression — the "last anointing" — meant death was at hand. And indeed death was at hand many days each month. There were also the lighter tasks of hearing confessions and giving out Holy Communion to those who could swallow. What was most important was giving the sick the chance to tell their story, something that neither the nuns nor the doctor had time to do.

Finally, one night after he found he could not concentrate while visiting patients, he decided he could no longer hide; he had to call on de Sacy, who could tell him what reports had come from Rome. Instead of leaving the information unchallenged, it made sense for him to be able to come forward with his version of what went on in Martinique.

In the dark he set out for the Jesuit church and residence which was seven blocks away. As he neared his destination, he noticed that several lampposts had tattered notices pinned to them. They seemed to increase in number the nearer he got to the priests' house. There hadn't been such posters in the vicinity of Notre Dame. Was there a connection?

He was able to read them despite the dim light. Miserably, he pored over the large print. He was not able to go though it all. It made him weak. He had to steady himself against the lamppost.

· · · · · · · · ·

EXTRAITS CONTRE LES JESUITES

Les demandes en condemnation solidaire, hazardees contre tous les Jesuites du Royaume, pour raison des Lettres de change tirees par le Père Antoine Lavalette, Superior de la Maison de S.Pierre de la Martinique[4]

· · · · · · · · ·

He could not read it all. His eyes blurred. The posters were rain stained; they had been there for some time, obviously.

What was this group condemnation all about? It was not easy for Antoine to walk the remaining distance to the Jesuit house. Should he go back and hide? Was this known beyond Paris? Had his name spread around the country? How could he face his fellow priests? He stopped dead. Would it be possible to slip into the residence without being seen by anyone but de Sacy? There were at least a half dozen priests living there. He could not go forward or backward. He simply could not fight this alone. So, he continued his way. At the front door, he hesitated again. He reached for the bell, but was frozen before it. Finally, he rang.

---

4 *Summary of charges against the Jesuits: Demands in connection with the group condemnation brought against all Jesuits of the Realm by reason of the letters of credit drawn by Père Antoine Lavalette, Superior of the Jesuit residence of St. Pierre , Martinique. (Source — 18th century pamphlet. National Archives, Fort du France,Martinique-1951.)*

After the third clang, a small window opened in the middle of the front door, showing the face of the brother doorkeeper. It was Frère André, Antoine later learned.

"What is it at this hour?"

"I have come to see Père de Sacy."

"Could this not wait until tomorrow?"

"I am a priest. I am a visiting Jesuit. My name is le Jeune," he lied. "Père de Sacy knows me."

Brother André raised the candle to the window to see whether his visitor was indeed clothed as a priest. Satisfied, he said, "I must consult with Père de Sacy. Pardon, Père, you must wait."

He waited impatiently. At last, the little window opened again. It was Père de Sacy peering out at him.

"Père le Jeune! I don't know any Père le Jeune. Where do you come from?"

"Jacques," whispered Antoine up close to the slot. "It's Antoine, from Martinique." It had been four years since they had seen one another.

"Antoine! Come in! Come in! I'm sorry, but it's been a while. I had no idea you were here."

The door opened quickly. Antoine and Jacques embraced.

"Brother," de Sacy turned to André, "The guest room is ready for Père Antoine, is it not?"

"Please, Jacques." Then turning to the brother anxiously, "Could you be so kind as to leave us alone? I wish to go to confession."

"Certainly, certainly," said André as he bowed and left.

"I cannot stay. I must go back to the hospital." Antoine said after the brother had gone.

"Hospital, what hospital? Are you sick?"

"No, you don't understand. Are you aware that I have been removed from being superior and Vicar Apostolic, and commanded to leave the mission?"

"No, we have not heard that. We've heard rumors that you were leaving the Caribbean and coming home, but we've been too busy having meetings about this lawsuit the creditors of Leoncy Freres and Gouffre are threatening to bring against all of us."

"Oh my Lord!" exclaimed Antoine in utter distress. "I feel terrible. My debts belong to the house in Martinique."

"That poster!" He was choked up. "That poster I saw on the lampposts! Is it all over Paris, all over the country that you are being accused on account of me? How can anyone blame you here in France for what happened to me?"

"That's exactly what our meetings are all about. They are blaming their bankruptcy on you. Since you can't be reached, they have directed their creditors to us."

"How badly you people must think of me!" interrupted Antoine, shaking his head. "Is it possible that some of the others in the house might drop in on us here? Can't we go to a private room where we can be alone, just you and me?"

"We could try the kitchen," suggested de Sacy. "Besides, no one will know who you are. Come, there is some tea on the stove. It should still be fairly warm."

There were still some fairly large embers in the stove, so de Sacy threw in a few small sticks while Antoine sat down at the kitchen table.

"One of the reasons I chose to stay at *L'Hôtel Dieu* is that I am ashamed to face my brothers after being removed from office. Now, what will they think if they face a lawsuit on account of me?"

"Maybe I can help you there," said de Sacy, trying to alleviate his distress. "I'm the only one who understands that your losses were caused by the pirate attack."

"But as soon as you start talking about the pirate attack, they will find about the sailors whom I killed."

De Sacy put the teapot on the table and poured tea into a cup for Antoine.

"Sugar?" he asked, as though he had not been shocked by Antoine's comment. Antoine shook his head. The pair began sipping tea in silence.

"Please don't tell anyone I've been here," pleaded Antoine.

"You know that's impossible. You may think that you can hide in *L'Hôtel Dieu*, but sooner or later someone will find out. It might just be a good thing for you to join us in these discussions about the lawsuit."

"How can I face them?"

"Did you ever think that we might need you here? You're the only one who knows all the details. The rest of us have been incapable of responding intelligently."

This remark made Antoine sit up. There was light in his eye for the first time. He took another sip of his tea.

"You will have to inform me about how this lawsuit started."

"It hasn't really started yet. There is only a threat so far."

"I don't understand."

"Do you remember the widow Grou?"

"Very well. She was very generous when I made an appeal for investments four years ago. And we have been writing to one another at least once a year."

"Well, she came to me a month or so ago to confide that she was in need of repayment on her loan to you. She came to me because I have been your intermediary for these ten, or has it been fifteen years, and I have been paying off your creditors once your shipments had been sold."

As the two continued to sip their tea, de Sacy began to recreate a scene played out while Antoine was still on his way back from Martinique.

De Sacy had been called to the parlor by Brother André to see Madame Grou. He had forgotten that she had come before to claim her credit on a loan. He had no idea of what was on her mind. On entering the parlor, he did remember her as one of Antoine's admirers.

What made it memorable was that on entering the parlor, before he could greet her or ask the purpose of her visit, her seven year old boy came running and shouting, "Mother, come see this picture."

"Child of God, you're embarrassing me. Come here at once." She had motioned to him.

Reluctantly, very reluctantly, Duval Grou had sat down beside his mother.

"Now stay here; don't be running about till we finish our business."

"But, there's a picture in that hallway of a woman who has a sword sticking into her chest and blood all down the front of her dress."

"Ssh, child. The priest is here to talk to us."

"But, it's so ugly!"

Madame Grou made a special effort to be patient.

"Remember that gospel story," she had whispered, "where Simeon says to Mary that a sword would pierce her side? That is what the picture was trying to tell you, son. It wasn't a real sword that he had in mind. He was trying to tell you that sorrow pierced her heart at the foot of the cross. Now, hush!"

The boy had been satisfied at least for the moment.

"I beg your pardon, Père," she stood up to greet de Sacy. "I had a little distraction here. I am Nancine Grou. And this is my son, Duval."

"I do remember you. Forgive me for not recognizing you immediately," de Sacy had said. "It's been some years. Please sit down. And how may I help you?"

"I was one of the early investors in your mission on Martinique, as I am sure you must remember now. I also deposited money to the account of Père Lavalette four years ago when he was here making an appeal for help to repair ten houses and some chapels that had been damaged by a hurricane. Some eight or nine years before that I gave money to your mission center here to build those houses, so I had a personal interest in their repair."

Now it came back to him. He had not been in charge at the time. But her name had always been prominent among the list of benefactors for the Caribbean mission.

"I don't remember exactly how long ago it was, but I did come to you with a letter of credit to redeem my initial investment. It was 15,000 *livres*, if I recall."

"Yes, yes, I do remember that distinctly," de Sacy hastened to say. "And you authorized me to contact the local representative of the Marseilles banking house. I received full payment plus interest. I abandoned that method shortly after and turned over all the claims to the banking house. I am sure you know that."

"Let me finish," the widow said. "Four years ago when I gave him 20,000 *livres* for the houses, he told me that a colonist had just turned over to the mission a plantation in Guadeloupe, I think it was. This plantation was certain to produce increased revenue with which he would be able to pay off all loans. This sounded so promising that I added another 10,000 to my loan."

De Sacy continued to listen politely.

"I was willing to grant him a two-year grace period. But now, we are well into the fourth year, and no payments. I have received a letter which he wrote some nine months ago explaining the difficulties he has suffered. I think I understand and I am willing to wait. However, now that the Marseilles bank has filed for bankruptcy, what I think doesn't matter. I am sure you are well aware by this time, that managers blame Père Lavalette for not paying his debts and causing the failure. So I am here to talk about the 30,000 that I am owed."

"Before we go on, Madame, I must make clear that I was only acting as an intermediary, not as any kind of a financial manager. Besides, when Père Antoine was here four years ago, I informed him of my intention to turn over all responsibility for handling his account to the local Leoncy office. It had become too much of a burden for me. Prior to that, Antoine had sent his shipments of sugar, molasses and cocoa to Bordeaux and Marseilles. Once these products were sold, the money was deposited with Leoncy Freres and Gouffre. Whenever a creditor came to me, I merely checked with the bank to find out what Père Antoine's balance was. I then sent the people to their office here in Paris. When the balance was not sufficient, I told the creditors to wait."

The widow Grou had been stirring uncomfortably in her chair, trying to keep Duval still and listen without interrupting de Sacy's lengthy explanation.

"This is all past history and totally irrelevant," Madame Grou said very pointedly. "I am in a somewhat embarrassing position. I was duly paid back with interest before. I am not here to collect money. I have every confidence Père Lavalette will pay me back again."

She continued, "But things have changed. That disgraceful poster that has been circulating! Many of us don't know what to think."

De Sacy leaned forward in his chair. "We are of one mind, Madame. All of us are worried about this threat from the banking house, or rather from the creditors."

"Before we go on, Père, I think there is something all the priests should know. I am not alone in thinking that there was incompetent management in the office of Leoncy Freres. We think that Père Lavalette is a convenient scapegoat. However, we will never be able to prove that. The important thing to remember is that the majority of those who have invested in Martinique are your friends. As Catholics, they would find it abhorrent to take you to court. But when money is involved, it's different. I am convinced that most of us will wait and not push to take the matter to court. However, someone is pushing a few of the creditors to take action immediately. I'm not sure who that is. It's imperative that you priests do something other than telling them to wait."

At this point Duval was impatient. The heavy conversation was boring.

"Isn't he ugly, Mama?" He had blurted this out before his mother could cover his mouth. There was another picture that caught his eye. On the wall was a sallow looking portrait of the face of a man in a black cassock.

"Shush, son."

It was a nervous moment for de Sacy. He had not meant to be stern to little Duval.

"That, young man, is our Holy Founder, St. Ignatius of Loyola."

"We better not prolong this, Père de Sacy," said the widow, looking down at her boy. The widow continued, "As I said, I am in an embarrassing position and I don't think I have made it clear. Believe me, I trust Père Antoine. The letter I received after a long delay explained his situation well. I am not blindly trusting, however. I, too, want my assurance. My main purpose in being here is to make sure that you priests are fully aware that a lawsuit is looming. Most of the creditors could possibly be persuaded to hold off."

"Thank you immensely for your advice. We have already had a meeting to discuss how we need to handle this matter. Fortunately, we still have some time to head off a court hearing."

"Only a few of the creditors know what I know from the letter Père Antoine sent me," continued Madame Grou. "They do not know as yet that he lost his cargo to a pirate attack. They need to know that he has found a safer route, even though it is a roundabout one and will take much longer. A payment of interest to each and every one would, in my judgment, win a delay."

For de Sacy, her views were comforting because he, too, trusted Antoine. Translating that trust into the shared confidence that would move his brother Jesuits to make a financial commitment to stave off court action would be the task ahead of him.

Fortunately, neither she nor de Sacy had any idea about the orders from Rome that had arrived at Martinique, and that now Antoine could do nothing about shipping sugar and molasses to Holland, or any other place, much less instill confidence in creditors.

In the kitchen, de Sacy's long narrative finally ended. Antoine was stunned; his tea had cooled to the point of distaste. One positive effect of de Sacy's bringing him up to date was that he was no longer thinking of his personal pain, his loss of his island home, his present exile. He was thinking only of the problem facing his brothers in the Order, and what to do about it. Their problem was his!

"How can I be of help? What can I do? I must do something. This is all my fault."

"The first thing you can do," replied de Sacy, "is get rid of the idea that you can hide in *L'Hôtel Dieu*. Everyone has been descending on me. I'm supposed to know everything. Second, you have to help me."

"Where do we begin?" Antoine asked.

"We have sixty days to respond to a mandate from the Consulate of Paris summoning me, Père Jacques de Sacy, to a pre-hearing. I am supposed to show cause why as head of the Jesuits of Martinique, I should not be held liable for 1,650,000 *livres*, deposited with Leoncy, Gouffre Freres by sixteen investors for your mission."

"How can they proceed against you? I'm the one to whom they were sending their money."

Père de Sacy shook his head.

"This is too much for one night," complained Antoine. "But, if you say I can't hide in *L'Hôtel Dieu*, what do you want me to do?"

Père de Sacy was silent for a moment.

"This is Friday. Nothing can be done over the weekend. We have called a meeting for Monday of thirty two Jesuits, most from here, but a dozen who have to come in from Picardie, Champagne and Marne. Père Larousse will be there as well. The point of the gathering is: what can be done about the summons?"

"Do you think they will abide my presence? And how can I help? We need a lawyer." Antoine was not exactly coherent.

"We need both you and a lawyer. We have invited an old friend, the Marèchal del Belle Isle."

"I don't want to talk about anything more right now," said Antoine wearily. "I better set out for the hospital."

He got up from the table and briefly embraced de Sacy who saw him to the door. It had been a difficult evening. There was more to oppress him than when he set out.

On his way back in the darkness, he avoided looking for any tattered posters. But there was no way he could divert his thoughts, and so after arriving at *L'Hôtel Dieu*, he lay sleepless for many an hour. It would become harder each night. His life had become bizarre. During the day he was faithful in visiting the sick, blessing them, trying to hear their confessions, which were more tales of woe than narratives of misdeeds. He anointed them with holy oil, struggled to comfort them, groped for the appropriate words. On occasion, he had to help carry the dead out to the wharf where the barges picked them up. All in all, to deal with the distress of others was an escape of a kind.

The following week brought a series of frantic meetings by groups of Jesuits around the city. It was truly disturbing for them to learn that as a group, they all were in danger of being hauled into court. There was a fierce discussion of how to deal with the crisis. Those in Paris were evenly divided on the issue of borrowing some money to hold off the creditors. However, the regional superior, Père Larousse, and three of his four advisors were adamant in refusing to become entangled in settling a debt not their own. They were the ones who would make the final decision.

Once the Jesuits in the provinces heard all the details, there was a majority in favor of borrowing money that might stave off a court trial. Their view was practical rather than theoretical. They claimed that the political atmosphere was not right for challenging the charges leveled against them, however unjust. But they also recognized that they had no voice in the final decision, so they did their best to rally the Parisian contingent around them. Their hope was to increase their majority by the next Monday, with members coming in from as far away as Lorraine and Normandie.

When the regional Superior, Père Larousse, got wind of this organizing, he demanded an immediate halt. However he soon realized he was being ignored, so he sat down at once to write a letter to Rome, informing the Major Superior that his men were violating the norms set down by their Holy Founder, St. Ignatius. They had become infected with the pernicious philosophy of the day, the republicanism taught by such people as Diderot and his coterie of so called philosophers. They were committing the unpardonable, trying to solve a problem by majority vote.

While this letter was on its slow journey to Rome, the committee whose numbers had now risen to thirty-eight, continued to exchange ideas. After a tumultuous debate, they reduced their committee to five, which included de Sacy and two professors from the College Louis le Grand, one from Normandie and one from Lorraine.

This group was commissioned to call upon the Marèchal del Belle Isle, a highly respected friend, who had a son in the Jesuit seminary. Their task was to convince the Marèchal to plead with the regional superior and his four advisers to follow a course of compromise. Now that they knew Antoine was in their midst, they put aside all hostility because they needed his experience to inform them about all the pertinent details. They wanted him present when they met with the Marèchal. Not all were happy with this decision; the debate that followed almost destroyed the whole endeavor. But finally, they came to admit that they needed all resources available. They were jeopardizing their chances with the regional Superior and his advisers, who would never allow Antoine near their door. But without Antoine's detailed knowledge of the financial history, the Marèchal would be incapable of pleading their cause to Père Larousse.

The news that he had been called upon to inform the Marèchal came to Antoine in a note brought by a messenger to the hospital one evening. Once again, he made his way over the seven blocks to the Jesuit residence. Once again, he tried not to look at the tattered posters which made him famous and infamous at the same time.

His entrance into a committee of five Jesuits was awkward. They were still not comfortable with the idea that the cause of their troubles was in their midst. But the serious matter before them made formalities as well as amenities unnecessary. He was invited to speak first.

"My dear brothers in Christ," he began to a skeptical audience. "I should inform you that I have visited the widow Grou and her son in order to learn about the possible lawsuit against us to collect what I owe. I realize that in your mind I am the cause of this possible lawsuit. But I want you to know that I have found an infinitely safer route for my shipments from the islands. I can promise the creditors who are considering this legal action that if they will be patient, they will be paid in full, with interest. In the meantime, I beg you to authorize a loan that will pay fair interest on the debt to each and every one of the creditors. Such a move would be pointless unless I am permitted to return to Martinique to take charge once again of the management of the sugar plantations."

Antoine embraced his old friend and sat down. The Marèchal del Belle Isle, one of whose sons he had taught many years ago at Louis le Grande before leaving for the Caribbean, was moved.

After a brief introduction, the Marèchal began to speak.

"I have been asked to present the legal aspect of your situation, as I see it. What Père Antoine has suggested makes perfect sense to me." He looked toward the Superior Larousse, who was not impressed.

"The first thing you should all know is that the Consulate of Paris is making a pretense of being a higher court. You have to know that it is not a court. It is a legal body that has jurisdiction over disputes between merchants, primarily disputes about the quality of the merchandise, delivery and payment, credit and debts, and such things.

"You Jesuits here in Paris do not qualify in any sense as merchants. You were never partners in any transaction. Secondly, the court must honor Grotius Law which is respected by all nations, even England. There are various clauses which pertain to international shipping, and one of them is that in any dispute or complaint the laws which govern the nation where the shipping contract was made take precedence. I have not had much experience with such matters personally, but the law is perfectly clear.

"So, the contracts made belong under the jurisdiction of Martinique. Any charge of violating a contract must start and finish there, not here. The island may belong to France, but it is not France. These contracts were made with individual ship captains who were working for specific companies. There were payments in advance, loading costs, costs of shipping, costs of unloading. The sale of the produce, credit for the sale and deposits were all separate transactions.

"I don't mean to bore you with financial details. My purpose is to show you that the Consulate of Paris has absolutely no right to handle this case, and of course, it has no right to charge you as a group for merchandise not delivered, or payments not made.

"There is something else in Church law, which I learned after consulting Bishop Emile Gregorian, and that concerns the independence of houses of religious men and women. The significance of this is that this independence is recognized by civil law as well. A whole religious order cannot legally be held responsible for the indebtedness of what an individual house incurs. But enough of this legal detail. Now, I want to talk to you as your friend and adviser, not as your lawyer, which I am not. I am personally somewhat mystified by this potential lawsuit. It should be thrown out of any court. But the fact that it hasn't is disturbing to me. I need to consult with a few of my friends about this.

"And now, I think it is imperative that we listen to Père Antoine so that we have some idea of what happened in Martinique, especially details about transactions and loans."

There was a stirring among the committee, caused by the obvious discomfiture of the Superior, Larousse. But it caused no hesitation for the Maréchal, who sat down and motioned to Antoine.

Out of the group before him, only de Sacy had any idea of what Antoine was about to present. Not all were hostile, obviously. But Antoine had to be brief, eloquent and above all, clear. He launched into his narrative. He had the advantage of the Marèchal's intimation that something irregular was behind the present financial threat.

In his explanation he stressed the key points: the poverty of the mission, the area that had to be covered, the illnesses of the missionaries. He did his best to make his audience see that setting up plantations was not an ill-conceived scheme. Moreover, he stressed the disillusionment of many colonists who were anxious to get back home with as much of their original investment as possible. Not all present were satisfied with his explanation of why he was recalled to France four years previously by the Governor's order. But they were sympathetic while listening to the narrative of the pirate attack.

And, happily, none of them had as yet heard the story about Noel and why he had met death at the hands of the privateers. Only de Sacy knew.

Antoine did a good job of arguing in favor of a new and safer route, however delayed. It made sense to say that the new route would be a step toward ultimately removing the threat of a lawsuit, and that he would have to return to the Caribbean to be in charge of lifting that financial threat.

When Antoine finished, he felt that he had achieved reasonable success. Of course, the handicap was that Larousse was there without his advisers, who would be key players when the final choice was made. His present audience was open and not particularly concerned about the Church law approach which de la Marche had proposed at their headquarters in Rome.

Antoine had another worry that he could not even share with de Sacy. His hope was that de la Marche had been so preoccupied with Church law and books and numbers that he had not looked into the nature of Captain Byrne's run up the east coast of Yanqui country. "Smuggling" was not a good word to bandy about when trying to describe what he and Isaac were doing in their struggle to get out of debt, especially to these priests who held Antoine's future in their hands.

Like a pastor eyeing his parishioners during his sermon, Antoine had been scanning the eyes of the Jesuits in front of him, a very critical audience at any time. He had not picked up any sign as to whether he had succeeded or not. The questions to follow would give him an idea.

"So," one of the committee began, "you're saying that the accusation of forbidden commerce is linked to the necessity of trying to put the mission on a stable financial footing?"

"Correct," nodded Antoine.

"But those of us who heard about your recall to France by civil authorities have been concerned about your credibility. If the government is investigating, you must have done something. This causes serious doubts in my mind."

"My answer may sound simplistic, but it is absolutely true. People can believe it or not. I have no way of controlling their reaction. The truth is that one colonist, St. Etienne by name, wanted to get out from under his financial burden and get back to France with a profit, just as two of his fellow colonists had done. He became furious over our refusal to handle his plantation. We simply could not undertake a wholly new obligation at that time. As a result, he retaliated with a clever legalistic charge that we were dealers on foreign soil, the island of Guadeloupe. Perhaps you don't know that the ownership of the island is under dispute with England. As long as the title is in contention, we are perfectly free to work there. What confused the issue was the report that a priest, above all a Jesuit, was running a commercial business in collaboration with England on French territory. This is what caught the public's attention.

"Please," Antoine continued, "there are two more major considerations which you have to think about. Keep in mind what I said about being called back to France because of a misunderstanding. M. de Cresols had a plantation whose annual potential is worth more than 200,000 *livres* in sugar and molasses. He turned that plantation over our Jesuit mission, of which I am in charge — at least I was in charge before de la Marche went to Rome. All Cresols wanted was to go back to France. He was tired of being a colonist. His only condition was a guaranteed pension of 12,000 *livres* per year. At the time, he was only using a third of his property, and that not very well. His offer to me was like getting a gold mine in Peru. Any French plantation owner in the Caribbean would have embraced this offer. But the only one who expressed jealousy, and did something about it, was M. de Cazotte. He is the one who went to the Governor, not because of any concern for Church law, but because he wanted in the worst way to get his hands on Cresol's property."

Père de Sacy turned to his companions.

"That's certainly not the way we heard the story. Our Superior gave us a talk in which he urged us to write to Rome to get Antoine out of Martinique because he was disgracing the Jesuits by his commercial dealings with England."

Before any one else could comment, Antoine went on excitedly.

"Before I came to this meeting, as I told you, I visited the widow Grou.

She is my friend; she is our friend. All she is asking of us is a reasonable guarantee. And, as Père de Sacy must have told you by now, she is also asking us to make similar guarantees to those who are willing to wait. In addition, she is asking us to borrow money to pay off those creditors who can't wait or who are unwilling to wait. So it is not all the creditors that we have to deal with.

"Furthermore," he rushed on, "there is something else you must hear, something she told me for us alone. She has been advised by a close friend, who is also one of the creditors of Leoncy and Gouffre, to plead her cause using an argument which should scare us all. She has been told, and she showed me the first draft of a letter in which the argument is that I was the Superior General of the Isles de Vent, and the Vicar Apostolic, the highest authority of the Church and of the Jesuits in Rome. In addition, the letter emphasized that I was named to my post by the Provincial Superior of Paris which means I represented all the Jesuits of France. When I had funds transferred from the ports of Bordeaux and Marseilles to Père de Sacy, he became my deputy. He, too, was appointed financial administrator by the Superior in Paris."

Antoine continued, "Do you see what this type of approach implies? Someone is trying to hurt us all by making us responsible for paying Madame Grou her 30,000 *livres*."

The priests present shook their heads in disbelief. Antoine went on quickly.

"Madame Grou would never have come up with an argument like that on her own, mons pères. Think about it." With that he sat down.

The room was silent. He waited for questions or comments. Since nothing was forthcoming, he got up and left the room.

As he went out the door he said to himself, "I've done all I could."

Antoine hadn't realized that though he thought he was talking to himself, his words were more than clear to the five priests. A vigorous discussion ensued, not really challenging anything Antoine had said, but searching for ways to persuade the Provincial Superior and his four advisers to make the final decision to settle with some creditors, and make guarantees with others..

The next day the group of five Jesuits arranged for an interview with the Marèchal del Belle Isle. Their plan was to have him with them as they approached Père Larousse. They knew that the Provincial Superior would not meet with them and his inner circle of four who were the decision makers. Larousse would probably not be open to their pleas alone and they could not bring in Antoine with them. They were convinced that there was no time for delay, so they made a special trip to Larousse's office, pleading for a special interview with the Marèchal at their side. The group gathering was refused, but Larousse agreed to see the Marèchal alone on their behalf. He was their only hope for changing the minds of the decision-makers.

Suspense reigned the following weekend and on into mid-week when the committee of five learned the details of the meeting. The Marèchal was received politely. However, Père Larousse was not to be persuaded. He was still unwilling to involve the Jesuits in any way in a debt not their own. He and his confidantes had received the same advice from all their advisors: money paid to the widow Grou, or to anyone else, and any kind of assurances given on the part of Jesuits would open the door to a wholesale commitment for the rest of his community. Any acceptance of Père Antoine's obligations would establish the legal link the priests had to deny, namely, that Jesuits in France were in any way liable for debts in Martinique. What clinched his opposition was that someone reported to him that Antoine was the source of the advice to cooperate with the widow.

The Marèchal informed the group of five that he could not convince Larousse that the priest's argument would hold up in a court room, or that an effort to give assurance to creditors would keep them from going to court.

The following week Père Larousse sent out a letter to all the Jesuits in and around Paris:

Sept. 21, 1761

My Dear Brothers in Christ!

Pax Christ!

In the matter of the pending lawsuit before the Consulate of Paris, it has been suggested by prudent men that we as a group head off a pending court case by settling matters with Madame Grou and her son, thus preventing a public hearing.

After taking the matter to prayer, and seeking the best advice possible, legal and secular, my advisers and I have decided to entrust our just cause to the jurisprudence of the court. It seems to us reasonable to place our confidence in the justice system.

In the event that Madame Grou pursues her intention and goes to court, we have every confidence that justice will be done. We have hired good lawyers who are willing to appear in the tribunal if necessary. They have solid arguments with which to deny any responsibility for debts incurred by Père Antoine in the Caribbean. The fact that some among us fear that we as a group may be summoned into court because of the investments and mismanagement of Père Antoine Lavalette, should not deter us. Any judge worthy of his reputation will dismiss this case immediately. I hope I have made it clear that this position is not mine alone, but the result of hearing the opinions of our lawyers who challenge the competency of the Court to rule here. It is their legal experience on which we depend and they are the ones who assert that our law here in France is not relevant to the dispute. Neither Père Antoine in the Caribbean nor the Jesuits are dealers in local merchandise.

Hence, after hearing the advice of my consulting team, it is my judgment to advise Madame Grou that at this time we cannot make any commitment to payment of what is clearly a Martinique obligation.

Your servant in the Lord,

P. Claude Larousse, OS

It was almost midday on a Monday in *L'Hôtel Dieu*, when two volunteer nurses came picking their way through the crowd of the sick seeking Père Antoine. At the moment he was baptizing a baby in the arms of a fearful mother. The child was only two months old and had a high fever. Fearing death, and the possibility that her daughter might not be allowed into heaven unless baptized, she had frantically sought out the priest.

The nurses came upon the pair in a corner. Simultaneously, they called out, "Père Antoine."

One began immediately to explain, "There's a priest at the wharf entrance looking for you. He says it's extremely important."

With a wave of his hand, he told them to wait. He was weary because Monday mornings were always a frantic. There were fewer volunteers on Sunday, the nuns had to hear Mass before going on duty and they also needed their day of rest after a tedious week. As a result there were always a number of patients that had come in with demands for immediate attention.

Actually, Mondays, tiring as they might be, were a blessing for Antoine. He was far from Martinique. He was the priest, the consoler, the healer. These were people who needed him. The nuns and volunteers had come to love him in a very short time. He was the first priest in a long while to live in *L'Hôtel Dieu*. The hospital had become his adopted home.

So it was with reluctance that he turned from the child and its mother. Instinctively he knew it was de Sacy, and that it was bad news — news he didn't want to hear. Unfortunately, it brought him back to the reality of money and debts and claims and hostility, matters that didn't belong in the hospital.

As he walked back through the large ward, he untied the white apron he wore to protect his cassock, and threw it over his shoulder. He had to ignore the hands raised to attract his attention. Even though he wanted to stop, he knew that his friend, de Sacy, was desperate. No one, not even priests, made the trek past the Cathedral of Notre Dame along the wharf to the hospital unless there was an emergency.

CHAPTER VIII

"**C**an we go out to the fresh air," was the only greeting that de Sacy offered when the two met.

Antoine nodded. He handed his apron to one of the volunteers and the pair went out.

"Look at this," de Sacy began. "Read it!" He handed Antoine a formal looking parchment.

Before Antoine could even begin to read the warrant, de Sacy burst out with great emotion, "Antoine, two gendarmes came to the door a short time ago. They served me with a summons. I am to appear in court tomorrow as a defendant, as representative of the whole Jesuit Order. Madame Grou is suing me for 30,000 *livres*."

Antoine tried to sound sympathetic.

"But, Jacques, you should not feel guilty. I have been trying to convince anyone who would listen to me that we should guarantee her what I owe, and then let me talk to the others. If Larousse had allowed me to make her an offer, we could have prevented this lawsuit. She knows perfectly well that the plantation in Dominique alone can bring in a half-million *livres* within a two year period even with the most careless management."

"But that doesn't help me. I'm the one who has to appear before the judge. What am I to do or say? You have to help me; you're the only one who can persuade Madame Grou to call off her lawsuit. There's still time."

"But I can't go to her and say, 'Nancine, please wait. Please be patient; give me more time. The Jesuits here don't owe you money.' She's heard this just once too often; she's not going to listen any more. She wants action. You and your friends have to go to Larousse and convince him to let me go back to Martinique. He's not going to pay attention to anything I say. He's just like de la Marche, who could not see anything but buying and selling. The situation is much more complicated. You can't solve any problem by blindly citing the rules of the Church out of Rome. There's a war going on. England is our enemy and they have legalized pirates patrolling the waters. French or Spanish crews don't have a chance. Only the Yanquis can challenge the English on the high seas. And I have a contact with the Yanquis. Jacob Byrne has outwitted the English customs officials in Boston and the vigilantes around Jamaica for ten years. He owns his ship, and believe it or not, he is my friend."

De Sacy was shaking his head all the while Antoine was talking.

"Have you informed Larousse of the summons?" Antoine went on, after futilely looking for a better reaction from his friend. He was desperately seeking a way to comfort him.

De Sacy shook his head.

"It's almost noon," said Antoine looking up at the sun over the cathedral spires. "You have a few hours to round up some Jesuits and get over to call on Larousse. That's the only advice I can give. Unless he will make some form of guarantee regarding the 30,000 *livres* in writing, I can't go near Madame Grou. And you can tell him, if he does write out a promissory note with a guarantee of payment that I can take to Nancine, there's an excellent chance that she will back off. She's a good woman. She doesn't need the money right now. She is thinking primarily of her son, Duval."

De Sacy was still deeply depressed and fearful. He didn't have a lot of time. He had to hire a carriage to get across the city to the provincial's residence. It would be impossible to get his small group together. Two were in college teaching at Louis le Grand, two others were in the parish of St. Remi and the fifth was thirty miles away, impossible to reach. He could not even be sure Père Larousse was available to see him on such short notice.

"I am going to be all alone in front of three judges," moaned de Sacy. "I may not even have a lawyer at my side."

"This has to be a preliminary hearing. They can't expect a defense team to be assembled in twenty-four hours," said Antoine, again trying to relieve de Sacy's anxiety.

The two walked on in silence up past the cathedral to the bridge where the carriages were parked.

"I can only say God be with you," said Antoine. "I will be in the court as soon as I can tomorrow. I have a funeral Mass. I'll try to be there around ten."

"The summons says 'Appear at 9:00 A.M. sharp.'" de Sacy said gloomily, as he left for the carriage station and waved a feeble farewell to Antoine.

It wasn't until 10:30 A.M. the next day that Antoine was able to leave the barge where the body had been blessed with holy water, incensed and dispatched down the Seine. He hurried as fast as he could to the Consulate of Paris. As he entered the courtroom, he saw what de Sacy and he had dreaded. The priest stood alone in front of the judges who were about to render an opinion.

"Reverend de Sacy, you have heard the evidence against you. However, before we pass sentence we wish to accord you the opportunity to speak in your defense. Have you anything to say?"

De Sacy was nervous and perspiring. He felt like a condemned criminal and had a difficult time trying to formulate his reply.

"Your honors, I feel it is an injustice to expect me to offer an adequate defense with so little time for preparing my response. I have been unable to engage one single lawyer to speak on my behalf. It is also unjust that I am held responsible for the Jesuits in France and in the Caribbean.

"I neither drew the letter of change for Madame Grou, nor did I endorse it, nor did I accept it. My role was only as an intermediary. When I received funds from Père Antoine through the merchants of New York or other cities, I deposited them in the name of our mission in Martinique. When Madame Grou sent me a claim for the money she invested in the construction of houses at St. Pierre, I withdrew the funds that were on deposit. I was in no way a party of the transaction.

"It is totally unjust," he continued, "to hold me and my brother Jesuits responsible in any way for payment of a letter of change that was not ours. I cannot say any more at this time, and I humbly petition the Court for an adjournment until such time as I can have a lawyer here to assist me." He sat down.

"Reverend de Sacy, it will please the Court if you remain standing."

The priest arose and stood before them again.

"It is the opinion of the Court that there have already been months of delay for this hearing, almost an entire year. You and your confreres have had more than sufficient time to prepare your defense. Your point about lawyers is not well taken because we have all the documents we need from your lawyers to plead your defense.

"And as for your second point, we have evidence to prove that your official title was Procurator General of the Missions. Said title was conferred upon you by one Père Camille Larousse, to whom you owe absolute obedience. As a consequence, there is a legal bond between the one under whose command all Jesuits work and the outreach to works in the Caribbean."

"This is not a proprietary bond, but an administrative bond," de Sacy almost shouted, in a futile effort to establish a vital distinction which Belle Isle had emphasized more than once to the priests.

"You have exhausted the time we allotted you. It would be out of order to prolong this debate," said the leading judge. "You will please remain standing until we have finished our final conference."

The three men put their heads together briefly. They all nodded in unison.

"Reverend Jacques de Sacy," began the lead judge, "we hereby hold you as Procurator General of the Jesuit Missions fully responsible for payment of 30,600 *livres* to the widow, Grou. Such payment includes court costs and interest. And we add that in default thereof the plaintiff can proceed against the houses and colleges, in short, against the properties of the said religious Order of Jesuits."

De Sacy shook his head in disbelief. Antoine put his arm around his shoulders. There wasn't much he could or wanted to say. They walked out of the courtroom together.

The following day, Père Larousse was indeed available to his fellow Jesuits. More than twenty-five priests descended on the provincial headquarters to listen to de Sacy tell his account of what happened the day before. What shocked them was in part the nature of the judgment against them, but mainly the fact that the news was all over Paris by the following morning. In a couple of days they would realize that messages were coming in from Provence and even Toulouse. What really disturbed the priests that day and during the weeks that followed was the nature of the message that was being repeated. It was not the widow Grou, but a poor widow with a child she could not support. It wasn't an individual priest who had drawn a single letter of credit, it was the whole Jesuit Order in France responsible for fraud. Père Antoine Lavalette's name appeared at the bottom of a new pamphlet that was being circulated. But it was not his name that caught people's eye. What stuck in their minds was: Jesuits guilty of defrauding a poor helpless widow.

That shock was followed by an after shock. Once the judges of the Consulate of Paris had established the precedent of making the Order responsible for Lavalette's obligation to the widow, they could not reasonably deny the claims of other creditors. Within two weeks, the sum rose to 400,000 *livres*, with much more to come. There was no way to tell the creditors to wait until the end of the war with England. Pursuing the banking house of Leoncy and Gouffre was hopeless, but going after one-hundred twelve Jesuit colleges and houses offered ideal quarry. Soon the amount sought rose to three million.

Evenings, Père de Sacy would seek out Antoine for refuge and to report on the almost daily meetings of the Jesuits with Père Larousse. From the very beginning, Antoine had suggested the name of the Marèchal del Belle Isle, member of the Parliament, highly respected and friend of the Jesuits. The reason he did so was that his colleagues were only talking to lawyers. They had called in the Marèchal very briefly and ignored his advice about settling with the widow. Now they were concentrating on their lawyers. Because of his acquaintance with his eldest son many years before, Antoine had set up a private interview with the Marèchal.

One evening after he had taken care of all the sick calls, he set out for the residence of the Marèchal. It was only a thirty-minute walk, and in the event Belle Isle could not see him, he would still benefit by the exercise. Above all, he would find relief from the oppressive atmosphere of *L'Hôtel Dieu*.

It was more than a happy coincidence that Antoine encountered the Marèchal at home. Not only was he available and delighted to see the priest who had been close to his son, he was relieved to have him at his side for an entirely different reason. At that very moment, he had been in conference with M. de la Croix, a lawyer, and one of the group to whom the Jesuits had been talking intensely ever since the judgment had been handed down by the lower court. Four of the priests had taken it upon themselves to meet separately with de la Croix as their adviser. Bigger meetings with the priests had become unmanageable, and self-defeating. So this group met apart, trying to do an impartial analysis of the decision against them and seeking counsel on how to plan an appeal. The problem was: to whom should they appeal?

There was a confusing procedure for appeals of decisions handed down by the Consulate of Paris. There was no consensus, even among lawyers, about that court's jurisdiction or its constitutional authority to adjudicate the case. Then there was the Parliament itself, which the lawyers had researched only to find that it claimed, amazingly, the status of a higher court. A third avenue of appeal was the Royal Council, the King and his inner circle of advisers.

It was an ideal moment for Antoine to come upon the scene. How to proceed in seeking legal assistance: this was the question. To whom do you turn for help to be rescued from an indictment? This was on the minds of the two men who welcomed Antoine into their midst.

After the initial greetings were over, de la Croix addressed Antoine.

"I am so happy you have come, Père Antoine. We have been discussing for some time now, the Marèchal and I, a rather puzzling aspect of the judgment decreed by the Consulate."

"Thanks be to God that you are aware of what we are going through," said Antoine.

"I am not alone," explained de la Croix. "Once the Marèchal informed us about your case, we were able to get a dozen lawyers interested. We've narrowed our group to three and we've only had a couple of meetings so far. We're deliberating over the method of appeal. So far we have settled on one conclusion and it is that the judgment is illegal. But where do we go from here? That is our puzzle."

"Sounds rather discouraging," said Antoine. "We desperately need your help in this situation that I have inflicted upon on my fellow priests."

"You have the Marèchal to thank for enlisting us on your side," de la Croix nodded respectfully to his friend.

"Not being a lawyer," interjected the Marèchal, "I had no idea how to proceed. I was apprehensive about what was threatening you. Fortunately, M. de la Croix and several of his friends were right there to help."

He gestured to the lawyer to begin.

"Père de Sacy told me that he was seeking legal help, but he didn't give me any details. If you could be so kind as to tell me what exactly your group has in mind, I would be very grateful. I have a very definite plan in mind that I would like to share with you, but perhaps it should wait until you tell me what you are thinking.

"As you can imagine," continued de la Croix, "we were totally taken aback by the judgment against you, but even more so by the fact that it immediately became a *cause célebre*."

"What stirred us all into action," the Marèchal intervened, "was that within two weeks, the amount involved rose to three million *livres*."

Sadness marked Antoine's face. It was the first time he had heard this.

"It was not the huge amount as much as the assertion of collective liability that really disturbed the advocates. It was the unprecedented decision that a commercial claims court could maintain that it had such extensive jurisdiction," de la Croix went on.

The Marèchal intervened again.

"I have tried without success to convince these legal minds that there is something sinister in all this, something hidden that has me puzzled. I'm not sure the lawyers are able to do any better. And that is where you come in, Père Antoine."

The priest sat there for a moment shaking his head. Then he quietly made a suggestion. "To go from the complaint of a widow seeking payment of 30,000 *livres* to the sum of three million in just a few weeks requires some looking in to. I think I have an idea of what might be behind this. It involves a Church dispute. When I get an opportunity, I will also go into deeper research about something Madame Grou told me."

"Which was?" queried the Marèchal.

"Suffice it to say that when she first talked to me she said that one of the main reasons she came to us was because there were a couple of men contacting different creditors, urging them to start a lawsuit. They were in no way connected with the bank. She told me that she couldn't remember their names. When I started asking around, I never received a satisfactory answer."

Antoine continued, "It is important for you both to know when next you talk to Larousse, that Madame Grou advised me to seek some kind of settlement not just with her, but with all claimants in order to prevent further trouble."

"It is getting late," the Marèchal interrupted. "Pierre de la Croix and I reviewed this dilemma for a couple of hours before you came. We will have to continue another evening." The Marèchal stood up.

"Where does that leave us?" asked Antoine, somewhat disappointed.

"At the moment, the lawyers who are at your side are saying that the judgment against the Jesuits is a departure from the judicial practice of the day. And in our opinion, it is illegal. The only persons who could be charged with liability were those who signed the letters of credit, or the co-signers, or those who benefited by the transaction. Jesuits in France did not fall into any of these categories. In addition, we're almost unanimous in our opinion that the Consulate lacked jurisdiction in the matter. We have said this more than once. To whom do we make our appeal is our problem now."

Thus did de la Croix sum up what the two of them had been talking about.

"I want you to know that I am deeply grateful for your participation." Antoine was also on his feet. "As for the appeal, I will present my plan the next time we meet. In the meantime, I beg you and your lawyers to contact Père Larousse. From what I have been able to learn from my few conversations with Père de Sacy, Larousse is convinced that we must appeal directly to the Parliament."

Before the threesome parted at the door, Antoine said, "You know, I am the one who will be blamed no matter what happens. I just can't wait for another meeting. I will send you a copy of the plan I suggest. I will send it tomorrow." The three men went out into the night.

Antoine walked on in the direction of the cathedral. He looked back briefly as he started off. Antoine watched as the pair dallied for a time chatting. Hopefully, they were talking about the implications he had raised. He began walking swiftly. He needed the physical exercise that might clear his brain.

After some blocks, he reached the Rue St. Nazare. Tallow candles hung from the casements in the houses along the way. People were still up. For some reason he had ignored *La Place de Grève* when he was coming, but now he could discern it in the shadows. Perhaps it was the mood he was in that made him stop and observe thoughtfully. This was the site of public executions, where criminals had been put to death. Here Damens had been beheaded twenty years ago after his abortive attempt on the life of Louis XV. At the time, the mob witnessing the execution had been unruly — so much so that a Royal Guard had been dispatched to watch the Jesuit residence beside the Church of St. Charles nearby. Certain parliamentarians, who were not particularly devoted to the King, had made a point of reminding the public that the Jesuit, Busenbaum, had taught that under certain circumstances it was legitimate to assassinate a King.

Antoine walked on past the locale, trying to pray. He was hoping that he might be granted the chance to return to the Caribbean, where he knew he could earn the money to pay his debts and deliver his fellow Jesuits from legal disputes. But *La Place de Grève* was not a place to stimulate hope, so he quickly turned back, heading for the river.

"*Restez-en la.*" Antoine was shocked by a sharp command. It was a gendarme who hauled the startled priest by the arm to the nearest lamplight. But once there, the embarrassed gendarme quickly apologized.

"*Monsieur le Curé, Je suis dans l'erreur.*"

Perhaps he was not that far wrong, thought Antoine, as he struggled to think of a reply. I am the culprit. He hesitated. At last he thought of something.

"Pouvez-vous me dire comment aller a l'eglise de Sainte Charles?"

The gendarme was more than eager to direct him with effusive apologies. Antoine turned and pretended to go back the way he had come. Once around the next corner he headed for the cathedral square and the hospital. He hurried along the quay to the door which was never locked. He always kept a candle hidden under the fiber mat at the entrance. This he lit from the gaslight which illuminated the vestibule. There was ever a danger of fire, so the big ward lay in darkness during the night. He had to pick his way carefully past the cots and mattresses. Moans and groans reminded him that there were others beside himself who were in pain.

A week passed. He found himself concentrating entirely on the sick. Once again it came home to him how important it was for a priest to listen. As he had said so often, the best medicine was to let them tell him about their children, their villages, their shops, their woes. He didn't want to admit to himself that his sudden interest in listening was something of an escape. It did take him away from the gloomy aftermath of the court decision. He worried about what de la Croix and the Marèchal were thinking, and what the Jesuits and lawyers were debating. Above all, he wondered in what kind of mood had they found Père Larousse. Would they be open to his plan for appeal when Antoine finally got up the courage to meet with them all again? Each time he thought about this cloud over his head, he postponed action for another twenty-four hours.

He found a rewarding diversion in chatting with the parishioners who lived nearby. They preferred to come into the chapel to hear Mass rather than go into the vast nave of Notre Dame which was mostly empty during weekdays. He also made it a point to walk up and down the quay watching the small boats loaded with produce that would come alongside the bank to attract buyers. Listening to the housewives haggling with the boatmen was another interesting distraction. Every other day, one of the sellers who pushed his hand wagon onto the bridge would lean over the rail and berate the competition. All of this activity was helpful in keeping his mind close to the hospital. But he could dodge his responsibilities only so long.

How was the debate going among his companions and lawyer friends? To whom would they direct their appeal at the Consulate of Paris? Had they made up their minds yet? Soon he would learn that many of the group were in favor of an appeal to the King's inner circle. The lawyers had uncovered a precedent in previous disputes involving religious orders and kings Louis XIV and XV. Instead of pleading clerical privilege, thus offending parliamentarians, many of whom were anti-Pope, they had approved the non-solidarity clause for orders when one of their members was in a legal tangle.

So it was that Antoine once again renewed his courage and sought a meeting with the Marèchal and the lawyer, de la Croix, desperately hopeful that the plan he had worked out might have a chance of being realized. They were only a few minutes into their conversation, however, when his optimism was dashed.

"I do not understand your superior," began the lawyer. "First of all he doesn't listen to the Marèchal who tries to convince him that you have a hostile jury in the parliament. Nor has he listened to me when I point out the validity of the non-solidarity clause. Why go into the lion's den?"

Antoine reflected for a while before entering the conversation. He had to remain optimistic. Both his friends were frustrated; they were in a perfect mood to hear a new idea.

"There's one thing you have to understand about my companions," he began. "They are always logical, or they try to be. I don't want to pretend that I have a superior insight into this affair, but my colleagues will be inclined to follow strictly legal channels instead of looking elsewhere for help."

"Mon Père, I am not sure I understand what you are trying to tell us," interrupted the Marèchal.

"Jesuits are logical," replied Antoine, "and they are looking at this matter of several hundred thousand *livres* from a strictly logical point of view. It makes no sense to hold Jesuits and their colleges and houses responsible for what happened to me. This was the same argument they used on Père de Sacy when he presented my argument to Père Larousse, trying to convince him to borrow the money to pay off Madame Grou. It was logical. And look what has happened!"

"I still don't know what you are driving at, Père. We are about to appeal to the Parliament to reverse the judgment against us. At least that is what Père Larousse has said to me."

"Yes, Monsieur Marèchal, that is correct. But what both puzzles and hurts me deeply is that I see myself as being used as an instrument for hurting all my brothers here in the country. I also see myself in total disfavor among most of the Jesuits and most of all, by Père Larousse. So what I want you to know is that I need you desperately, since no one will listen to me. I want to pursue a wholly different course in this matter and no one will listen to a proposal if they think it comes from me."

The Marèchal shook his head.

And the lawyer added, "I am afraid I don't see another course in a legal dispute."

"If I understand you correctly, Père Antoine," continued the Marèchal, "you think you have a convincing argument. You don't have much time. After our last gathering, Père Larousse assigned his assistant to begin drafting a formal appeal to the Parliament."

"But, there is another route. If you both are patient with me, and above all, if you keep an open mind while listening, I think I can show you that my plan has merit."

"All right, go ahead. We promise to hear you out." The Marèchal turned to his friend, who smiled in agreement.

"I hope you won't be shocked, but I want you to think for a moment about Madame Pompadour."

They tried not to be prudish, but their reaction was immediately cold and wordless.

"I know how you feel," Antoine hurried up to say. "But hear me carefully. As a priest from the faraway Caribbean, I'm not supposed to know this. But because of my friendship with Père de Sacy over the years, I do know that the Pompadour is on our side and that any politician or noble who wants to go anywhere must curry her favor."

"So, you're suggesting that we ask Jeanne Antoinette to intercede for us and forget approaching the Parliament entirely?" asked the Marèchal.

"Precisely," said Antoine. "First of all, such an appeal, if successful, will give us time. And my hope is that during this delay, Père Larousse will let me go back to Martinique."

"Père," the Marèchal felt he had to intervene, "we don't want to offend you, but there is a war on. The odds against your delivering any shipments to France are astronomical. Besides, Jesuits are not exactly popular in the realm, so how do you propose to get an interview with the Pompadour?"

"Getting her attention will not be hard, believe me. But, give me time. Before you worry about that, I have to show you that my plan avoids any war risks."

"I do find that very difficult to believe," put in de la Croix.

Antoine stood up. It was the critical moment. "One year's cultivation of Cresols plantation on Dominique will provide enough to hold off all the leading creditors."

Antoine hurried on before they could express their skepticism.

"What neither of you knows is my situation in the Caribbean. I have not been able to describe it to you or anyone else. With the existing arrangement back there, I have to risk very little. Hostility to the King is not something that is exclusively French. The Yanquis in the English colonies hate the monarchy and their Parliament more than anything else. Have you ever heard of the Molasses Act?"

Both men shook their head.

"According to that act, Yanquis cannot manufacture molasses. They must ship their raw sugar to England, after being forced to buy it from Jamaica or the other English islands. Because of this, Yanqui ships come down to our area to buy raw sugar and molasses. Sometimes they settle for the sugar and make their molasses back home. What that means is that both the plantations on Martinique and Dominique have assured customers."

"How does that affect your problem of shipping to France?" de la Croix challenged.

"It totally removes the hazard of shipping on the high seas."

"That, I don't understand," said the Marèchal.

Antoine, still standing, began gesturing to hold their attention. "You're forgetting my arrangement with Captain Byrne. I am sure I told you about him. He is the one who carries our sugar up to the colonies. Now, instead of shipping it all the way up to Boston, he can deliver it to New York where it is sold. My associate, Isaac, has relatives there in the shipping business. They handle the transaction. The money or letters of credit are then sent to Holland on Dutch ships. Another thing you don't know is that the English merchant marine as well as the privateers avoid Dutch crews. Unlike their French and Spanish counterparts, the Dutch will not give up their cargo without a fierce fight. There is always danger of loss, but with this arrangement, there is only a financial transaction which can always be protected or renewed, whereas shipments cannot."

For the first time, the Marèchal became convinced that letting Antoine go back to the Caribbean made sense. Up to that point, he had been somewhat patronizing when the priest brought up the idea. Certainly, once the shipping danger was minimized, it was only a matter of credit exchange across the sea.

"I hate to raise an objection at this point," said de la Croix. "You have presented quite a case, and I want you to know that I am with you as never before. However, as a lawyer I see another difficulty. There's another word for the kind of trade you are engaged in which I am sure the English government has used more than once to describe your activity."

Antoine had to smile because there was no defense to what de la Croix suggested. "Smuggling?" he asked.

"You know I support you, Père," de la Croix emphasized, "but a plea to the Pompadour in an effort to defend a priest engaged in smuggling may not strike the Grand Chambre as a worthy cause — to say the least."

"I agree, but everything is a risk. I say that we must take that risk and hope that Madame Pompadour will only think of Père de Sacy and not me."

"Where does Père de Sacy come into this?" the Maréchal was puzzled.

"Before I answer that," replied Antoine, "I repeat that we have to take a risk. We're dealing with unjust indebtedness which threatens the functioning of our schools and colleges here in France. We are doing a marvelous job of education; even our enemies have called us the 'Schoolmasters of Europe.' We have one-hundred twelve Jesuit schools and colleges in this country alone. In my judgment, they're all in danger of being closed. Without some kind of appeal, the Jesuits can never pay off my debts."

Both men were silent. They were impressed. Even though Antoine had been far away, he had a better vision of the whole picture than most of those who had never left France.

"Now, as to why I want to talk about Père de Sacy. I think I have made it clear that I want us to appeal to the Grand Chambre, the inner circle of the King, not to the Parliament. In particular, I want to have Père de Sacy make a direct plea to the Pompadour."

Both men were taken aback by this proposal. So much so, that they didn't even raise a question. They seemed ready to listen to a surprising narrative.

"Several years ago, Père de Sacy had been an assistant chaplain at the court. While beginning his working at the parish where he is now, he was also on call for special feast days at the Royal Court. It so happened that the head chaplain became ill on Easter Sunday, and asked him to take his place for a private Mass at the Poisson home outside of Paris. After that, he was invited back on several occasions and the family asked him to begin instructions for the First Communion of their daughter, Jeannette, who had just turned sixteen. He became something of a regular visitor to the family home, and as a result was much loved by Jeannette." Antoine had no trouble keeping the attention of his audience of two. They were fascinated; they had never heard this story before.

"It had been a delightful time for de Sacy. He enjoyed the lavish hospitality of the wealthy family. At times, he abandoned his parish duties for more than a week. The day of her First Communion was a social event, a social introduction, with holy water and incense and an array of lighted candles. She was a charming sixteen year old. Her beauty was enhanced by a flowing white dress and a lace veil. During this period, Père de Sacy managed to keep 'custody of the eyes,' most of the time, but as Jeannette filed down the aisle to the admiration of the select congregation, even the priest had to observe that here was a matchless beauty.

"What de Sacy was not aware of at the time was that once the pious ceremony was over, the reports of the charming beauty had somehow reached the King. Plans were afoot a year or two later, for the family carriage to be driven through the Parque d'Etoile on a Sunday, where His Majesty Louis XV was known to park the royal carriage and take a leisurely stroll. De Sacy soon became aware of the subsequent relationship, as did all of France."

He continued, "Once Jeannette had been invited to be the royal consort, relations between her and de Sacy became somewhat distant. Even when she received the sobriquet of 'Madame Pompadour,' which no one dared to use in the royal court area, she did not forget him. On several occasions, at royal banquets, for instance, she had him give the invocation. Mostly at Christmas time, but often at Easter, she sent for him to say a Mass in the chapel of Jeanne d'Arc.

"Notably, in the great gossip story of a Paris morning, it was none other than Père de Sacy who received notoriety. She had called him in the middle of the night, dispatching King Louis' private coach to the Church of Sainte Germaine, rousing the priests' household, waking up the neighbors because of the noisy cavalry escort, demanding the immediate presence of the priest at the palace. King Louis was dying!" Antoine paused for breath.

"But before Louis met his Maker, he had a few things on his conscience. He wanted to go to confession and receive the last rites before that final moment. According to the gossip that was all over the city in the morning, the Pompadour had come into his bedroom to console him as he agonized. He had already been informed that she had called the chaplain who was on his way with the holy oils. Actually, he was in terrible pain from stomach cramps for having stuffed himself with half-cooked beef. He is quoted as saying to

Jeanette, 'Get out of here. The priest is coming.' According to witnesses, the melodrama ended with her drawing back from the side of the bed, saying haughtily, 'Oh, then, shall I call Her Majesty the Queen to be at your bedside?' He replied, 'Go way, I'm dying.'"

As long as his two friends were captivated by his narrative, Antoine decided to hurry through what for the most part was familiar. They didn't need to hear again that not only the formidable Duc de Choiseau, but any one else who had ambitions of rising higher in the realm, had to court her favor before even thinking of approaching the King.

The Marèchal and de Croix had been absorbed listeners. Now Antoine had to be quick. "We, too, must court her favor. You see that I have a sound approach. I need you both to get Larousse's attention and persuade him to let Père de Sacy speak for us to the Pompadour. We're not trying to evade anything. All we need is more time."

"I really would like to have you accompany us," said de la Croix. "You can do so much better than the Marèchal or me."

"You do not understand, Monsieur. Apparently, I have not made it clear to you that neither Larousse nor his advisers will listen for one moment to anything that comes from me."

"That is unfortunate," said the Marèchal. "You have certainly been eloquent."

"Thank you. But make sure you present the case for my going back from the point of view of Père de Sacy. He is the one who appears as the defendant and he is the one for whom the majority of Jesuits have the highest regard. Even Larousse will admit that."

The interview was at an end. The three began to leave. The final word came from Antoine. "I will be waiting at the hospital for the outcome of your meeting with Larousse. I will be praying hard."

Their meeting occurred on a Friday evening. Most of the next week went by without any information from his two friends. It was an ordeal for Antoine. He found diversion by listening to the daily news. Happily, the Town Crier came by now and then. His services were not often in great demand at the Hotel de Ville which stood across the plaza, beyond the bridge, a block from *La Place de Grève.* By coincidence, one morning after calling out the news, the mantled crier noticed the priest on the wharf for his daily stroll. Antoine had stopped for a moment, entranced with the flamboyant news announcer and his powerful bass voice that reverberated over the river. He made it a point to get up earlier the following morning to make sure he heard that booming voice again. When the crier came on the scene, it was pretty obvious that the priest had timed his morning exercise to coincide with the proclamation of the latest news. After a bit, the morning news was an occasion for a chat between the two.

At most any hour of the day, there was a small group going in and out of the cathedral who later gathered in the square. They were the ones who believed that lighted candles would keep them and their prayers alive before the altar of Mother Mary until the flame went out. Waiting to sell to them candles, rosaries, medals and food were the merchants with their push carts. The cathedral square was a natural spot for anyone to pass the time of day. This was an interesting early morning preliminary to Antoine's infirmary visits. Especially now, he desperately wanted to pick up some gossip, anything that might let him know what might have happened when the Marèchal, de la Croix, and Larousse got together.

Perhaps because he admitted that it was foolish to hope for the kind of news he was looking for in the Cathedral Square, or because he could no longer stand the suspense, he sought out one of the bread sellers. With several coins he lured the seller to run an errand for him. Another coin would be available if the man could get a message and reply to the home of the Marèchal del Belle Isle.

Two days more went by before Antoine received a reply and a Sunday evening hour appointment to meet with his friends. The thrilling part of the reply was that Père de Sacy would share in the meeting, and it would be held at St. Germaine's. Although it was only a matter of hours that he had to wait, the suspense was more painful than a week's wait.

That Sunday night was probably the brightest night of his life. Antoine had been through many depressing nights and days brooding over his dismissal from Martinique, his yearning to return, the shock of the impact of his indebtedness, resentment of his brothers in Christ, and the apparent hopelessness of winning his appeal for time. He was greeted by a smiling trio. They recounted their successful endeavor in detail.

One aspect that Antoine had thought not possible was that Larousse had allowed de Sacy in to their talk. Elated though he was, and not wishing to doubt success when it was before his eyes, he did want to know what exactly changed the mind of his stubborn superior.

Amazingly, all three of his friends disclaimed credit for the attitude change. True, Père de Sacy had surprised the man with the details of his friendship with the Pompadour, and the absence of risk for the future in transferring funds from the Caribbean. But most of the credit — they were at one in this — was due to someone they didn't know, who made Larousse aware that the Jansenist[5] element in the parliament was not only hostile, but well organized and prepared to reject any compromise in dealing with the Jesuits. This was a stunning realization. Obviously, since the last attempt to persuade him, Larousse had thought more and more about the horrendous prospect of raising three or more million *livres*. The reminder about the Jansenist feud forced him to recognize that the Jesuits didn't have too many options for seeking help. Any recourse to the Parliament would be problematic, at best. These considerations, together with what de Sacy emphasized as the relative ease with which funds could be transferred from the other side of the Atlantic, became the turning point in the discussion.

The following weeks were all sweetness and light in the Jesuit camp. The Pompadour received the request from her former spiritual tutor graciously. She specified a date when he could come and talk to her. It had been almost a year since they had spoken. The day all the Jesuits in Paris had awaited finally arrived. Priests and lay brothers were all watching as the royal carriage pulled up before the residence of St. Germaine. Père de Sacy marched out in a brand new cassock for the important moment, as the uniformed attendant opened the carriage door for him. All eyes followed the fancy liveried pair of white horses as they trotted down the street and turned the corner en route to the Palais Royal.

Upon their arrival, a member of the palace guard came down the long flight of stone steps and bowed to the distinguished visitor in black, whom he then accompanied slowly back up to the entrance. Together the two walked across the immaculate tile floor of the empty hall to another flight of stairs with elaborate marble banisters. At the top stood his hostess with a warm smile for the priest who had given her First Communion. She was not the unofficial Minister of State, nor Madame Pompadour, she was "Jeannette," and he was Père Jacques as he took her hand. They walked together into the parlor.

"Père Jacques, it has been a while, hasn't it?"

"Indeed, Madame Jeannette, it has, and I trust you are well."

She touched his shoulder. "Please, mon Père, it was once just Jeannette."

Through the rest of their conversation, he was careful to follow her hint.

---

5 *Jansenists were followers of the Dutch theologian, Cornelis Jansen (1585 – 1638). They believed in predestination and denied free will. The Jesuits opposed these teachings and were able to persuade the Vatican to call for their condemnation.*

"I have heard that you have had some bouts with bronchitis," he began again as they sat down side by side.

"These palace buildings were built to be looked at, not lived in," she replied. "They are so drafty. You can't sit before the fireplaces all day. And even when you do, as soon as you leave, you get a fearful chill and begin sneezing like a horse. But tell me Père, what is this urgent request that you have for me?"

As briefly as he could, de Sacy outlined the crisis, the need for delay and the solution that included Père Antoine's return to the Caribbean islands. It was surprisingly easy. The previous months of anxiety were dissipated in a moment. A personally signed note would be delivered to the Duc de Choiseul at once. It would be in his hands by that afternoon for communication to the King and his Royal Chamber.

Jeanette related news of her family to de Sacy. Her father had died; her mother was at last reconciled. It had been a painful ten years with her mother, who had been mortified by the machinatons of her husband, in collusion with an uncle in introducing her daughter to a new career. A younger sister, Marguerite, had developed a serious case of influenza. Her brother was now a vice-admiral on a warship in the Atlantic off the Azores. Her youngest brother, Dolman, was the only family living on the estate.

Often during the year she spent weekends at the family estate, getting away from the burden of affairs of state. She reminisced about the week de Sacy spent preparing her for the First Communion. There was a tone of sadness in her voice throughout her chat, but when it came to her promise to help de Sacy in his distress, she was firm. She was definitely in charge. She stood and allowed the priest to take her hand and bow in farewell.

She smiled wistfully, as she stood at the vestibule of the castle door. She was remembering another time, no doubt, when she and the priest were busy poring over the catechism and getting ready for the sacrament.

CHAPTER IX

Instead of heading back to the parish, de Sacy asked the driver to take him to *L'Hôtel Dieu*. Antoine should be the first to hear. Larousse and the others could wait. As de Sacy expected, Antoine's reaction was one of joy and immense relief.

He went into action immediately, as though all had been solved. He followed de Sacy back to the residence. He had stored some of his belongings in the attic. There were his saddle bags and what the people called *alforjas*, the rough woven bags he used to hang on the saddle horn with his breviary, rosary and Mass book, along with a spare shirt. He anticipated with relish the moment he would ride into the village as the children came running. He would toss the small leather ball for the boys to kick around and the jump rope for the girls. Later he would ring the hand bell, calling for the ball and jump rope. "Children! Time for catechism!"

He accompanied de Sacy along the wharf to the Pompadour's private carriage. By the time the two priests climbed in, a curious crowd had gathered. Antoine was so wrapped up in his own enthusiasm that he pushed de Sacy into the carriage and ignored the people. When they arrived at the Church of St. Germaine, a cluster of onlookers including a few of the priests, gathered quickly to greet the two blackrobes emerging like royalty from the luxurious carriage.

The days that followed were indeed days of good humor. Antoine gathered the few clothes he wanted to take with him. Several Jesuits descended on him to wish him farewell and a safe journey. Some were a so effusive that Antoine had to wonder whether part of their warmth was a sign of good cheer, or of the happy prospect that he would no longer be a burden to them in France.

But the day before Antoine was to leave for Marseilles, a depressing note came from de Sacy. One of the theologians in the archdiocesan seminary had upset Larousse with a caustic reminder that it was an order from the Pontifical Congregation of Religious in Rome that had mandated Lavalette's recall. Where did a minor superior of the Jesuit Order suddenly obtain the authority to countermand a directive from Rome?

This news upset all the Jesuits in Paris. Just when they thought they had extricated themselves from a complicated lawsuit, they found themselves stymied by a question of authority. Unfortunately, the authority was from the throne of Christianity. Two weeks went by filled with consultations with experts on Canon Law. Then another two weeks. Poor Antoine's dream seemed blocked. However, the threat of possible bankruptcy and the closing of Jesuit schools drove the Companions to a series of meetings with a desperate sense of urgency. One team came in from Limoges with a solution. Larousse was not sending Lavalette back in any capacity of authority. He was not defying any command. He was resolving a financial problem in the payment of a debt.

The seminary watchdog who was all set to go to Rome personally with his complaint, was called off at least temporarily by the group from Limoges, who spent most of two days pleading and arguing with him. Once they had mollified the complainer, they went directly to the hospital. They helped Antoine pack and loaded him on the carriage bound for Marseilles.

In one sense it was not a thrilling journey because of the dusty trail and the rocking, bumpy horse-drawn ride. But when he thought of his destination, of the harbor at St. Pierre, Martinique, the sugar plantations and his people, all thoughts of the discomforts of the bouncing ride on the dirt roads were forgotten. It was good that Antoine was quite far away because a new stage in the drama was developing.

· · · · · · · · ·

Once again the striking scene of a royal carriage pulling up in front of the priests' house caught the attention of all nearby residents and passersby. It was a Saturday afternoon, market day. The number of the curious was not really large, but still unusual for the quiet neighborhood.

To his great surprise, again the vehicle came for Père de Sacy. This time there were four uniformed escorts. They pulled up around three in the afternoon. It was confession time. De Sacy was nonplussed being interrupted while hearing confessions. Pulling back the curtain of the confessional, he was handed a parchment.

It was a request from the Pompadour to come immediately. Was it another sick call? Perhaps like the one that had made him famous? Was King Louis really sick this time?

He had to assure the secretary that he would be in the office, but he had to finish hearing confession. Next, he had to apologize to the line of people who were waiting to go to confession. He hurried over to the residence to get a substitute. He could not keep the Pompadour waiting, not now. Was she backing out of her promise to help solve the Martinique problem? What could be so urgent that she wanted to see him immediately?

It was not long into their interview before Jeannette Poisson unburdened herself. She began her pouring out her soul to him like the penitents he had been hearing earlier that afternoon. She hadn't forgotten the precious moment when she knelt before him to receive the host. The smell of the incense, the glow of the candles, the Gregorian chant of Thomas Aquinas' communion hymns. It had all come back to her that afternoon in the parlor when de Sacy had come pleading for his Jesuit brothers. During the intervening weeks, the vision of the chapel on the family estate would not leave her. Once again she wanted to kneel at the communion rail and receive, like the little girl in white she once was, she was turning to her Jesuit friend. She hoped he wouldn't think that she was demanding a favor in return for her intercession on behalf of the Jesuits, although certainly there were many who would think that was what she was doing. She begged him to think otherwise. Seeing him again and chatting as they once had, caused her to yearn to be at peace with the Lord. She and Louis were no longer intimate; he had younger diversions.

"Dear Père de Sacy, can you help me?"

This time they parted with an embrace, the curé and the Mistress of the King.

Determined to undertake his commission, de Sacy directed his royal chauffeurs to the Chancery of the Archbishop. This was not the way to court a favor, calling on the prelate late on a Saturday afternoon without warning or invitation.

As it turned out the Archbishop received him, mainly out of curiosity for the motive behind such a sudden and plaintive appeal. He had known de Sacy for a long time and knew he would not appear without warning unless there was something serious afoot.

As de Sacy had dreaded, the Archbishop's first reaction was negative, though not unfriendly. But he did not stop shaking his head, even as he was promising to help all he could. His skepticism was valid, indeed. Rome was Rome. The odds were against them. The prelate agreed totally with de Sacy when he stressed what all of Paris knew: that the Pompadour and the King were no longer in a sexual liaison. Louis wanted her at his side when he was immersed in political and military turmoil. They were still close to one another — very close — but now in a way the Roman authorities might condone. Solemn counselors to His Holiness, however, were sure to stress that the point was not whether they were together. The point was that there had been a scandal. This could not be readily overlooked. The Archbishop did seem to relent a bit when de Sacy launched into a discourse about the Jesuit dilemma, the Martinique problem and all it entailed. All this accomplished was that the Archbishop promised to consult with his assistants for advice. He would then forward their opinions to Rome. In the meantime, there would be an abundance of advice. The whole nation would be watching: priests, bishops, laity; particularly the Jansenists, and with them the self-righteous, gathering their cloaks about them like the Pharisees of another era, who shook their fingers at one who dined with tax collectors and other sinners.

Poor de Sacy! It seemed that ever since Antoine returned, he was spending week after week perspiring over one dilemma after another. He was tired of saying to himself: "Why me, O Lord!" But he repeated his complaint again and again amid the discomfort of an awful carriage ride all the way to Italy. He both feared and abhorred a trip on the sea. But he had to get to Rome to plead the case of the Pompadour before the Sacred Congregation of the Sacraments, so the carriage was his only option. Before he went before that tribunal, he had to contact the Superior General to pave the way for what he needed, a favorable hearing for the Pompadour's request.

His trip to Rome and the frustrations of going back and forth in the Vatican were a taxing ordeal. And what was more dreadful was the result: total failure in the face of the advocates of the strict observance. It did not matter whether the Pompadour and Louis were living together or not. There was the scandal of having been the King's mistress. There was but one condition for forgiveness and that was that she would have to leave the court. Only then, would she be allowed to kneel at the communion rail again.

The solemn faces of the members of the Sacred Congregation of the Sacraments showed no emotion as de Sacy cited the father's forgiveness in the story of the Prodigal Son. He risked offending his hearers by referring to Rembrandt's portrayal of the smug, elder son looking down with disgust at his prodigal brother, the drama of the foolish pardon on his face. He really deserved high praise for the way he cited many scripture passages with a message of forgiveness. Though mercy may have been considered the greatest of God's works, it was not so for the ascetics who served on the panel reviewing the Pompadour's plea to receive communion at the Court of Versailles. Nor would the Pope (who evaluated the petition privately) let it be forgotten that the petitioner had been mistress to Louis XV.

It was said in certain circles that for the first time in many decades, the devout Catholics of France, as well as the not so devout were on the side of the Pope for his pronouncement that the Pompadour must leave her position of influence before being permitted to receive Holy Communion. The disastrous results of foreign policy in the sea struggle with England and the Seven Years' War were laid at the door of King Louis XV, especially because of his penchant for listening to Madame Jeannette.

For Père de Sacy, the return from Rome was even more tedious than the journey there. He was afraid to face Jeanne Antoinette because he knew that even the peers of the realm feared her fury. The lowly Jesuits did not need her to join the ranks of the hostile politicians. His forebodings were happily allayed, however, when he actually faced her to detail what had transpired in Rome. She was the soul of politeness with him. She knew what he had been through. She knew how sincerely he had tried to win the permission she sought. No matter what had transpired in the meantime, the day of her First Communion from his hands in the family chapel dedicated to Jeanne d'Arc would ever be a precious memory.

It was a few days before de Sacy learned that she had saved her outbursts of wrath for the King's ear, and directed them at the Jesuits. De Sacy was the only exception.

The Pompadour was no student of history, but she did know that there had been a fierce dispute that started in the past century, and continued into the present. It was a dispute that was ever in the public eye. She knew that the Jesuits had directed an attack on the followers of one, Jansenius, and his adherents. Port Royal, on the outskirts of Paris, was the local center where many of the upper class attended Mass. The Jesuit challenge of Jansenist doctrine had won out over the most influential segment of the Catholic hierarchy and gained the approval of both king and pope in a most Catholic crusade. It had seemed to her and the people she had dealt with that the controversy was silly — a bickering over whether we had free will or not — something like that. She knew how weary Louis was of that dispute. The popes themselves had written several letters to the kings of France, begging them to use their royal authority to help crush this religious war between

Jesuits and Jansenists. What remained uppermost in the mind of the Pompadour was that the Jesuits won the condemnation of the Jansenists from the Vatican, with the total approval of the monarchy.

If they could do that, they certainly could have gained the Pope's ear for a simple request by a woman who wanted to go to Holy Communion again, especially now that she and Louis had different bedrooms. There was no doubt in the entire court, with its salacious nose for scandal, that there really was no liaison now.

So it was that the Marèchal del Belle Isle and the lawyer, de la Croix, had to take up the defense of the priests once again. They had lost their patroness. There were two options left. One was a direct appeal to the King and his Royal Council; the other was to go to the Parliament. They had to challenge the judgment of the Consulate of Paris that had condemned them in the name of Père de Sacy. This poor priest had not recovered from his disastrous trip to Rome before he found himself summoned by the Abbé Giroux to show cause as to why the Jesuits had not begun to honor the judgment of the lower court in Paris. The court demanded that they indemnify creditors in the payment of Lavalette's debts, whose sum was now stated to be 3,500,000 *livres*. It was imperative that the Jesuits address the demand immediately or the matter would be brought before the Parliament Committee on Justice.

It was absolutely essential to the trial before them because for some unknown reason, the Abbé Giroux and his Committee had gotten into the fray against the Jesuits. It was important that Antoine be present as a material witness to events and transactions in the Caribbean. De la Croix was adamant in insisting that he could not present a realistic defense without Antoine. A special courier had to be dispatched on horseback to bring him back from Marseilles.

Reluctantly, de Sacy complied with the lawyer's imperative. How sad it would be for Antoine to be recalled just when he was to return to the island he loved. But de Sacy could not waste any time on sentimentality. Antoine had been gone almost two weeks now. He had to be contacted. What would they do if he had already left?

At the moment, Père Antoine was going to and fro along the docks of Marseilles. He had been spending time exclusively on the ships that were coming from the Caribbean with sugar. It had taken him a week or more to learn that these ships were transporting most of their cargo to England where they got higher prices for the sugar.

Only after another frustrating week of talking to seamen and ship captains did he find the *Valienté*, bound for Cap Francois, in Nueva Isabela, the spot where he had sought refuge after the pirates had robbed his ships. Captain Honore Liguidi was happy to offer him passage to the island which Columbus had baptized with the Queen's name. But first he had to load his ship with flour, paving stones and slate destined for what had become the commercial center of the Caribbean.

Captain Liguidi was also waiting for a shipment of wine from Bordeaux. The delay was fateful for Antoine. But for the wine, he would have been on the horizon the following day. As it was, he was torn. He should have followed his first hunch! He had come down to the docks the very first day with all his belongings, seeking lodging. He had gone to the Church of St. Hilaire, some eight blocks away from the docks where he had found lodging. It was here in the rectory that the rider-messenger from Paris had delivered the note from de Sacy, begging him to return.

If it had been anybody else, he would have thrown the note away. His first reaction was to say, "I'll go back to the docks. I'll leave on the first ship. I don't care where it is going." But then, to whom did he owe loyalty? Was God calling him back to the sophisticated environment of Paris where he was hated or to Martinique where he was known and loved? How could he deal with this? Where was God?

It was the last day before the *Valienté* would put out to sea. He had to make a decision. The interior struggle was intense. Success was at hand. Defiance and escape were uppermost in his mind. But there was the final plea of his friend, de Sacy. At last, Superior Larousse was convinced of the peril they were in. And the lawyer had been adamant in demanding the presence of an eye witness. They faced a kind of extra-judicial court trial with political enemies as the jury. They absolutely had to have a black cassock in the tribunal to dramatize that, in a way, the Church itself was on trial. With the evidence he could bring to this tribunal, there was always the chance of prolonging the defense and the prosecution. Any excuse for delay held out hope that the Pompadour might forget her grievance, and once again change her mind. Nor could he forget that there was also the Royal Chamber, the coterie around the King to whom other religious orders had gone on bended knee.

Then, too, there was the information which de Sacy had passed on to him. Larousse hinted that he might use his power to direct the Church authority in Martinique to deny faculties to Lavalette. Escape would be meaningless if he could not say Mass and hear confessions or function as a priest. He had to do both — take charge of the plantations and function as a priest — to bring the people to his side.

During the final day before departure, Antoine had been pacing back and forth along the docks. So engrossed was he, that he failed to notice that he had been doing this for almost two hours. Painfully and reluctantly, he came to the conclusion that he had to return to help the cause. He had no choice. It was his cause, too.

The tedium, the dust, the discomfort of the carriage ride back to Paris coupled with the misery in his heart, made him want to die. For the first time in his life, he wanted to find some way to end it all. In the face of the pirate swords, death had been of no account. Now, it was something he yearned for. Was there no oversize rut or fallen tree branch or a mud puddle sufficient to turn them over as they were hurtling along in the night? Anything that could deliver him from the burden life had become would be a welcome alternative.

His better self tried to break through the depression. Another, whom he was supposed to model, had faced failure. He had knelt alone in the garden, while his so-called friends snored indifferently. He, too, had known failure. He was supposed to carry on the tradition of Moses, but his compatriots accused Him of betraying both Moses and the Prophets. Antoine didn't need any reminders. He was called to see beyond the cross. He had preached this to others: through anguish you rise to the stars *"Per aspera ad astra."*

Unfortunately, there were no road hazards sufficient to block his way to Paris. So it was that after a back-breaking ride, Antoine's carriage came rumbling over the bridge across the Seine into the shadow of the Cathedral of Notre Dame. He was five days into the journey, arriving shortly after sunrise on a Friday morning. He descended from the carriage with creaking joints and aching back. He began to walk around the block of the priests' residence in an effort to get rid of the stiffness. He finally went to the room de Sacy had prepared for him. He didn't have much time to rest and he didn't want to stay there. He wanted to set out with his knapsack for the hospital. He would have gone there first if it had not been for the urgency with which de Sacy had begged him to return at once from Marsilles. His instructions were that immediately upon his arrival, no matter the time, he was to send a messenger to the residence of the Marèchal and to the lawyer, de la Croix. A reply as to the time and place of their gathering would be forthcoming. There were no more adjournment possibilities because the speaker at the parliament had arranged for the first hearing on the following Monday. That left them the weekend to confer. It was imperative that the trio meet before formal litigation began.

Antoine had another carriage ride with which to contend. He had to hurry off to the Marèchal's residence where his two friends had been waiting anxiously. Happily the ride was soon over, and proved a short respite from the business at hand. His friends were relieved in a sense, because their excuses to the parliamentary panel had become flimsy. They had had to assure a secretary in person that they would appear the following Monday. They didn't want to court any further hostility with one more delay.

The Marèchal was deeply moved as he looked on the countenance of the priest. He read the sadness and the disappointment, especially now knowing that the only route to relief was through the Parliament. This would mean the whole nation would eventually hear more and more of Antoine Lavalette. How to comfort the man?

The Marèchal got up and embraced him. There was more bad news to impart to the forlorn priest. He had to tell him. After all, his son had told him many times that his favorite teacher at Louis le Grande had been Père Antoine. Antoine taught the history of theology class and had been the first to clarify for his students the roots of Calvinism from which Jansenism had sprung. Père had made clear what no one else had ever made clear: there was a problem in the Adam and Eve story. It certainly was a problem because a kind of religious warfare had been born between the Jansenists and the Jesuits in a debate over whether it was just or not for the whole human race to inherit Adam and Eve's sin. Now it seemed like an attempt to appease the Jansenist faction in the Parliament by targeting their Jesuit enemies in the person of Antoine.

The Marèchal was genuinely compassionate. Why did such things happen to a priest? He was too talented to have been sent to the Caribbean. He should have been kept in France teaching theology. Now, as a public trial loomed before the august legislative body of the nation on account of him, his depression and guilt were too obvious to ignore. The Marèchal wanted to do his best to console the man.

"Père," the Marèchal put his arm on the priest's shoulder, "I know you find yourself in a most embarrassing position, but try to see something more here — something that goes far beyond you — something for which you have no culpability whatever. Please, don't try to carry the whole burden of guilt on your shoulders. I hesitate to mention it because it sounds so unbelievable. Anyone who knows what I am about to tell you is in danger of his life. I do not exaggerate! I don't fully understand it, but this thing of Jansenist supporters in the Parliament is very serious. This is the situation: the Marquise d'Ammecourt, who as you may know recently died, was married to a woman who is a first cousin of the Abbé Giroux, a powerful voice for the Jansenist party. D'Ammecourt died in his carriage vomiting blood, several hours after a luncheon with members of parliament, among who was the Duc de Laurent. The rumor that has spread among the Roman party (a rumor which of course is categorically denied by the Jansenists), is that D'Ammecourt came into possession of a copy of a letter written by the Abbé whose purpose was to enlist other members of the Jansenist Party in a specific plot to expel the Jesuits from this country! D'Ammecourt was allegedly on his way to the office of your Père Larousse to warn him of what was afoot."

The Marèchal shook his head in disgust. Then he went on, "We are dealing with pure evil and deception, now intertwined with life threatening plots. Poor D'Ammecourt had no idea he had become a target in the midst of chicanery. Somehow because of his closeness to you Jesuits, he knew of the fierce debate within your inner sanctum between Larousse and the rest of you. This battle developed while you were gone. In the six weeks of your absence in Marseilles, Larousse had announced to your colleagues that the only avenue of appeal was the Parliament. To get the protection of the King's Council or that of Madame Pompadour implied guilt. He saw this line of approach as a subterfuge, a device to seek patronage, not justice. The Society of Jesus had nothing to fear from the truth. The Sons of St. Ignatius were duty bound to face a tribunal in which they sought justice, not favoritism.

"M. de la Croix and I were not invited into your inner sanctum. We only learned of the internal controversy about going to the Parliament after D'Ammecourt's death. Then rumors began to circulate. Once we were informed about the details, we went immediately to Larousse to warn him. Unfortunately, we were too late. He had ignored all opposition and written a formal letter to the Abbé Giroux seeking legal recourse from the judgment of the Consulate of Paris."

The Marèchal looked at his compatriot and then back to Antoine.

"Of course, there is no way to prove what I have told you, because the letter which was to be delivered has long since been destroyed. Nor has Père Larousse believed me when I told him about it. I am telling you this for two reasons: one, so you recognize that there is something going on that has nothing to do with your failure to honor letters of credit; two, to emphasize that there was something suspicious about a lower court going far beyond its usual jurisdiction of regulating commercial transactions. We have pointed out this breach of ethic and etiquette in the Madame Grou case currently before the Consulate of Paris. It is imperative, that you and Père de Sacy do all you can to alert your confreres that we, Monsieur de la Croix and I, believe that your existence as a religious order in France is under serious threat."

De la Croix and Antoine were shocked by the suggestion that murder might be involved. The Marèchal had guarded his secret even from his close friend until Antoine could return.

De la Croix's reaction was one of irritation as well as shock.

"You have kept this from me, M. Marèchal!" said de la Croix, exasperated. "I heard about d'Ammecourt's death, but nothing about your interpretation of it. I find it hard to believe something so grim. Besides, as you indicated, you really don't have any proof."

"I don't have the documentary evidence nor testimony," said the Marèchal. "But I do have a clue you cannot ignore. You have heard about the house arrest of the Marquise de Laurent, the cousin of the Duc?"

"Who is he?" asked de la Croix.

"The Marquise de Laurent is a known friend of the Jesuits. He was a companion on the journey with d'Ammecourt on their way to Larousse's office when the fatal attack occurred. After D'Ammecourt was disposed of and the incriminating letter destroyed, the cousin of the Duc was put under house arrest.

"All of this," added the Marèchal, "is hearsay. All we really know is that the Marquise de Laurent has been denounced before the Royal Council for engaging in a plot of some kind that enlists English ships for help against the pirates in the Mediterranean."

Both Antoine and de la Croix were unable to respond to the astounding report.

"What do we do for evidence of all this?" asked le Croix.

"Well, my only evidence is that all of Paris knows that the Jesuits have no more loyal ally than the Marquise de Laurent. For him to be accused of complicity in a plot and confined by house arrest is too absurd for the opponents of the Jansenist Party to accept. What is more, this treatment of the Marquise," the Marèchal became very emphatic here, "may not be surprising to the unquestioning public, but it surely is to anyone familiar with affairs of state."

"As you can guess, I am shocked, and still a bit offended that you did not confide this to me before," de la Croix interposed. The lawyer, as could be expected, was approaching the situation in search of all the legal arguments he could find. That there was something else to be considered besides a legal complaint, had not dawned on him quite yet.

De la Croix was upset with the Marèchal for withholding this item from him because even before Antoine had left for Marseilles, he had sought out the priest for a private interview. He had wondered about the underlying cause of the long standing feud between the Jesuits and the Jansenists. What specifically puzzled him was why a powerful faction in the Parliament called themselves the *Parti Janseniste*. True, many of them were clergy, but he was still trying to figure out why these legislators kept a name significant to what had been basically a Church dispute. How had a theological faction become a political bloc, above all, in the highest legislative branch of the country?

Antoine was the only one to whom he felt he could go. Antoine had the background to give him the answers. Later, of course, he would realize that he should have asked the Marèchal to accompany him. However at the time his impulse was to get some kind of explanation immediately for the deep seated hostility that was mixing politics with religion. He had sought out a specific day and time. Antoine had made arrangements to fit in with his hospital duties.

"Père," began le Croix, when they were together, "I feel I cannot be an active, intelligent partner in our cooperative endeavor, until I understand what is behind this insistence in the Parliament that this group call themselves the *Parti Janseniste*.

"When we held our lawyers meeting after the consulate decision, a member brought up the issue of the controversy with the Jansenists. We were aware in general of the theological debate that has gone on for decades, but none of us had a really clear idea of the basic cause of the dispute. Nor were we able to understand the report that certain members of Parliament were trying to get their hands on the appeal from the lower court — even before any appeal had been made. Besides, all involved are Catholics. It appeared to most of us that the members interested were not truly concerned about the legal issue. They seemed to be carrying a vendetta of some kind.

"Though there are a few Protestants engaged in this matter, the majority are Catholics. So, what has been confusing is that two parties who share the same faith are at odds on disentangling a problem which is really a theological issue. We haven't reached the point of conflict just yet, but it seems to me that Parliament is ignoring the impact of war and piracy on your failure to deliver shipments to France, and the subsequent financial debacle of the Marseilles bank.

"Then perhaps you can make clear what this is all about," the lawyer added. "From childhood, we have heard about the arguments between the

Jansenists and the Jesuits. And as we grew up, we've heard caustic remarks about the rivalry. Was it Diderot, or Voltaire, someone like that, who said he wanted to see the last Jansenist hung with the entrails of the last Jesuit?"

Antoine nodded.

"And I have always understood the dispute to be over salvation and damnation — religious quarrels. But today, we have a political party that keeps the name Jansenist. It's been something of a mystery to us as to why these legislators keep the name of Jansenius alive. He lived in the last century and he was part of a theological dispute."

"Remember, Monsieur de la Croix," remarked Antoine, "people of all ages have been fascinated with the idea of the last judgment. Stars falling from heaven, the sun darkened, no moon, death, hell, heaven. Luther was looking for certitude about his salvation. He won most of Germany, the Netherlands and Scandinavia. John Calvin convinced the Swiss to leave the Catholic Church over the same question: Are you saved?

"I hope you are prepared to be patient," Antoine went on, "because I really need time to give you a small lecture. In case I lose you along the way, remember what I am trying to do is answer the question that you raised: How does a political party grow out of a theological quarrel? That is really the core of the matter."

"I promise to listen with patience," said de la Croix respectfully.

"The most prestigious university in all Europe in the last century was at Louvain in the Netherlands. The most prominent professor there was a man whom everyone knew as Baius. He dedicated his life to the study of St. Augustine, who, he claimed, taught that after the sin of Adam in the Garden of Eden all mankind was condemned to death, pain, depravity. That sin became the Original Sin, the origin of all sinfulness, and it was transmitted through sexual intercourse by parents to their children. Whether justly or not, this Baius was accused of also teaching that God knows all things in advance, including what choices his creatures will make. That being the case, it didn't really matter what choices persons made here on earth. They were predestined to be condemned or saved at the last judgment. They really had no choice. That's an oversimplification, of course," added Antoine.

"That's basically how the fierce debate over the Theory of Predestination took hold on the university campus. A bright, newly appointed professor at Louvain accused Baius and his followers of being advocates of John Calvin, the heretic. Those loyal to Baius countered by saying that the Jesuit was glorifying an earlier heretic, Pelagius, who was blamed for teaching that all of us are perfectly free to choose to follow God's commandments or not. We do not need any special help from on high to do what God wants of us. What further sparked the debate was that the Jesuits claimed St. Thomas Aquinas for their side, while opponents invoked St. Augustine as their patron in heaven.

"Two newcomers entered the fray, Luis de Molina, on the side of the Jesuits, and Cornelius Jansens, on Professor Baius' side. Both factions immediately sought the attention of Rome, seeking to achieve the condemnation of the opposing doctrine. With the help of clever repetition, the Jesuits named their opponents Jansenistic- Calvinists. The name Jansenists stuck. In retaliation, the Jesuits received the nickname of Pelagians."

Antoine paused. "Have you had enough, or do you want more?" he asked.

De la Croix was not exactly pleased.

"All you have done is give me some interesting details of what appears to be a theological dispute between Jansenists and Jesuits which started in the last century."

"With your indulgence, I will continue and try to link the Church conflict to the political," Antoine replied patiently.

"The first link is Richelieu. He was a bishop before he became Cardinal Minister of State. You may think this is ridiculous, but he actually condemned a Jansenist doctrine as too strict. It had to do with what was required to obtain forgiveness in confession — contrition or attrition. Contrition was perfect sorrow and regret for having offended God by one's sins. Attrition meant you were sorry for a lesser motive. You regretted your sin because of fear of God's punishment. Then there was the more delicate issue of whether husband and wife committed mortal sin if they entered into marital relations from a motive of pleasure only, forgetting to seek only the procreation of children. The more lenient positions on these and several other moral questions were favored by the Jesuits; the stricter views were held by the Jansenists, and a prominent one in particular, the Abbé of St. Cyran. Richelieu had St. Cyran arrested and jailed, allegedly for his over strict interpretations, but the real reason was revenge for a pamphlet the Abbé had written against the Cardinal for his helping to finance the deployment of troops of the Protestant leader, Gustavus Adolphus, against the Catholic Augsburgs.

"A further reason for St. Cyran's being thrown in jail was that he had used his influence in Rome to block the annulment of a marriage for the King's brother which Richelieu had been working hard to obtain."

"Are you still with me?" asked Antoine.

A little more light glowed in de la Croix's eyes.

"So you see how those who saw themselves as loyal to St. Augustine began to view the monarchy in the person of Cardinal Richelieu as hostile to their cause?" Antoine paused again. He still had the avid attention of de la Croix, surprisingly enough.

"It's impossible to summarize in a short space the bickering that went on after Richelieu. What complicated the issue and caused many to be disgusted with both the Jesuits and the Jansenists was a kind of theological tug-of-war to enlist the approval of the pope, a competition which bothered the King and his Council of Advisers because of the pope's continued demand for the King's help in a battle the pope could not win.

"First, the Jesuits would send their indictment of Jansenist doctrine to the Vatican; then the Jansenists would reply by sending their accusations of unsound teaching. Then, the Pope would respond by asking the King to help him intervene. Depending on which cardinal wrote on behalf of the Pope, Louis was either failing to protect the faithful from the evil of John Calvin, or he was undermining established Catholic teaching by tolerating lax Jesuits who taught that free will was superior to divine grace.

"Finally," Antoine was self consciously looking at the lawyer for signs of boredom, "finally, Louis turned the tables and demanded some kind of decree from the Pope to stops the endless bickering. And so, that's how a new encyclical called *UNIGENITUS*[6] came to France, allegedly for the whole Church, but no churchman anywhere doubted to whom the message was directed. Basically, the encyclical letter condemned what the Jesuits termed, the 'gloom and doom of Jansenism.'"

Antoine stopped again. "Clear?" His friend was still with him.

"I don't have to repeat what you already know. France is not Spain or Italy. The papal decree solved nothing. The bishops demanded to be consulted, and they were angry that they had not been.

"It may be 40 years ago," Antoine said, "and you may never have heard of it, but members of the Gallican party closed down the Parliament to walk in the funeral cortege of a then prominent cardinal — Cardinal Noailles. You may also never have heard that the dispute was not about whether babies who died without baptism went to hell or not, or if you could receive Holy

---

6 *A celebrated Apostolic Constitution of Clement XI, condemning 101 propositions of Pasquier Quesnel.*

Communion with imperfect sorrow for your sins, or whether you could go to a dance right after receiving Holy Communion. It was a dispute over whether the Bishop of Rome — the Pope — could overrule a cardinal.

"Remember, John Calvin received his first benefice here in France. You don't need me to point out what effect this type of dispute had on the papacy, especially in the light of what both Calvin and Luther had done to Church unity.

"And of course," continued Antoine, "you know where the Jesuits stood because of their vow of total obedience to the Pope. On the other hand, Noailles was the leading Jansenist theologian at the time. He was not bashful in demanding a Church Council to challenge the Pope. You know who won that battle, but you may not know that as a result of that defeat, the successor of Noailles barred the Jesuits from Paris for ten years."

Antoine felt that he had dominated the scene too long, so he stopped and waited de la Croix's reaction.

"Actually, I found it very interesting, Père," de la Croix admitted. "What is more you made it clear to me, as no one else has, what the basis really is for the underlying hostility."

This lengthy theological discourse had occurred well before the d'Ammecourt tragedy, before even Antoine had gone to Marseilles in what he hoped would be escape from turmoil. However, the Marèchal made it something of an issue when he saw how miffed de la Croix was at being kept ignorant of the d'Ammecourt debacle. They were even, in a sense. The Marèchal had been excluded from Antoine's valuable explanation of the Jansenist controversy, but de la Croix had been uninformed for a while in the d'Ammecourt incident.

CHAPTER X

A week went by, then two, with no follow up action in the Parliament to the Jesuit malfeasance charges. The financial liability question seemed to have mysteriously disappeared. It was as though Antoine's long discourse about the roots of the hostility were pointless. The Marèchal was suspicious; de la Croix was baffled. The priests as a group, which included Antoine, believed a rumor that the Bishop of Beauvais had intervened on their behalf, deploring the disgraceful attack on a religious order by the most prestigious legal body of the land. Reliable parliamentarians attested to this report and attributed it to none other than the Abbé Giroux, the royal appointee of the Clerical College of Deputies in the Parliament. A further announcement came from the Speaker that the Abbé was on his way to Rome for a papal consultation on another matter. Hence, conflict seemed to be held in abeyance.

Optimism grew each day, even in the mind of the Marèchal. He had been informed by his friends that the daily debates in the assembly were now focused on the financial woes created by the war — whether to increase the taxes on cognac and how much. When it wasn't finances, it was bitter wrangling over the specter of losing influence in India and Canada. It was as though the Jesuits had ceased to be of interest to the politicians and the crusade against them had somehow been forgotten.

Nonetheless, the Marèchal remained skeptical. He decided to take advantage of the moment and pursue the report that the Bishop of Beauvais was truly interested in their cause. That meant that all the bishops should be approached to make certain that the issues sparked by the lawsuit be removed permanently from parliamentary oversight. In the mind of the Marèchal, no one was more revered than de Sacy. He could be the chief coordinator, using his diplomatic skill to get the bishops firmly on their side. It was vital to start with Père Larousse. Another reason why de Sacy should be the man.

The Maréchal wanted his Jesuit friends to be freed from the implications of this grave situation. Why had the Parliament taken up the adverse judgment of a court whose jurisdiction was mainly commercial disputes? His struggle to find a satisfactory answer had been rewarded with the shock of realizing the deep seated hostility — even hatred — that Antoine had explained in his discourse on the history of the Jesuit–Jansenist feud. Now he was prepared to view the Abbé's absence as quite possibly a temporary reprieve.

The lawyer, de la Croix, was not enthusiastic about the project. Whatever the odds, the law was the law. He believed that they should seize this opportunity. In the absence of the Abbé, they should extract a resolution from the members of the Parliament which would declare the illegality of any attempt to charge the Jesuit Order with liability for Lavalette. However, he thought it best not to challenge the Maréchal's enthusiasm for an appeal to the bishops.

De la Croix's skepticism about their ability to stimulate the support of the bishops had one good effect. It spurred the Maréchal to think and plan carefully. The result was that he had the idea of reaching out to the parishes in Paris and beyond. The point was to get the faithful in the pews sympathetic to a plea on the priests' behalf.

He spent most of one evening trying to convince de la Croix of the need to conduct some kind of campaign. Even though the apparent armistice might be permanent, the priests needed the bishops with them and all the parishioners they could reach. A clear majority of the bishops were their friends. Over half of the present members of Parliament were diocesan priests. They would have to give their bishops a hearing, even though their hearts were not in it. Nothing would be lost by having more sympathizers than they needed. No precaution was too much when the Jesuit ministry, so vital to Catholic education, was under attack.

"The bishops have to be publicly on our side," the Maréchal said in his exhortation to de la Croix, Antoine, and de Sacy. He was adamant before Larousse and all the Jesuits when they were finally able to assemble.

Another period of waiting ensued. Visits that were painfully dusty and bumpy, in bad weather and in good, filled the interval. De Sacy had done a stellar job in convincing his confreres that each and every bishop had to be interviewed — one on one.

In the meantime Antoine went back to the hospital, spending busy days in serving the sick. There were nights when the chaplain was simply too tired to walk over to the Jesuit residence to query de Sacy on how the campaign was faring. When he did go, he learned that Père Larousse needed some convincing, and that he kept putting off an interview with Belle Isle. Finally, he gave in. He assembled as many Jesuits as he could for a discussion of the proposed approach to the bishops.

It was obvious that Larousse still did not think that this was the proper procedure. Nor did he view the situation as sufficiently grave to seek episcopal assistance on such a scale. 'Why disturb the peace?' was at the root of his attitude. All was tranquil now; Lavalette was a hospital chaplain, not raising any eyebrows. Enjoy the present. The Gospel was on his side as well. It told you not to worry about the morrow; be like the lilies of the field, and trust in God. He had found it very difficult to share the Marèchal's apprehension that this period might be just a lull in the battle.

At last, his excuses for not moving on the idea of an appeal to the bishops for support ran out. It took a personal interview, set up by both the Marèchal and de la Croix, to make him relent.

De Sacy did not leave Antoine during the interval. He filled in details by sending him a copy of the questionnaire that had been sent all over the country, as well as the recorded votes of the bishops after a poll had been taken. Antoine received it at the hospital.

Four questions had been formulated:

1. In your opinion does the Society of Jesus perform a vital function in our country?

2. What is the manner in which the Jesuits conduct themselves in your diocese?

3. Are the Jesuits obedient to their bishops and loyal citizens to His Majesty?

4. Do you consider it fair that all the Jesuits in our country should be held liable for debts incurred by one of their number in faraway Martinique?

Energetically, priests and lay brothers made their rounds to the chanceries with their survey, and made a second trip to collect the replies. Forty-four bishops out of fifty-one gave them positive recommendations.

Armed with the results of the bishops' approval, and a carefully drafted critical analysis of the lower court's decision holding the Jesuits responsible for Antoine's debts, the Marèchal made an eloquent plea to the legislators. A lot of soul searching had gone into the decision to include the analysis, but both de la Croix and the Marèchal were at one on this point. The judgment of the lower court was an essential adjunct in any statement proposed for the bishops' approval.

Obviously, this added detail revealed the hand of the Marèchal. Despite the success of the bishops' poll, he still could not give in completely to the idea that this period was anything more than a brief period of grace afforded by the absence of the Abbé. At the risk of seeming intransigent to many Jesuits, he demanded an extra copy to be placed in the hands of all the deputies in the Parliament. The prestige of the bishops' approval, plus the analysis with its sound legal arguments ought to be sufficient insurance against the more hostile minority in the Parliament.

In the weeks that followed, there was no reason for Antoine to go near the Jesuit residence. He was waiting for a response from the superior to renew his permission to head back to Martinique. The immediate threat was behind them, but the indebtedness still remained. If he could be allowed to return to the Caribbean to deal with that, there would be no need for legal or parliamentary action.

Unfortunately, Père Larousse acted as though the indebtedness had also disappeared. There was nothing Antoine could do about that. Once again he threw himself into his work as hospital chaplain. There were others far more miserable than he.

His escape did not last ten days. Unfortunately, a note from de Sacy heralded a storm. There were rumors from Rome of a different interpretation for the absence of Abbé Giroux. Giroux had headed a select delegation that gained a private interview with the Pope. Antoine was trying to put his heart back into ministering to the sick and dying in Paris, while hoping to return to Martinique. Meanwhile, four men in Rome with portfolios under their arms stood in the anteroom of the Vatican waiting for a Papal audience. Finally a member of the Swiss Guard opened the door. He ushered the small group into the Vatican chamber and announced their presence to Pope Clement XIII.

"Your Holiness, I present to you:

"M. Diego Carcao, legate of the Duc de Pombal of Portugal.

"M. Jacinto la Plaja, legate of His Majesty, Carlos of Spain.

"M. Giorgio Pacomo, legate of His Majesty, Giuseppi, King of the Two Sicilys.

"Abbé Francois Giroux, legate of the Parliament of Paris, in the name of Louis XV of France."

After the formalities, each of the representatives approached the throne to kiss the ring of Pope Clement and duly bowed before the two cardinals flanking the Pope. The Abbé came forward as spokesman.

"Your Holiness," he began with another respectful bow, "my colleagues have done me the honor of designating me to speak on their behalf. As representatives of the four most Catholic countries of Europe, they have bestowed their choice upon me because I come from France, the eldest daughter of Holy Mother the Church. As you know from previous correspondence, we are here to discuss a grave matter which concerns all of Christendom. We speak as one voice for the Catholic countries which we represent. We urge you to hear our petitions for the removal from our midst of the Society of Jesus, for being a harmful influence to our citizens as well as to our fellow members of the Church."

He made a dramatic pause. Then he took a vellum page from his portfolio.

"I have here a document signed by one-hundred ten Jesuits, excuse me, one-hundred ten members of the Society of Jesus, which establishes their total support for the Gallican Articles[7]. It is true, Your Holiness, that this document was signed in the last century and was also later repudiated. But it revealed the thinking of the French members of this group. The fact that it was repudiated does not really exonerate the original signers. They were under severe pressure to reject what they had affirmed, that is that a Council was superior to the Pope. My purpose in resurrecting this document is to graphically illustrate the question: How could Catholic religious have signed such articles in the first place?

"Let me present this to you." The Abbé approached the throne and handed a highly illustrated written page to the Pope who turned it over to his Cardinal Secretary.

"It is not necessary for me to comment on this blatant contempt for your sovereign authority over the Bishops of France. Nor do I think it to be irrelevant that this occurred in the last century. I submit this as evidence of an important page in history, indicating the Order's disregard for authority in the past. It seems vital to me to reiterate the charge that this group still maintains its independent views. I would like to present to you a situation, a source

7 *Gallican Articles: The principles enunciated by the French Roman Catholic Church in 1682, claiming limited autonomy as opposed to ultrmontanism.*

of dismay in my country, caused by an individual Jesuit, named Lavalette. However, I would rather yield to my colleagues to allow them to present you with evidence from both the civil and the ecclesiastical realm to corroborate our contention that the existence of the Society of Jesus is a definite threat to our public welfare. I call upon M. Diego Carcao of Portugal."

"What I have here is a coin, Your Holiness," began the M. Carcao. "Engraved on it is the head of Nicholas I, of the Jesuit Kingdom of Paraguay." He handed the coin to the Pope who examined it then passed it on to his associates.

"I also have a more detailed account of the Jesuit's kingdom which you and the Reverend Cardinals can read at your leisure. For the moment, I only wish to emphasize that these priests have lured some 40,000 Guarani Indians to abandon their labor on plantations in the south of Paraguay to move northward to a zone quite isolated from other settlements. This move caused immense hardships to Catholic landowners of the south, which I need not go into at this moment. In addition to enslaving these simple natives, they organized a rebellion among them when a decree from the King of Portugal moved Brazil's border southward and declared their land legally forfeit. It is clearly proven that Jesuits themselves took part in this armed rebellion. And now, I ask you...."

Before he could continue, the cardinal on the Pope's left interrupted. "Isn't there some disagreement as to just what happened in that border dispute between Brazil and Portugal? I have heard different versions. And I have heard that the philosopher,

Voltaire, spoke of the Jesuit work with the Guarani as the greatest humanitarian effort of this century."

"Certainly," countered Carcao. "With all due respect, Your Holiness, I wouldn't trust any statement of a known enemy of the Church, who wanted to see her erased from the face of the earth, as though she were an infamous woman."

"I am just saying," replied the cardinal, "that there is more than one version of what happened thousands of miles away from us many years ago."

After this exchange, Carcao handed his portfolio to the Pope for his perusal.

Next, the Abbé presented M. Plaja of Spain, who began politely. "Your Holiness, the portfolio that I wish to present is self-explanatory. It contains an account of the way in which the Jesuits have exploited the general permission of our King Charles to maintain a private army. With their native recruits, the priests have repulsed generous offers of employment from our Spanish colonists. I feel I have explained the situation clearly enough so I can leave the matter for you to read at your leisure.

"There is another topic which weighs heavily on me — one on which I prefer to hear your views. Unfortunately, I have not had the time to write out my thoughts on this subject. It concerns China. It is only during these days when we have been preparing to have an audience with you about the Jesuits working in our kingdom and colonies, that I have learned from the Abbé Giroux some astonishing facts about the Order's missionary works in the Orient. With your permission, I should like to present what I have been told. I promise to be as brief as possible."

Pope Clement looked at his cardinal aide for a moment. The cardinal shrugged his shoulders in acceptance; the Pope nodded his approval. It was obvious that he was in agreement with the critical attitude of his guests.

"I learned for the first time that just a little over twenty years ago, Pope Benedict wrote an encyclical, *Ex quo singulari*[8], in which he not only condemned Jesuit practices in China, but imposed a mandatory oath for all missionaries going to that country. The oath required them to promise never to take part in the rituals which the Jesuits had approved. This is obviously something with which you must be familiar.

"The Abbé described for me how the Jesuits approved burning incense, lighting candles, placing food in the center of each table in the homes of the deceased, as though they could still eat and smell. In the center of each table were little wooden tablets with the names of the dead persons on them with dates of birth and death, and marriage as well. These tablets were called 'spiritual tablets.' The Abbé told me that the Dominican and Franciscan missionaries had denounced these practices to Rome a hundred years ago. The Jesuits claimed that superstition was totally in conformity with our teaching and devotion to the souls in Purgatory.

"I was amazed to learn, Your Holiness, that these rituals were endorsed by a priest named Mateo Ricci, who refused to wear a cassock like other priests. Instead he walked around with the ceremonial square bonnet and the silk robe of the Confucian scholars. Rather than devote himself to teaching about the gospels, he made a name for himself by introducing the latest European advances in astronomy and mathematics. For this reason he was given the name of 'Doctor from the Great West Ocean.' Referring to Confucius, this Ricci wrote a series of axioms in veneration of the man which he

---

8 *Bull of July 11, 1742 in which Benedict XIV suppressed the Chinese Rites.*

entitled *Wisdom of the Orient*. In perfect Chinese — he spoke the language fluently — he used such words as 'heaven' and 'Supreme Lord and Ruler,' referring, of course, to Confucius. The reaction of the time, according to the Abbé Giroux, was that other Catholic missionaries wrote to Rome saying that if Mateo Ricci were not checked, the Chinese converts to Catholicism would have statues of Confucius on the altar beside those of Christ."

At this point, la Plaja bowed and started to go back to his chair. But before he did so, the Abbé hurried forward.

"Please excuse me for interrupting, Your Holiness, but M. la Plaja omitted one of the most significant aspects of what you here in Rome refer to as the 'Chinese Rites.' The most severe ecclesiastical punishment ever imposed on a religious order was the prohibition against receiving seminarians for a two-year period. This was the penalty the Jesuits paid for the ceremonials they had espoused. I think it is imperative that we remind Your Holiness of that fact."

"I am quite aware of that, thank you," responded Pope Clement.

Next, the Abbé presented Giorgio Pacomo of the kingdom of the Two Sicilys.

"My government," he began, "has become aware of Jesuit involvement in the shipping trade in the Caribbean though our contacts with Montecristo, one of the ports which Columbus touched in his journey to the new world. I am not sure that Your Holiness has been informed about the importance of the Caribbean islands to the sugar trade. I have explained this at length in the portfolio I am about to give you. Suffice it to say that the colonists from England who settled on the east coast of North America get their sugar and molasses from the islands of the Caribbean. They do so in violation of English law. Another word for this kind of trade is smuggling. It is a dangerous trade, involving piracy and killing. It is certainly not the kind of work to which a priest is called. I am not sure you have heard that the Jesuit priest, Lavalette, actually engaged in a battle with a pirate ship in which he personally fired a cannon killing three men. On top of that, we know that he so won the admiration of the pirate crew that they offered him a position as chaplain on their ship!

"Another point which I have explained in some detail is that this kind of trade is a vital source of coinage for the American colonists who find themselves handicapped by paper currency, the only kind of money their English lords allow them.

"It is not for me to recall the gospel scene where Jesus condemns the money-changers in the temple. But it is my duty to inform Your Holiness that the reputation of this priest, Lavalette, as a money-changer has reached the shores of Sicily."

After handing his portfolio to the pontiff, the legate Pacomo took his seat.

Allowing for another dramatic pause, the Abbé Giroux stood up and walked slowly to take a stance in front of Pope Clement.

"I will no longer impose on your time, Your Holiness, but in closing our testimony, there are a couple of points which we as a group have failed to bring out. One is the issue of commerce — buying and selling at a profit. We have no need to point out to you and your colleagues that this activity is forbidden to priests. We have included ample evidence of that in our written reports. There is another item which we forgot to include. Of the two partners in Lavalette's buying and selling and smuggling, one is a Jew and the other is a Protestant. I conclude our representation to you by asking how we can tolerate a religious order that allows one of its priests to associate with Jews and Protestants?"

As the group prepared to leave the papal chambers, the Pope spoke. He said that he and his two cardinal associates would give careful attention to the testimony that had been given.

This puzzled Carcao, Duc de Pombal's legate from Portugal, who had been chosen at the last minute to represent his country at the papal audience on the Jesuits.

"Do you think we convinced him?" he asked the Abbé as they descended the long staircase out of the Vatican. "He didn't seem to show any reaction at all to what we said."

"Don't worry," replied Giroux. "Your Pombal has been in contact with the most likely candidate to be his successor. There are good reasons to believe that he will be less defensive of the *Jesus-ites*, and more open to what we have in mind."

"Pombal never mentioned that to me," confessed Carcao.

There were details that the Abbé kept from those who had accompanied him to see Pope Clement. He would reveal them another day. He had another agenda that his colleagues had served well for the moment. They were no longer necessary. He left them and made his way back to France. He had spent almost six weeks visiting the offices of cardinals. He was anxious to get back to Paris. Finally he arrived, late one Sunday night.

Early the next morning he was in his office at the Parliament. By noon, all members in the immediate vicinity of Paris had been informed of his return. Riders on horseback were galloping to the provinces to summon those who had gone home. There was to be a mandatory convocation. Few members had any idea of what his mission had been. In his capacity as clerical counselor to the Parliament, he had sufficient authority to arrange for a special session. Once assembled, few members were surprised that again the Jesuits were under scrutiny. The speaker recalled the motion to hold the Order liable for Lavalette's debts. The minority was taken aback because it had only been a few days since they received the bishops' endorsement with the detailed analysis prepared by the Marèchal.

It had been a tense day for all the Jesuits in Paris who were waiting for an explanation of what was going on. The absent Abbé had returned and summoned a special session of the Parliament. It was several days before the news reached Jesuits in the provinces that all their efforts to gain for support from the bishops appeared to have been cast aside and there was a new and threatening development.

They were told that the clerk had made a perfunctory acknowledgment of the folio he had received from the bishops. Several members had sought to be recognized by the chair. They had been ignored. A dozen members of the Roman Party stood up shouting: "Point of order." They, too, had been ignored. Instead, the clerk read from the legislative rules of procedure to confirm that the Parti Janseniste, because of a previous request, had priority for the rostrum. The Abbé Giroux, as official coordinator of his party, was recognized to speak. Action on "in defense of the Jesuits" that was based on the bishops' testimony was adjourned indefinitely.

What became obvious was that the Speaker had clearly anticipated any efforts to place the Jesuit appeal on the agenda once the Abbé had returned. His reasoning was flawless. The issue for the priests was complicated by the request of the bishops for special consideration of their statements. Hence, it was a matter for the clergy. Two good reasons for isolating the appeal were presented. First, the committee of the clergy should consider the matter before it was sent to the laity. Second, the majority party was also entitled to evaluate the petition. Moreover, ninety-five percent of the majority party were clergy. Thus the Speaker had successfully confined the matter to committee, which was to say it was not just adjourned, it was tabled.

Two amendments by the Roman Party demanding immediate consignment of the appeal to committee, and the limiting of hearings to one week only were voted down. A narrow majority then succeeded, after some shouting and offensive debate, in winning a vote to permit the clergy committee to use their discretion as to the amount of time they needed before any further action could be taken.

For Antoine, the interval that followed was not a problem. Not because the parliamentary strategy did not merit some serious scrutiny and reflection, but because he could once again escape by throwing himself into his hospital routine. Part of this routine involved visiting the homes of those who had been released from their sick beds and those who had lost dear ones. (This, of course, brought back memories of his visits to the villages on Martinique.) In addition, he also served as an intermediary for families who wanted to commit relatives to the care of the nuns. This provided occasions for meeting with the nuns and comforting the sick people. It occupied his time and helped him put away the specter of the majority in the Parliament who were toying with the fate of the Jesuits.

Antoine's respite from controversy lasted about six weeks. One afternoon a messenger brought a note from de Sacy advising him of another important gathering that very night. There was nothing in the note that aroused anxiety in Antoine. Yet as he approached the parish residence, he realized that something was definitely afoot.

The parlor windows were ablaze with candlelight. To his great amazement, Antoine entered a room filled with more than a dozen Jesuits, most of whom squatted on the floor. Larousse, his advisory team, and both the Marèchal and lawyer de la Croix were there as well. To his further surprise, no one seemed to notice him, not even Larousse. How could it be that the presence of the culprit in all of this raised no eyebrows? He found a corner for himself and saw before him a different Père Larousse. He was a man shaken by a peremptory summons from the Clerk of the Parliament to submit a copy of the Jesuit Constitutions within forty-eight hours. The shock had obviously not worn off. The unbelievable had become believable. The original charge of the Order's liability for Antoine's debts was not up for consideration. Rather, the Order itself was on trial. Its book of rules and regulations were to be scrutinized by legislators, which was unheard of. Larousse was reaching out for help as never before. Now he saw his need for de Sacy who had contacts with the Pompadour, the Marèchal with his reputation and friendship with King Louis, and de la Croix for his legal expertise. He also needed his brothers in Christ because never before had such a summons been received by the Jesuits.

Larousse was at his wits' end. He wasn't making a lot of sense when Antoine came in. He talked about appealing to the King for justice, for protection. He seemed to have forgotten that he had consistently opposed that kind of appeal.

Antoine tried to listen to the discussion that ensued. It was difficult to be patient. It was embarrassing for him, especially because he could see himself as the primary cause. He felt he had to intervene. He asked to be recognized.

There was an awkward pause. Larousse and company were not about to listen to anything Antoine had to say. With a gesture, the Marèchal overruled them.

"Mons Pères, as I am the culpable one," Antoine began, "I deserve to be heard. First of all, I totally agree that we have to seek the protection of the Royal Court, this time of the King himself. Before we do so, I think we should make a written and oral appeal to the Parliament so that we have a public document to present to King Louis. In this appeal we have to declare that I am the person responsible for this situation. Moreover, I will throw myself on the mercy of the judges for my failure." He paused, almost tearfully.

"How can anyone demand our book of rules in a case like this? You are not the ones who tried to transport sugar on Caribbean ships. You were not in Martinique. I propose to go before the Parliament as the one who is guilty. You must let them proceed against me, not you."

"We know all that," burst in Larousse. "We don't want to hear it again. We're not here for a public confession. We have forty-eight hours to respond to a demand of the Parliament asking for our rule, the Constitutions of our Order. That is the issue now."

"Please, with all due respect, Père Larousse," insisted Antoine. "What I am trying to say is that we demand that the legislators look at the commercial issue first, something they have neglected to do for weeks and weeks. I propose with the help of the Marèchal and other parliamentary members that we seek permission to speak and give evidence, which I understand can be granted. In my presentation, I can emphasize the propriety of taking first things first. In the event that the Abbé Giroux and his friends prevent me from speaking or reject my appeal, we will have a better case to present to King Louis, and it will be in writing. The parliamentary clerk will see to this. What is more," Antoine directed a meaningful glance toward Père Larousse, "we will not be trying to cloak ourselves in royal protection. We will be seeking royal authority to demand the hearing of the original charge against me. At the same time, we will be highlighting the fact that Parliament has taken up a second and third action before dealing with the first. Further, the King will be moved by a plea of mercy; no court in the land could ignore such a plea."

What Antoine did not realize was that his proposal was worthless unless someone in the Parliament could be called on to help. Proper procedure required that the original charge had to be put on the agenda first. This was imperative lest it be buried indefinitely, and vital because of the new and radical tactic which Abbé Giroux and his friends were trying to rush through — the demand for the Jesuit book of rules.

So it was that the group of priests approved his going personally before the legislators. Larousse, in spite of himself, was touched by Antoine's effort to divert the blame. This action offered relief from the disturbing prospect of turning over the Constitutions of the Order to public scrutiny. The Marèchal offered qualified approval. He hadn't been present in the visitors' balcony when the vote was taken to demand a copy of the Jesuit rule book, nor were his friends present in sufficient numbers to insist that they had not finished with the prior claim: Antoine's debts as a Jesuit liability. It was only the day after the vote that the Marèchal had a chance to see the docket at the clerk's desk and find out what stratagem had been adopted. Listening first to de la Croix's advice, the Marèchal decided to put his faith in this procedural challenge. It would be cruel to dampen the spirit of Antoine, for whom they had come to have deep affection. It would be interesting to see the reaction of the legislators as they had to make a decision in the face of such a gallant effort by a beleaguered priest. It would be difficult for anyone with a conscience to invoke procedural rules in such an emotional scene.

It was not easy for the Marèchal or de la Croix to conceal their feelings as their guest took his place between them in the assembly the following morning. They found the atmosphere most uncomfortable. They would have preferred open hostility to the polite tolerance they were shown. There had been an unusual pause in the legislative house after the Speaker had announced this novel agenda, but no one made a move. The hushed moment seemed to Antoine's two protectors to have the aspect of an elementary school play, where Antoine was ingenuously presenting a script before an adult audience.

Silence pervaded the chambers. Antoine became nearly tearful as he blamed himself for the bankruptcy. No other audience could have remained as stoic as this assembly. Antoine begged them to see him as the guilty one, not the Jesuits.

The Abbé received the plea graciously and thanked Antoine profusely for his noble effort. He promised to enlist all his co-religionists to carefully reflect on his petition. Then he dismissed the session for the day.

When the three visitors left, the assembly members prepared to leave. But once the Jesuit contingent had gone on their way, the legislators filed back into the chamber and the session began again.

The ugly, hunched-back Abbé took over the podium. He dominated the scene, not only because of his deformity, but because of his stentorious voice. He gesticulated frequently, swinging his cape as he turned right and left to emphasize his points. His voice literally bounced off the walls!

"It is well known," thundered the Abbé, "that the Jesuits are recognized both inside and outside the Catholic Church as obedient men. They are obedient to their Father General in Rome, and it goes without saying, to the Pope. They are very obedient to his Majesty the King, especially when it serves their interest.

"It is also well known to all that this merchant priest, Père Antoine Lavalette, has been engaged in business transactions and investments for more than a decade. He has engaged with pirates, Protestants and Jews. All of this with the approval of his superiors.

"This priest, Lavalette, was named Vicar-Apostolic of the Windward Islands. This title means that he was the official representative of the Catholic Church in that area of the Caribbean and also the highest authority of the Jesuit Order. Such an appointment must have the approval of the Vatican itself and his Father General. Contrary to what he has just presented to us under the aegis of our respected colleague, the Marèchal del Belle Isle," the Abbé dramatized his deformity at this juncture by bowing awkwardly to the table where the Marèchal and the two guests had been seated, "Père Antoine Lavalette cannot be treated as an isolated perpetrator by this tribunal. There is no denying that his commercial activity was inextricably linked to the chain of command within the Catholic Church and his religious order.

"As a consequence," the Abbé made an even more dramatic pause before going on, "the reality is that now it is irrelevant to spend any more time on this matter. The whole structure of the Religious Order of Jesuits is on trial here. Therefore, it is our duty to carefully evaluate the rules and regulations of this congregation with a view of seeing whether it should continue to exist among us." With another sweep of his cloak, the Abbé strode from the rostrum. As he left, he made a comment to the clerk with a sardonic smile.

Later on in the week, a friend of the Marèchal quoted what the Abbé whispered to the clerk. "Wouldn't it be an irony of history," he had said, "if one cripple were to destroy the religious order that came into existence at the hand of another cripple?"

What did he mean by this remark, the lawyer wondered several days later.

"Ignatius of Loyola was a soldier," the Marèchal explained. "In a battle in the Pyrenees with the French, he was hit in the knee by a deflected cannon ball and limped for the rest of his life. He is the one who founded the Jesuits. That's what the Abbé was referring to.

"It was a caustic way to refer to the Order," added the Marèchal. "Jesuits have always venerated the memory of the time he was bedridden after the fractured knee. While he was recovering from his injury, he demanded surgery on the knee because there was a protruding bone. He wanted it sawed off so he could once again appear on the dance floor in the tight fitting hose of the courtier. The resulting prolonged convalescence was so tedious that he was willing to read anything available. The only books at hand were of a religious nature. Reluctantly, he settled for the *Lives of the Saints*. The road to recovery led to a conversion of his mind that in turn led to the priesthood and the founding of the Jesuits.

"It's a sentimental story. The Abbé had it clearly in mind when he concluded his speech. The barb was uncalled for."

The following morning there was gathering of Jesuits anxious to hear how Antoine's appeal had fared. Père Larousse was there with his four consultants. The group had little time to dwell on the rejection of Antoine's plea. The matter of the Jesuit rule being submitted to legislative debate preoccupied them. They had been given forty-eight hours to comply with the mandate. The deadline would be at 5:00 P.M. on this very day.

"I shall do all I can to enlist the help of my lawyer friends," began de la Croix. "I do think there is still time, no matter what the odds. I also believe that a carefully drafted legal plea based on statutes and precedent will persuade a good number of the legislators to reconsider the underlying agenda."

"I thank you for your effort, M. de la Croix." The Jesuits were attentive as the Marèchal intervened. "I cannot but believe," he went on, "that there are enough fair-minded men who will attend to their conscience and have the courage to stand up against what appears to be a coordinated effort to go beyond legal boundaries. I don't think we have enough time to engage more lawyers." He bowed respectfully to his friend de la Croix.

"Drafting a new plea and getting another hearing should still be on our agenda, however desperate that may seem. Right now we have this 5:00 P.M. deadline."

His audience listened somberly. Many of them still clung to the hope that his emotional appeal would win the day.

"My counsel is to get another copy of your rules to the King as fast as possible. I will personally deliver the copy to the Royal Secretary. Perhaps I will get a chance to see him face to face. If not, I will beg the Royal Council to take up a study of your rules. I have a friend in the group, Comte Denis Destriches. I believe he will come to my aid. What we need is a carefully worded royal decree requesting a postponement until such time as His Majesty and his council have perused the rules and considered the allegations put forth by the Abbé."

"I am still confused, M. Marèchal," Larousse interposed. "Our Jesuit rules are a matter of church discipline. The parliament has no right to inspect our way of life. How we live and work is strictly a church matter. Isn't there any way that we can block this demand at once by an order of the King?"

"An authoritarian block is not the way to go now for many reasons," replied the Marèchal. "Considering the relations between the King, his advisers and members of the Parliament, a royal decree will only serve to alienate and entrench our opponents."

The Marèchal turned to de la Croix. "You have some friends in the Parliament. Don't you agree that a royal decree will offend rather than help?"

Before the lawyer had a chance to reply, Larousse exclaimed excitedly. "Two of my consultants say I must hand over the book of rules and two others say no. I do not know what the legalities are here, or what my obligation is, or what the diplomatic strategy should be. Now you tell me I must send another book of rules to the King's Court. I do not know what I should do, nor do I know what is best. Our Constitutions are a private matter. I don't want the whole world to see them."

"Technically speaking, you are perfectly correct, Père Larousse." De la Croix did his best to calm the priest. "Mon Père, I understand your distress. However, as a lawyer, I see the situation now as completely extra-legal. The leaders of the Parliament see themselves as a court. They are not a court, but they pretend to be. This is clear from their demand to hand over your rule books to use as evidence." He finished by saying, "The only avenue open to us, in my opinion, is to grant what they demand."

There is obviously some duplicity here," added the Marèchal. "I don't think the Jesuits are ready even to suspect what that is. My advice is to hand over your rules; and at the same time, commission me to go before King Louis with another copy. This way, we appear docile and submissive while we are seeking the protection of King Louis."

De la Croix intervened again. "Père Larousse, I totally agree with the Marèchal. Several lawyers I know have been researching this matter ever since the Abbé returned. I have brought it up before, I know, but this type of claim has been made in cases involving the Franciscans and Benedictines. The Royal Council with the approval of the King has consistently invoked the 'non-solidarity clause' of church law which has been recognized as a precedent in other disputes of this nature. Individual houses of religious women and men may share a common tradition, but they are only administratively linked. No one can claim financial and property ties just because these houses have a common saint as their patron founder."

"But what about our obedience to legitimate civil authority?" One of Père Larousse's advisers raised this question: "Is it appropriate for us who claim to be models of obedience to be seen as defiant and evasive?"

"That is not the issue at all," responded Larousse. "Our book of Constitutions has nothing to do with civil law. It is a guideline for the way to perfection. It tells us how to live closer to Jesus. I really don't see how the rules can be used against us, even though you, M. Marèchal, seem to be hinting that something more sinister is behind the demand."

A serious debate followed in which the Marèchal and de la Croix did not participate. The issue was now in the hands of the Jesuits themselves. The debate could be terminated only by the Superior, who had the final word.

Unfortunately, Père Larousse was not informed of what occurred the following day when the Abbé Giroux had the podium, and was waving the rule book in the air during another special session. It was probably just as well, because Larousse would continue denying the evidence before him, and he would be the last of the priests to realize what was really about to happen.

Because he had so many friends in the Parliament, the Marèchal learned of another special session to which he had not been called — one that followed the delivery of the rule book. Fortunately, a confidential memo reached his home after the gathering had been hastily assembled. The Marèchal had hurried into the special meeting just as the Abbé was pounding the podium with the copy of the book that Père Larousse had personally put into his hands.

"I submit," the Abbé was saying as he continued to hammer on the book, "that the issue is not how many miles separate France from Martinique, nor how many separate Jesuit houses we have here, but rather the Jesuit rule that links them together in an iron bond.

"For this we have only to look closely at this book of Constitutions. This book reveals to us that the obedience to the Superior General and to his subordinates is absolute. The famous, or infamous as you wish, Inigo de Loyola, wrote a letter which every Jesuit must read each month, in which he cites as a model the example of the monk who watered a dry stick for weeks. He was not to reflect on whether it would grow or not, only his obligation to obey his superior.

"This is the kind of obedience Jesuits are called to observe. It is referred to by their founder as 'blind obedience' — unquestioning submission. This type of total submission is made by vow to the Pope. This is not a monarchical system as we have here — respecting our beloved King Louis. It is despotic rule. This is harmful to our nation. This type of servitude makes of its members indentured slaves of a foreign body residing in Rome. This priest, then, Père Lavalette, has brought this nefarious system to light. He had the dual authorization from Rome, both Pope and Father General, to act as he did. Hence, I say to you, my comrades, compromise is out of the question. For the good of France this group should be banned permanently. And I call upon all here present to vote accordingly when next we call a plenary session."

The Abbé took his seat, but not before wiping his eyes as though real tears were present.

This was a Friday. As the Marèchal left the assembly to which he had not been invited, he found it impossible to be hopeful in any sense. The following Friday there would be one final assemblage. During the week there might be a few committee meetings. The summer vacation would bring an eight week break. Such an interval without some kind of defensive action might be irremediable. It was imperative that they unite their friends with members of the Roman Party, and a group of eminent Catholics to make a personal call upon King Louis to emphasize the urgency with which they needed royal protection. The Abbé and his loyalists had to be sidetracked somehow. Their charges could not be left unchallenged for two months. As usual, the Marèchal had to seek out his friend, the lawyer de la Croix. His help was vital. The people he hoped to assemble before the King and his council were of such diverse temperaments that they would need detailed briefing. Perhaps even the Marèchal and de la Croix would not be able to provide shelter in this storm.

CHAPTER XI

While the Marèchal was spending the weekend recruiting a board of appeals for a special mission to the palace, another clandestine meeting was going on in a remote corner of the Parliament. It was a Sunday afternoon session. Extreme precautions had been taken so that no unwanted members would be present. Their goal was to prepare the agenda for the forthcoming final session.

It would be several months before the priests and their friends would learn exactly what the Abbé said during that meeting.

"I have called you here as the heads of our principal committees because so far we have allowed some wide ranging issues concerning the Jesuits to occupy our time," said the Abbé. "I wish to bring up a consideration which is absolutely basic to any evaluation of the presence of this religious order in our midst.

"We in this assembly have been considering secondary issues, such as the financial liability in the Martinique affair, the book of Jesuit rules, and slavish obedience demanded of anyone who would be part of this group. However harmful their teachings and practices may be, both politically and theologically, they are not the key factors that we face.

"There is a question of legal title that no one has as addressed; this question overshadows all other allegations. It is simply this: where did they get the right to exist in the first place? There is no more fundamental question than that." At this point the Abbé raised a scroll containing documents whose pages were yellow with the years.

"This Parliament," he intoned, "the highest legislative tribunal in the land, has never authorized the Society of Jesus to teach in this country. Historical documents," he waved the scroll over his head, "will show that both in 1561 and in 1603, there were two distinct opportunities for this body to approve the Jesuits as our teachers. This opportunity was denied. Instead there was a delay and in 1618 the Jesuits opened the College of Clermont by virtue of a decree of the Royal Council, the intimate friends of the King. This decree was vigorously opposed by the University of Paris as an affront to their reputation and an infringement on their prerogatives."

The Abbé paused for effect. He looked over the heads of his listeners to the only layman in their midst. Their visitor had slipped in unnoticed, attired in academic gown and hat.

"Let me present to you, Dr. Christophe de Ravignan, Regent of the University, who has kindly consented to be with us this morning."

All present bowed, and the honored Regent stood and doffed his cap.

"He is here," the Abbé had continued, "to answer any question and resolve any doubts you may have on what I am about to say.

"Despite the opposition of the leading scholars of the day, and the unanimous opposition of the faculty, the King and his Royal Council approved the right of the Jesuits to open a college in Clermont, which they soon baptized with the name of Louis le Grande. Incidentally, many of you may not know that Père Lavalette, who has caused such a stir in our country, once taught there before distinguishing himself as a missionary in the Antilles." This was an appropriate moment for the Abbé to pause, just in case the innuendo had not registered.

"From that site, protected by the King, the Jesuits have expanded their academic domain until they now run one-hundred twelve schools and colleges. In England they have been called the 'School Masters of France' among other insults. Yet, they have never been granted legal status. They exist here only because of Royal protection, as I have endeavored to bring out and as Dr. Christophe will verify. They do not have a truly legalized position in France. Consequently, I want your active and vigorous support when I bring a motion to this floor in plenary session later on this week. Because of the moral harm of their teaching which includes authorizing regicide, their vagaries on the subject of freedom of the will, their insistence on blind submission to their rules, and finally, the financial debacle they have caused in Martinique and here in Marseilles, we will propose that their claim to existence in our country be reconsidered."

There was no need for a dramatic flourish, according to later witnesses. His audience had not expected such a broadside attack. However, according to the final version, no one was taken aback by his final statement:

"They do not belong in our country!"

The day following the secret session brought further bad news. The Marèchal had suddenly become ill. Most of his friends thought it was the startling news about the challenge of the Jesuits' legal title to exist in France that had been the last straw. To this outrage was added the burden of many months in his role as protector. However, unbeknown to many, he had long been a victim of gall stones. Tragically, he was not available for advice at the most critical moment facing the priests. What good would it do to scurry around organizing support for their plea seeking royal protection if the very validity of that protection was under fire? The Marèchal's grave illness could not have occurred at a worse time.

Without the Marèchal, the priests were in a panic. They were without resource as the fated Friday approached. Then, perhaps more devastating than the feared summoning of the final session, was the sudden announcement that there would be an adjournment of the gathered body for eight weeks.

Instead of leading the charge as everyone expected, the Abbé stunned everyone by announcing he would make a personal call upon the Jesuit Superior, Père Larousse. Even the most skeptical had to admit that the Abbé could turn on the charm, although they were still confused about what exactly was brewing.

To the relief of all concerned about the Jesuits' plight, the Abbé's surprise visit seemed plausible. A church dispute had to be relegated to an inferior spot. Ministers of State needed time to reevaluate the progress of the war. Select members of the Parliament, including the Abbé of course, were to meet with the King and his council that same week to discuss some aspect of foreign policy that had not been made public.

In one sense, it was a timely break. The Jesuits needed time to investigate the legal archives of the past century and sift through royal decrees so as to be able to discuss the Abbé's contention intelligently. Only then could they be in a position to defend themselves.

In classical mythology there was a dangerous strait which demanded careful maneuvering by Roman ships passing between the boot of Italy and Sicily. On one side of the narrow strait was a rock called Scylla. On the other side was a whirlpool, Charybdis. This was the kind of predicament that now faced Larousse. His dilemma was to stand up to all the charges or sign the document the Abbé was presenting to him now.

"To seal the spirit of compromise, Père Larousse, and totally extricate the

Jesuits from the surveillance of the Parliament, and to put previous hostility behind us, once and for all, I urge you and your confreres to once again sign the Gallican Articles," the Abbé encouraged.

He hastened to add, "I know how this threatens you. The last thing you want to do is offend the Pope by declaring that the Church here in France is in any way superior to the Vatican."

Larousse paused a long time before answering.

"I don't have to remind you what happened when one-hundred twelve of us signed those Articles in the last century. When our Father General heard about the signatures, he was furious; likewise, the Pope. We had to make a public retraction and that caused a furor here in France. Both the Roman Party and the Parti Janseniste were against us — because we signed and the other because we retracted."

"I cannot help you there," responded the Abbé. "I am simply saying that if you want compromise and peace here, and if you want to divert the hostility and suspicion of those members of Parliament who see you as loyal only to Rome and not France, you should once again sign the Articles. You can let the authorities in Rome fight it out among themselves." The Abbé was about to leave. He acted as though he were only asking a small favor of the Jesuits.

"Just a moment," Larousse interposed. He was trying to cope with the surprising presence of an avowed opponent apparently seeking a compromise. He recalled the statement made famous at Troy, 'beware of Greeks bearing gifts.'

"I never did see the version that was signed years ago." This was the best he could offer at the moment. "Before I can enlist my comrades, I have to carefully read what it is you think we ought to put our names to."

"It's very simple and non-threatening if you ask me," said the Abbé. "Here is a brief summary." He extracted a single sheet of paper from a small bag.

As trusting as Larousse was trying to appear, it was a bit disconcerting to find the Abbé with a copy of the old document in hand.

"The King is independent of the Pope in temporal matters," the Abbé began slowly. He looked up to detect any reaction, and then continued. "That should be easy enough to sign again. We are all familiar with fights over the revenue from church benefices, but my recollection is that our bishops solved those disputes in favor of the local church."

"Number two," he continued, "This is far more delicate. The Church councils, the gatherings of bishops around France, are channels of teaching *on a par* with that of the Pope."

"The words, '*on a par*,' have to be very carefully interpreted," said Larousse hesitantly. "Those three words are not to be interpreted to mean that in a dispute the hierarchy's views are to prevail over the Pope's."

"Number three," the Abbé went on, "The authority of the Pope must be exercised in cooperation with the bishops of France."

"Well," Larousse hesitated again. He was trying to be as diplomatic as possible, given this unique opportunity. "This is more delicate in the light of controversies we have had over Catholic dogma. It has been going on for decades. We would have to debate a statement like that among ourselves before signing. This will take some time."

"As your fellow priest, and confidante," said the Abbé softly, "I think it is imperative that you take a stance like this to offset the hostility caused both to bishops and Catholic laity by this whole Lavalette-Martinique debate."

Never did the Jesuits need the presence of the Marèchal more. He could have blunted the impact of the Abbe's powerful presence on Larousse. A healthy Marèchal would have exposed the veiled threat in the Abbe's words, and would have underlined forcibly the fact that the rationale of their book of Rules was a club being raised over their heads, while their dependence on the King's favor as a legal basis to exist was another.

The temptation to sign was great, indeed. The Jesuits were in deep trouble. The fact that their book of Rules had been demanded, and their authorization to teach in France had been challenged were sufficient warning to the Order to seek some kind of reasonable compromise.

"Number four," read Larousse, "Papal decrees are not absolute; they must be submitted to the Catholic faithful of France for some kind of consensus."

Larousse had to be very careful about his language because the Abbé was taking some notes. "I think we could accept this with reservations, provided the discussion is about opinions that have been debated. Something like limbo, for instance, is open to discussion because what happens to infants who die without Baptism is open to conjecture. On the one hand we all hold that Baptism is necessary. But, on the other we have the majority of the human family who never heard of Baptism. It doesn't make a lot of sense to condemn a vast number of the human race to a secondary destiny, especially, when you are teaching that God's mercy is above all his works. So, we believe that there are areas of doubt and uncertainty in our teachings that allow us some latitude in deciding what are mandatory decrees, and what are open to discussion."

Larousse was thinking out loud, desperately trying to find the right words to use to maintain the Abbé's approval and provide him with a reaction he could pass on to his friends. Dealing with Rome had to wait.

"As I mentioned before," he continued, "it's almost a century since more than a hundred of us accepted similar statements. I don't really condemn those who signed them. I think they were mostly thinking of whether the Pope, because of his status as monarch over the Papal States, has temporal power on a par with our King."

Larousse was struggling to find some sort of compromise that would please the Abbé and still not make himself a target of Rome.

"But don't forget, Père," the Abbé reminded him pointedly, "all the Jesuits who signed the Gallican Articles retracted at the insistence of your Father General."

"You are perfectly right," agreed Larousse. "But in all fairness, I think you could explain the retraction as an action taken within the Jesuit Order. It was a diplomatic move to placate the Pope and the cardinals of the Holy Office in the heat of the moment, rather than a studied change of opinion. Remember the last century saw some very bitter exchanges between the Vatican and the Court over temporal matters, but also over the tenets of Jansenism. There was savage debate over whether what the Pope condemned was the actual teaching of the Jansenists. Bishops and priests, as well as the King, were all trapped in a theological wrangle that lasted for decades. It never was solved."

"You must keep in mind, Père," said the Abbé, "that I am here on a mission of compromise. I am not trying to resurrect those theological debates. I realize I have been very intemperate in my criticism of your Order on several occasions. I regret that, but I must be able to return to my colleagues with your commitment to signing these Gallican statements, and assure us that there will not be another retraction."

Of course, Larousse could not possibly guarantee that. He tried to sound firm.

"I will do all in my power," he assured the Abbé, "to urge my brothers to not only sign these statements, but add a further appeal that these signatures be allowed to stand because of their importance for our relationship here with King and Parliament."

"You can be sure that the reward for your cooperation will be that the charges in the Lavalette affair will be dropped and the squabble over your rules and regulations will be forever interred."

The Abbé stood up to leave, and extended his hand in farewell.

Larousse escorted him to the door.

"I am deeply grateful for your taking the time to call on us, and for your message. It has brought us hopeful news at a trying time."

Once the Abbé was gone, Père Larousse went to his office and closed the door. Before consulting with anyone, he had to ponder what had just happened. Gradually he realized that it was too much for him to sort out alone.

In the weeks that went by, the Jesuits were not interested in whether the fleet of Charlemagne was in danger from the English, nor how their army was faring in India or who was asserting claims in Canada. The criticism of the Pompadour as war minister did not affect them in any way. They held a series of intense meetings all over the country. Happily, they did not have to worry about imminent gatherings of the Parliament. That, at least, gave them time to deliberate, but it didn't give them any release from the dilemma they shared with their Superior, Larousse. For the first time they had to face their problem without being able to lean on the shoulder of Belle Isle. Even with an angel from on high they could not figure out a way to sign a document that taught that a council of bishops in France had higher authority than the Pope. In two weeks the debate became insufferable. Finally, out of sheer exhaustion they reached a consensus: sign the forbidden Articles here in public assembly, and at the same time send a message to the Vatican and to their Superior in Rome, pleading duress, and lack of freedom — both grounds for invalidity. They were trying to do the work of the Church; if they did not sign, their work was in danger of being stopped altogether.

No priest could hold that the bishops were above the Pope. But if the Abbé and his cohorts were to learn of their secret alibi letters to the Pope and Superior, their cause was doomed. Nevertheless, they went ahead.

While the signed dusty copy of the Gallican Articles was on its way to the Speaker's desk in the Parliament, and the apology-explanation was simultaneously on its way to the Vatican, the Marèchal de Belle Isle died.

In the eulogy during the funeral Mass in the Cathedral of Notre Dame, Père de Sacy stirred up resentment by declaring that had the Marèchal lived; he would never have put an ounce of faith in the Abbé's suggestion. He would have abandoned the priests for good at even the suggestion of pursuing a route as historically ill-fated, as that of their predecessors in the last century.

At the end of the funeral, Père Larousse made a special announcement. It was more a plaintive appeal. They must initiate a crusade of prayer among students and faculty of the schools and colleges. They must reach out to all the parishes throughout the country. They had to beg the bishops, the pastors and the faithful to join them with Masses, rosaries and vigils. By this time it was common knowledge throughout the country that the Order was under attack. That their very existence was in jeopardy was not so commonly known.

Antoine was back at *L'Hôtel Dieu*. He had to walk over to the church for the funeral of their beloved defender, and listen to the acrimonious complaints of the priests filing out after Mass. Still, he could escape to the hospital routine, where others could not.

It was not easy, although the focus was no longer on him and what he had caused. It was some relief to feel that people were no longer talking about him. His life was on a bit of an upswing. With the exception of the funeral, he hadn't gone near the Jesuits for several weeks. Everything he learned came in second hand. He was needed here. It had been too difficult for Mère Elisette to keep a resident chaplain, as she had told him more than once. He was vital, something he needed to hear at this stage of his life. The ailing and the dying were comforted by his mere presence. For many, his smile was enough to make their day. He visited every bed, every cot, every patient, even those whose mattress was the floor. They said 'thank you' in so many different ways. The relatives of those he buried in the cemetery of St. Genevieve showed their gratitude for his words. But most of all, his presence at paupers' graves was its own reward.

He didn't feel guilty when he discovered he could smile again. It had been a long time since he had even been tempted to laugh. There was the old man who asked him when he was going to be dismissed from the hospital. In a fit of anger over his illness and being confined to this place of smells and groans, the old man had thrown a cup of lukewarm tea in the face of Mère Elisette. She had not reported him. He was amazed and totally humbled as Antoine talked a little about the dedicated life of those who saw Jesus in their neighbor. And then there was the woman who in a rage, demanded to leave. Her glass of lime juice had somehow been replaced by a cup of urine.

He was called upon for more sorrowful tasks as well. Perhaps the saddest of all was to attend pregnant women who had come to term. He had not been in the hospital long before he came to know the head physician,

Dr. Coudray. Their friendship was therapy for Antoine, who carried his own burden of sadness because of his financial debacle. The doctor carried a far heavier burden, the constant loss of women and babies in childbirth. The doctor needed the priest at his side as they confronted the terror of the younger women especially as their hour drew near. One tragic day they embraced one another in tears after two women died within a half hour of each other.

"I should leave here," Coudray was finally able to say. "I am unable to stop these deaths. I can't stand it anymore. There is a monastery outside of Paris where they want me to look after some monks. That's where I belong, not here."

It was a complete change of roles for Antoine. He had to forget everything connected with the Abbé Giroux and the Parliament and Leoncy Freres. For the first time in a year he had to listen to some one else tell a tale of woe.

"I have been searching for several years for a way to stop the mortality rate in the lying-in room," he was sobbing on Antoine's shoulder. "I have redesigned the room in the form of an ellipse with flues on the walls. More light, more ventilation I was told. I even put small chimneys above the flues to provide an upward draft to eliminate the harmful odors which my colleagues claimed were the cause of the deaths. It was the lack of circulation in the high ceiling that made the air fetid for childbearing.

"Then," he continued in a broken voice, "I got an idea from the hospital of Port Royal. Flowers, trees, a garden, exposure to air and light was the answer. I moved the lying-in room to the plaza away from the river. It made no difference.

"I devised a vapor spray of sulphur and saltpetre with which I fumigated the area where we put the women who were nearing term. We have no place to build a separate room for waiting. I even tried another vapor of juniper juice and vinegar that a doctor from Bretagne claimed was the answer. I have also tried aromatic baths shortly before delivery which I was told would prevent infection. Nothing works."

This was not the only time Antoine listened. As time went on, he was able to tell the doctor something of what he had been through. It was this sharing of woes that made them a team in the service of the sick. For Antoine, it was a godsend. He was now a hospital chaplain, doted on especially by Mère Elisette, but loved also by the other nuns. And besides Coudray and Elisette, he had parishioners like he had in St. Pierre, Point Carbet and throughout Martinique. They might not be as healthy as Uncle Loize and Marie Celeste, but they were his friends nonetheless. Here, he was not the man who had to be investigated from Rome. And as the days went by, he would awake from time to time with no thoughts of debt or legal appeals. And he very much wanted to believe that the signature of his brother Jesuits on the Gallican Articles had won pardon for him as well.

His feeling of tranquillity was further enhanced by the report from Père de Sacy that the Abbé Giroux had taken a leave of absence again. No one seemed to know where he had gone. Antoine was surely the most relieved of all the Jesuits. He hoped the memory of his name on a lamppost on an evening long ago would disappear. In any case, the routine of *L'Hôtel Dieu* was gradually helping him to put most of the ugly scenes behind him. He could even release the pain of not being permitted to return to Martinique.

Nearly a month went by. It was now almost August and a windy day. The news was that Parliament was making preparations to gather again. That was news he didn't want to hear.

Then it happened. He was on his usual walk just after midday. He had put aside this period of time for himself. He thought of it as a bit of free time, a break from the usual routine.

This day, however, was different. He had barely reached the quay when he saw Père de Sacy and the Superior, Larousse, coming towards him, leaning into the wind and holding on to their clerical hats to keep them from being blown into the Seine. He spotted them long before they saw him. He stopped still.

"How are you, Antoine?" asked de Sacy when he came close. They all three stood uncomfortably in the breeze.

"I must see you at once," said Père Larousse before Antoine could reply.

"Let's get in out of this draft," said Antoine as he led the way back toward the hospital. On entering the hallway, de Sacy insisted that they sit down immediately. He was shaken by something. At this time in the afternoon, the benches where patients usually waited were not occupied. De Sacy did not want to go any further, so the three of them sat down.

"What is it?" asked Antoine. There was a pause, in which no one said anything.

Finally, Larousse took a letter from his pocket.

"I received this from Rome. It was addressed to you in my care. The Father General did not have your correct address. I read it. I am sorry that

I did so, but I can't take back what I did. It was a mistake; you should have been the one to open it."

Larousse handed the letter to Antoine with a pained expression on his face. His friend, de Sacy, looked helplessly on.

Antoine took out the letter from its envelope and began to read.

There was no comment. An even heavier silence fell on the three of them. Antoine read the letter through. He looked up a moment, and then reread the letter.

"I need some fresh air," he broke the silence. He got up and left them sitting as he started to walk out along the wharf. He did not return. The pair of priests, after an awkward wait, finally stood up and left.

It was an ordeal for Antoine, but he had to keep rereading the missive, which he found difficult to believe.

> *"It is with profound regret, that I am obliged to inform you that because of the direct intervention of the Pope based on information he received from the Reverend Leon de la Marche, papal visitor to Martinique, and as a result of the allegations against you presented by His Majesty, Louis XV's government, in addition to the notoriety which has arisen from your commercial enterprises that have violated Church Law, you have been dismissed from the Society of Jesus."*

There was no need to read on further. Antoine walked back and forth along the quay, the letter at his thigh, flapping a bit in the breeze. It was better that he was alone. Later, de Sacy would apologize ineffectually, for not waiting to offer some consoling words. He had felt completely inadequate at the time and totally incapable of formulating any comforting words for his abandoned friend.

Antoine assured him that he had not been offended by his leave taking. It had been a moment when conversing was impossible. He had to be alone.

That night, *L'Hôtel Dieu* was no longer the house of God, at least to Antoine. He was racked with nightmarish dreams.

He was on the single sailed dory running swiftly before the wind, blowing him and his pilot out to sea. The panic on the Carib's face said "Huracán" better than words. There was a deadly wrestling match between Bratel and the tiller, trying to keep the dory from tipping, and at the same time hold a course that would catch the tip of Point Carbet. Otherwise, there was the open sea.

Then the scene changed to the last hurricane — the time they lost the sugar harvest. His cassock was blowing out behind him. A slave worker held him fast lest he be blown down in the mud. He was half crazy as he embraced a cane stalk, trying to keep it from being leveled in the gale.

Next it was the fire of 1757. He was one of a long line of blacks passing wooden buckets of water in a desperate effort to save the slave quarters from the blaze.

Now he was beside a cannon. The pirate ship was approaching. It had just fired a shot across the bow. He was lighting the fuse to return the fire. But then it was not the ship, it was a battlement. It was a Basque soldier on a wall. The cannon ball went hurtling through the air. Someone beside him shouted. "You got the little bastard; you hit him in the knee."[9]

Antoine sat straight up on his mattress. His voice was hoarse. He must have been shouting for some time. Mère Elisette was there sitting on the bed, reaching out to comfort him. She had caught de Sacy before he left and knew what had happened. She had seen the look on de Sacy's face and pressed him for an explanation.

It didn't matter how she knew. She was there beside him, hugging him.

She had been attending a dying woman, and was about to call Antoine anyway — to administer the last rites. Then she heard him shouting wildly behind the chapel altar in his sleep. Instinctively, she rushed in to comfort him. His reaction was instantaneous. Before he completely recovered from his nightmare, he found himself in a passionate embrace. Tears were pouring down his face.

"Antoine! Antoine! There are others who love you. Priests can be so cruel to one another."

It must have been the word "priests" that stirred a reaction. Both of them were in their night clothes, she wore a light kimono. They suddenly broke free from their embrace, like two little children caught in a pantry. Drawing back guiltily, they stared at one another in the dim candle light that filtered through the dormitory door. She rose to go.

"Please," he begged. He held out both hands which she clutched tightly. It was a pathetic gesture to keep her close. This lasted for several minutes.

"I cannot stay. But I can pray that God be with you," she said, breaking the hand clasp reluctantly.

---

9   *Reference to Ignatius of Loyola, a Barque soldier and founder of the Society of Jesus who was wounded in battle. He took a cannon ball to the knee.*

It was a gloomy week for Antoine. The hospital routine was purely mechanical. At the end of the week, he went to the parish to seek out de Sacy for confession. It was a struggle to make up his mind to go to the Jesuit residence. He was no longer one of them. He was not welcome. But he had to be able to pour out his frustration, his anger, his desire for vengeance, together with his sense of helplessness. Without Mère Elisette as confidant, however, he could never have gotten up the courage to make his peace with God in the confessional.

The confessional brought no peace. It was a repeat experience of what had happened between him and Dr. Coudray in the maternity ward. Expecting the sympathetic ear of a confessor, he found de Sacy equally as depressed as he was. Actually, de Sacy could not find words of advice or consolation. His depression was in part due to what happened to Antoine, but it had become further complicated by the latest report which their friend, de la Croix, brought from the Parliament.

In a way, it was providential for Antoine to realize that de Sacy was more in need of comfort and consolation than he, unbelievable as that might seem to an outsider. Once again, Antoine found he had to change roles from one to be consoled to consoler. Perhaps that was the way God wanted it. He had to admit that he was the beneficiary, because it was now impossible to feel sorry for himself.

What was crushing to Père de Sacy in the de la Croix report was that the Abbé was back. He had been on a mission to Rome once again. Any hope of compromise was gone. Once again he took up the sword, waving it fiercely against the Jesuit rule book and their legal claim to exist in France. The motive for his trip to Rome was unclear, but rumor had it that something else was afoot in *La Place de Grève* — something that concerned the Jesuits.

There had also been a message from de la Croix that proved to be quite a shock to all the Jesuits. A goodly number of black robes had been lured into complacency, a sense of relief that there was no longer pressure on the Order. For people like de Sacy, however, there was no escape from a pervading mood of gloom. Somehow he could not shake his apprehension. Consequently, he had been of no help to Antoine. They left the confession box together and headed for the kitchen. Perhaps a bit of wine rather than late night tea could help them. They needed something more than small talk for their depressed spirits.

Their strained conversation was interrupted by the appearance of the lawyer, de la Croix. De Sacy took the opportunity to escape, which he did as soon as the pleasantries had been exchanged.

"I know it's late and you have to get back to the hospital," began the lawyer when they were alone. "But I must talk to you. I have a lot on my mind. I'd be happy to walk with you over to the hospital. I don't want to be interrupted by the priests here."

"I need some advice," began de la Croix when they were outside, and on their way to *L'Hôtel Dieu*.

"I can't be of much help, now that I have been dismissed from the Order," replied Antoine, thus upsetting his listener.

"I am appalled," apologized the lawyer. "I didn't know. Please forgive me." He stood there forlornly.

Antoine had enough to depress him. His first inclination was to move on and leave the man, but his priestly intuition stopped him.

"I don't see how I can be of help with Jesuit problems now," said Antoine. "But I can try."

"I'm sure Père de Sacy has given you the news about the Abbé returning from Rome and again starting the procedure to drive the Jesuits out of France."

"I didn't even know that the Abbé had been in Rome again, let alone that he was back."

"All the members of the Parliament have received printed copies of proposed legislation to bar the Jesuits from the country on three counts: one, general liability for the unpaid debts incurred by Leoncy Freres; two, unauthorized legal status here in France; and three, causing controversy for Catholic citizens."

They walked on in silence. "What deception!" Antoine said after an interval. "And all because of me! But what can I do now? I am no longer a member of the Society. The only strategy I can think of is to go personally before the King's council to plead for protection for the men I have hurt."

"I'm not here to talk about strategy. I am weary of that. We've been snarled in that kind of activity for almost a year. I am here for another reason. My faith is threatened. I was truly shaken to witness this priest renewing an attack on fellow priests immediately upon returning from Rome. He lied to us previously; he has twice pretended to have abandoned charges against the Jesuits. His true motive for setting out for Rome, we know now, was to enlist the Pope in the cause of expelling you from France."

"You mean them, not me," Antoine added with a note of sarcasm. But he quickly added, "That is sad indeed."

"That was a slip; pardon me," de la Croix said quickly. "I have a deeper problem. I see your ouster as part of a hateful campaign among priests in the Catholic Church — of which I am supposed to be a member," he added. "And I see the hypocrisy and deceit in a priest who has a prominent position in our Parliament, a position which is designed to bring harmony and compromise to legislative debates." De la Croix paused. "What do I tell myself in such circumstances?"

There was another lengthy pause as Antoine reflected on his answer. Reluctantly, he saw that perhaps, once again, reaching out to his companion in distress might just be the best therapy for him.

"One of the reasons I got out of teaching the history of theology was that I was tired of the hairsplitting theories and detailed analyses in doctrinal matters. What you have to keep in mind is that religion is probably the greatest source of controversy in the world.

And fighting over the Bible is perhaps the best example that we see before us in our time, whether the argument be in Germany, England Switzerland...here in France...anywhere."

"That's doesn't help me at all."

"We went through this before, remember? I tried to explain to you how a religious group could develop into a political party." Antoine could not go on. "How can I do this with more clarity?" Antoine asked himself aloud. "I'm not trying to justify the Abbé, nor condemn him. What I'm trying to get across is that you shouldn't blame the Church for some of the theories and practices that priests propound. The Abbé is convinced that the Bible is on his side, or more exactly, on the side of the Jansenists. But beyond theory, he is convinced that their position has been misrepresented to both Pope and King by the Jesuits."

"It's a confusing mix," added Antoine. "You have the Catholic Church, the Monarchy, the Parliament, all claiming to represent the people and all claiming authority. Add to that the fact that all factions claim God is on their side. Wars have been fought and people have died because of this kind of controversy. The tragedy for me is that I am tangled up in all this, and I would like to find some place to hide." He stopped. They stood there looking at one another in the darkness.

"I don't know whether I have been a help or not."

"Yes, indeed, it helps to some degree," replied de la Croix. "I think I have imposed on you enough," he added. By this time they were near the bridge. Notre Dame loomed in the darkness.

Long after de la Croix had departed, Antoine remained on the bridge, the famous Pont Neuf. He stared down at the flowing water for a long time. At last, he turned slowly and walked toward the end of the bridge and then headed for the hospital.

He barely got into the hospital when one of the night volunteers caught sight of him. An old man was suffering intense abdominal pains and wanted the priest immediately. It was indeed a blessing for him. He was happy to forget the lawyer as he hurried to the tabernacle for the Sacred Host and the oils with which he brought peace to the dying, the peace of solemn words and blessing.

CHAPTER XII

The following morning while things went on as usual in *L'Hôtel Dieu*, there was an outburst of curiosity among the hospital workers. Everyone near the bridge was talking about what was going on in *La Place de Grève*, just a block away. Mule drawn carts were hauling firewood and their owners stacking the logs in front of the Gendarme's headquarters. There was to be a huge bonfire in *La Place de Grève*. Someone was to be burned at the stake. But who? The rumors flew thick and fast. In no time the word was out that a priest was to be burned alive. The Parliament, it was soon learned, were preparing legislation to punish all the Jesuits, not just one. Some said that the priest at the stake was from Martinique where he had committed crimes. Others said they had it on good authority that the Jesuits would be expelled from the country, and that firewood was only for the books that Jesuits had written against the King and the laws of France.

The rumors continued. After all, Damens, who had attacked the King had been executed in *La Place de Grève*, and the Jesuits had taught him that it was morally just to kill kings.

Speculation increased with each load of firewood. There surely was enough to burn several people. The unloading, arranging and stacking went on for three days. Finally, it was rumored all over Paris that at the height of the morning marketing, after a fourteen-story pyre was in place, the Abbé Giroux, swinging his cape dramatically, came into the plaza and began inspecting the pyre and the pyramid of logs along side. He made a point of dallying beside an isolated single stake that was mounted on a platform.

The Abbé offered no information to the curious. He hobbled over to where a carriage awaited him. Then, he left for the Parliament.

The following day, he and his cohorts in the Parliament went on debating the fate of the Jesuits. To call what he was orchestrating a debate seemed problematical, even to his loyal confreres. This was a one-sided series of presentations. The speaker, under the tutelage of the Abbé, saw to it that the opposition had very little time for rebuttal. Three key accusations were repeated in varying language: **one**, the Jesuits had no legal authorization to be teachers in the country, royal favor did not constitute legal authorization unless confirmed by the Parliament; **two**, their books and their history were proof that they undermined the authority of both church and king by their perverse interpretation of free will and their doctrine approving regicide; **three**, they had not as yet taken steps to indemnify the creditors of Leoncy Gouffre Freres for the bankruptcy caused by the illegal commerce of the missionary Lavalette in Martinique, whose dealings had total approval of the highest Jesuit authority in Rome.

Invitations had been extended to the public who filled the balcony during each session. After two days of haranguing and after the Jesuit supporters had been allowed limited time, the roll call was begun to submit the matter to a vote. It was at this moment, that a friend of the late Marèchal de Belle Isle, highly respected by all, was recognized for a period of ten minutes only. M. Emile Huguet was the leader of the Papal Party, as they were called behind their back. Not only was he respected, he was also persuasive. He held the attention of the assembly in such fashion that the chairman did not dare to intrude, even when he exceeded his allotted time. Each time the chairman looked toward the Abbé for a signal to intervene, he was cautioned to hold back. It was imperative that total deference be shown to M. Huguet. He seized his opportunity well because he fully perceived the atmosphere in which he pleading. His main thrust was original and creative. He appealed to the Catholic conscience. This was significant because practically all members present were Catholic. At one juncture he raised the document signed by the vast majority of bishops whom the Jesuits had canvassed on foot. They had expressed their solidarity for the religious order that had served the Church so well and provided a first-class education to so many.

Huguet was a better polemicist than Belle Isle could ever have been. His genius was to suggest without offense that the root of this bitter wrangle was the controversy over what St. Augustine taught. He even brought a polite smile to many by dramatizing how the Pope had intervened between the Jesuits and Dominicans many years ago. The incident that had finally led the Pope to forbid all future public debates about free will, Huguet insisted, was when a Jesuit used a pun, deliberately confusing the Latin word *canis*, a female dog, with the last name of his debate opponent, the Dominican Friar

Melchior Cano. This insult, plus the retaliatory remark, accusing all Jesuits of being Pelagians — heretics who denied that we needed God's grace to keep the commandments — ended the arguing. This topic of debate had become rather popular — drawing Catholic audiences in several big cities in France and Italy.

So restrained and so thoughtful was Huguet's presentation that he offended no one in the entire assembly. He concluded, "We must consult with His Majesty over a matter in which our Catholic heritage is deeply involved. Your parliamentary considerations about legal charges against the Jesuits cannot be resolved by the political process alone."

Huguet's speech had the notable effect of impeding Abbé Giroux's attack. He could not believe that anyone, especially some unknown laymen, could so deftly change the mood of the legislators.

As Huguet's speech had progressed, the Abbé became furious with himself. In his rush to the assembly he had forgotten the most important document in his arsenal. And the more quietly eloquent M. Huguet became, the more the Abbé cursed himself for having left behind the rough copy of a one-hundred fifty year old declaration by Pope Gregory, which was now in the hand of his successor, Clement. It was a decree being prepared for promulgation throughout the whole Church. It was the result of many meetings. It had been launched with the help of the four representatives of the Catholic monarchs whom he had painstakingly organized to appear at the Vatican. If he had it in his hand to read as planned, M. Huguet's reflective plea would accomplish nothing. Perhaps this was not the moment. There were too many people in the balconies. Straddlers among the membership needed time to forget what Huguet had said.

Call off their meetings. Let the members mull over the pious ideas that Huguet had spoken. Let them alone for a while. No harm in letting them think over how the Catholic faithful might be affected by all this. There would be no time allowed for discussion, he was determined about that. All the members needed was to hear the edited version of the Pope's encyclical letter. He could schedule that in a day or two.

The Abbé found that he didn't have to worry about the interval after Huguet's speech. The town was totally distracted. The people lost all interest in the Parliament. They were caught up in speculation about the mountain of logs in La Place de Grève. No one who crossed the bridge on the way to the market or the Cathedral of Notre Dame could possibly not notice the log pyramid.

In the evenings that followed the crushing news about his dismissal, Antoine was in the habit of eating alone in the kitchen. After a meager supper, he would take a stroll by himself in the darkness. It was exercise and escape.

The curiosity that still reigned about the purpose of the bonfire drew him inexorably to the site. Even though, he came by regularly the place during the week on his midday walks, and often spoke with the men unloading their ox carts, he could not resist coming by in the evening as well. He had a morbid fascination for what this project might mean.

He had questioned each and every one in the plaza and everyone else he could contact, but to no avail. The uniformed soldiers who guarded the log pile had become his friends. They had no idea as to what was being planned. It was a frightening notion that a human being might be put to death in such a horrible way.

One evening on his walk, he heard a couple of men talking.

"The gendarme told me a Jesuit priest is going to be burned alive for writing a book against the King."

"No," exclaimed his companion. "They're not going to burn a priest. We would all have known about that before this."

"All I know is what the gendarme on duty told me this morning."

"But a priest! Impossible!"

"He told me that they burned a Jesuit priest in Portugal, and they're going to burn one here, also. That's what he said."

Antoine stopped still. His leisurely walk ended. He changed direction immediately and headed for the Jesuit residence which he had been avoiding. It would be a painful visit, but he hoped he could find de Sacy available. Perhaps he could get in to contact de Sacy without being seen.

It could not be that a Jesuit had suffered such torture! Surely, this was false. But why this fearful pyre of logs? Was he himself in danger? After all, he was the culprit. The lawsuit against the Jesuits was his fault. Certainly they would never be able to pay the millions of *livres* he owed. Was the Parliament considering him as the criminal to be punished? He had not been threatened so far.

Antoine began to walk even faster.

Happily, he found de Sacy just coming from the church. But this was not a moment for greetings.

Breathlessly, he blurted out, "Is it true that a Jesuit was burned at the stake?"

De Sacy nodded.

"But why? How is that possible? Such a terrible punishment!"

"We don't know the details. There's a Minister of State in Portugal, named Pombal. I am sure you have heard of him. He hates us with an infernal hatred. He drove hundreds of Jesuits out of the Portuguese possessions in Brazil and Paraguay. In Portugal he has thrown at least one hundred priests and brothers in jail. Just what this priest did, we don't yet know. Père Alonzo Bordoni is here from Rome to help us deal with our crisis. He's also here to plead with the King on our behalf. He has enlisted M. Huguet to speak to the bishops for us.

"My understanding is that he knows all about what has happened in Brazil and Portugal. He's going to be staying with us here in the residence. I'm sure he will be open to your questions. As for the Jesuit who was burned at the stake, his name was Gabriel de Malagrida. That's all we know so far."

"And when does this Bordoni arrive?"

"Antoine," de Sacy smiled, "you've traveled enough by passenger coach. You know better than to ask a question like that."

"Do you think Père Bordoni would allow me to see him?"

"I don't see why not. But you will have to catch him early. We're expecting Jesuits from all the provinces. Everybody wants to see him. We're collecting straw mats from all over so that everyone has a place to sleep."

"So the frightening news has spread all over!" exclaimed Antoine.

"It depends on which bad news you're talking about," commented de Sacy. "All reports about the impending parliamentary session are ominous. We have heard lately that the Portuguese have been joined by Spain in their persecution of us. We're very anxious to learn what is true and what isn't."

"Could you plead my case with Père Bordoni? Now that I am not in the Society, he may not want to see me. However, I still have an immense obligation to all of you. I don't want you destroyed because of me. Believe me, I can still stave off the creditors, at least the big ones. Just give me enough time to get back to Martinique to work with Isaac and Jacob on behalf of the mission. You'll see. Everyone will see."

"Antoine," de Sacy raised his hand in restraint, "all of us are waiting for a chance to ask questions of Bordoni. I will do my best to get you an opportunity to see him. And I will personally come and invite you. But be patient.

There is too much on our minds right now."

Happily, the Jesuits didn't wait long. The Roman visitor came in one night, weary and late from his long trek. Despite the exhaustion and the stress of the moment, he was the soul of attentiveness. He got up early the next morning and held interviews all day long. Unbelievably, after all had gone to rest he made himself available to Antoine, whom he received with great cordiality. De Sacy had sent a note to *L'Hôtel Dieu*.

Antoine was truly touched by the consideration shown by Père Bordoni. The lateness and inconvenience of the hour were one thing, but the fact that the visitor from Rome agreed to see him at all was quite another. Once in the room with Père Bordoni, he burst out with the question that had been consuming him.

"What can you tell me about the Jesuit who was burned at the stake?" He was truly fearful as he asked this question.

"You know who Pombal is, don't you?" began Bordoni.

"All I know about him is that he hates Jesuits."

"That is, of course, an understatement," confirmed Bordoni. "You probably have not learned that Pombal removed six hundred Jesuits from their missions in Paraguay and Brazil?"

"I have heard nothing like that," said Antoine.

"A very saintly missionary by the name of Gabriel de Malagrida was one of those thrown in jail in Lisbon. In the course of his incarceration he became somewhat demented. He was in his eighties after all. After he saw the destruction of our great work in the Reductions of Paraguay, the jail life was too much for him. He began writing pamphlets from prison against Pombal, identifying him as the anti-Christ."

"Is this Pombal so vicious that he couldn't recognize that the man was not in his right mind?"

"Yes, he is. But just after the devastating earth quake of 1755, Père Malagrida wrote a pamphlet. His theme was similar to the themes that run through the Bible. The earthquake was the punishment of God for the sins of the people. Who was the leader of the people?"

"Pombal," suggested Antoine quickly.

"At the time," continued Père Bordoni, "Père Gabriel was of sound mind. He meant no harm to Pombal, but a perverse mind knows no logic. He never forgave Père Malagrida for what he interpreted as a direct accusation of responsibility for the catastrophe. There were other hidden political motivations and chicanery involved, but those details are really not that important."

"But was there no trial — no chance for Père Malagrida to be defended?" asked Antoine. "No chance for pardon, for escape from such an awful death?"

"The trial was a farce because the judges were intimidated. Pombal's wielding of power in Portugal has been fraught with such unbelievable cruelty and brutal incarceration of nobility, as well as peasants, that no one dares to face him."

Antoine shook his head in disbelief.

"I don't want to continue this ugly story," Père Bordoni went on. "Père de Sacy tells me that you are personally worried about the preparations of the pyre in *La Place de Grève*, and wondering whether there is to be another Jesuit burned."

"I most certainly am. I could not believe that a priest was burned in a Catholic country. I don't know what to believe now."

Bordoni listened respectfully. It was quite obvious that Antoine still could not accept the fact that a priest had been burned. But the visitor also sensed that Antoine, after being dismissed from the Order, might just possibly be feeling so guilty about all that had befallen him that he might well believe he was a prospective candidate for the stake.

"Père Antoine," he began, "you have been in the Caribbean too long. You have not had the opportunity to be informed about what is happening in France and in Europe. The Jesuits are caught in a movement that goes well beyond us.

"Above all, I must allay your fears that any one of us is threatened with the bonfire. The Abbé, with the help of his cronies in the Parliament, is preparing a special show for the public. I'm sure you know about his trip to Rome to intimidate Pope Clement."

Antoine nodded.

"That's a whole other story," Bordoni continued. "But the main thing is that not only France, but Spain, Portugal, Parma and Naples are putting pressure on the Pope to get rid of us."

"That can't be true," exclaimed Antoine in disbelief.

"And not only from their kingdoms, but from the Church as well," added

Bordoni.

Antoine found this remark so devastating that he was unable to reply.

"I'm sorry," apologized Bordoni. "I should not have brought that up. Let's go back to the bonfire. All that's going to happen now is that the Parliament will gather in its formal attire with trumpets to accompany them, and they will have uniformed soldiers toss books by Jesuit authors, like Bellarmine and Molina and Suarez, into the fire."

"So, no one will be burned," said Antoine hopefully.

"That's correct. But there is a positive note here so you don't leave depressed. The book burning was scheduled for two months ago. The reason for the delay is pressure from the Curia, in Italy. Our General has been frantically contacting every cardinal in Rome to protect us from what appears to be our demise.

"Maybe, as a beginning, I should tell you the crudest story of all, so you get an idea of why I am here. It is common talk around Rome that ministers of our four Catholic countries have told Pope Clement that if he does not take action against us, they will leave the Church, just like Luther and Calvin."

"Surely, the Pope was not swayed by that outrageous kind of approach," Antoine said, distressed.

"There are many things in France you are not aware of yet and one is that Pope Clement was not a well man. Even in good health he was not the type to stand up to constant badgering by diplomats."

"But, we still have many friends in Rome that can help us, don't we?"

"Yes, of course we have, but I just wanted you to know the kind of machinations that Pope Clement has inherited. There's another complication that intimidates even our most loyal friends now. I will tell you about that later. You've been with us these many years, and I totally sympathize with you. You deserve to know just where we stand. Tomorrow or the next day, Abbé Giroux will present a copy of an encyclical from papal headquarters which is being prepared against us for Pope Clement to sign. Among other things, it will say that we Jesuits are a source of constant controversy in the Church of God. That will be the signal for all the long robes to rise and march out to *La Place de Grève* with a contingent of soldiers, accompanied by blowing trumpets and a cart loaded with books by Jesuit authors."

"I am so relieved to hear that it is only books to be burned. You can't imagine how worried I have been since they started piling logs. But," he added, "how do you know all this?"

"We still have friends in the Parliament; they are far from the majority, but they are friends."

"The news that you bring is very depressing," commented Antoine, "but at least it's only books that are to be burned."

"However, the message they are trying to get across by the book burning doesn't help our cause," commented Bordoni.

"Thank you, for your explanation," said Antoine. He seemed to have missed the implication of Bordoni's comment because he hastened to add, "There is something else on my mind. I'm wondering if you would consider it."

"Yes?" asked Bordoni.

"I am asking that I be authorized me to go back to St. Pierre for one purpose: to focus on the sugarcane fields of Martinique and Dominique. I know this is a strange request, considering that I am no longer a member of the Order. But I assure you that all I need is time. The war is ending, and even if it were still on, I have a safe route to the Caribbean. The English do not interfere with it. I have two very competent assistants, Isaac Judah and Captain Jacob Byrne. In one year we can deliver enough milled sugar to make a significant down payment to the most insistent creditors. This way we will show the Parliament that the Jesuits have taken steps to pay off the creditors of the Leoncy bank."

Bordoni's response was evident in the way he began to shake his head.

Antoine rushed on.

"I know that technically I do not belong to the Order, but nevertheless I still have an immense obligation to help and serve. I can do it. All I need is your authorization or perhaps that of someone from Rome."

"Père Antoine," Bordoni took a long look at Antoine and sighed. "What you suggest makes sense to me. But unfortunately, at the time that you came back to France, Père de la Marche's report had been sent to Rome and given to Père Larousse also. The emphasis was on the commercial aspect — the priest in business — rather than on the widow Grou's threatened lawsuit. She was willing to call off legal action, provided she had some kind of reasonable guarantee. Père de Sacy presented your proposal as eloquently as anyone could. Suarez and Bellarmine could not have done any better. But unfortunately, Père Larousse delayed forwarding your plan to Rome. He should have sent it immediately, to counter de la Marche.

"Now, it's too late. I mentioned to you before, you have been on the

Caribbean mission too long to be informed about the vicious rivalries that have been going on among various political and religious factions in France with the Jesuits in the middle."

Bordoni paused; he was choked up, actually. He was suddenly a different person — no longer the formal visitor from Rome under the cape of authority. He began to pour his heart out on the topic that had been tearing him apart for the last several years, that of the terrible injustice to the Guaraní and Jesuit missionaries in Paraguay and Brazil.

"I was going to tell you this later, when all the Jesuits were gathered. But I must tell you now. I and several others in administration in Rome were strongly opposed to your being dismissed from our Order. What happened to you in Martinique was a result of piracy and a war between England and France. This is not to say that you were totally without blame. Unfortunately, it occurred in a timely fashion for the Marquise de Pombal. He took advantage of what happened to your bank account in Marseilles. He cleverly linked it with the Reductions in Paraguay."

"How could anyone do that?" inquired Antoine. "I know very little about what was going in the villages of Paraguay."

"You would have to know more about Pombal to understand. He exploited the bankruptcy and court action and the parliamentary debates here in Paris for his own ends."

"How could he do that?"

"It was"t simple," Bordoni said. "He had to distort what the priests and brothers were doing with 40,000 of the Guarani tribe in Paraguay. The lay brothers were training them in a variety of trades, farming and as nurses and gendarmes. The priests taught them reading, writing, music and drama. Even our critics, like Voltaire, have said the Reductions were a Utopia for the indigenous. It was a cooperative endeavor. It delivered the people from the dominion of the landholders."

"But, where do I fit in a situation like that?" asked Antoine somewhat puzzled.

"You don't fit there. But you do fit as a scapegoat for the Jesuits who have been frustrating the wealthy. Remember, Paraguay is far away, and it takes a long time for news to cross the seas. What was actually going on in the villages of Paraguay was re-edited on the voyage to Europe, especially as it got close to Italy.

"Portuguese landowners had been complaining to Pombal for years.

Forty thousand natives were prime cheap labor. Spanish planters had joined the Portuguese in trying to raid indigenous villages. Jesuit trained militia fended off the raiders. This, of course, became a Jesuit army for publicity purposes. The most aggravating element was that the priests had garnered a royal decree from the King of Spain which made it illegal to raid the villages. Ordinarily, this would not have been enough, but the decree also empowered the priests to demand help from the Spanish military for enforcements whenever they might need it. Besides, their contacts on the Iberian Peninsula and in Rome put the local Viceroys on the spot. Thus the plantation owners, both Spanish and Portuguese, had to find another way.

"They made use of the financial scandal of Leoncy Freres in nearby Marseilles to make their distant tale more believable. Finally, and this may seem like a little thing, the Jesuits not only trained teachers for their schools, they forbade them to teach either Portuguese or Spanish," Bordoni concluded.

"Thank you," said Antoine. He had been gripped by the story. "But I still don't quite see how my bank failure could help their cause."

"The idea that they want to sow," explained Bordoni, "is that we are interfering with the business world. As priests, we are supposed to be missionaries only."

Bordoni paused. "Have you ever heard that one of Pombal's deputies went to Rome and had an audience with Clement?"

Antoine shook his head.

"The Jesuit Reductions, as they were called, our Missions to the Guarani, became the 'Jesuit Kingdom of Paraguay with gold mines.' This actually appeared in the written report that was handed to the Vatican."

"Oh, my!" exclaimed Antoine.

"So, you see, when the word got to Rome that a Jesuit was carrying on a commercial operation in the Caribbean, it affected the banking business in France. Pombal had more ammunition for blasting the Order."

Bordoni paused again before continuing. "The last thing I want to do is offend you. You see now how misrepresenting you as a financial entrepreneur has been an ideal weapon for Pombal in his campaign to discredit our Paraguayan missionary effort. It is also a political move to reach out to Rome to defend his devout Catholic plantation owners.

"If we had taken advantage of the opportunity the widow Grou gave us," continued Bordoni, "and kept her lawsuit from reaching the courtroom, Pombal would never have had the kind of publicity he needed to claim that there was another Jesuit commercial operation going on in Paraguay."

"I guess it's too late," said Antoine gloomily. He stood up to leave. "I am deeply in your debt for allowing me to see you. Thank you so much for your information. You will excuse me. I must get back to the hospital."

"At this hour?" said Bordoni, a bit surprised. "What could demand your attention now?"

"We have a body that has to be transferred to a barge on the Seine. There will be a few relatives there who want me to say some prayers and bless the corpse."

"I guess others have their woes, too. But couldn't this wait till morning?"

"The boatmen don't like to have a barge loaded with a corpse during the day. Sometimes if people die during the night, they begin to smell by noon time. If relatives are around, or if they're waiting for night services, we can't sprinkle the bodies with sulfur. That's why the preferred time for dispatching bodies down the river is late at night."

"I understand," said Bordoni, "and thank you for your offer to do what you could to help us in our time of crisis."

"Please," begged Antoine, "could I come to see you again before you leave. I really want to be informed about what is happening. I owe so much to the Jesuits."

"Tomorrow is the drama at the Parliament. I think that will consume my whole day. There will be conferences with all the men who are here in Paris. The point will be to review what will take place tomorrow. This is Tuesday. How about Thursday evening, after Litanies, about this time?"

"Fine! Thank you, again," said Antoine. "I am so grateful."

The pair parted. Antoine went out into the night, heading for the wharf beside *L'Hôtel Dieu*. He went to his little room, then to the chapel, coming out with his ritual book, holy water and newly lit incense. The incense served a double function, one pious and holy, the other practical, considering the odor from the already decomposing body. Along the wharf were a half dozen torches stashed amid a dozen or so mourners, waiting for their chaplain to give the final blessing. The captain of the barge and two crewmen stood with hats in hand. The mother and father of the deceased were there. The mother was weeping. Her son had been only fourteen. There were five brothers and sisters, a few relatives and friends. This was an unusual crowd for this time of night. There were still a few curious watchers who stopped on the bridge to look down on the eerily lit assembly. Antoine's words were beyond their hearing as he intoned the Dies Irae. "Dust thou art and unto dust thou shalt return," he continued in the vernacular, concluding with a few words of promise from St. Paul.

> *"Unless Christ be risen from the dead, our faith is in vain, but we have the Apostles' witness that the tomb was empty. Also…the angels pointing to the embalming cloths telling them that He is risen. He is not here. He goes before you into Galilee."*

Antoine embraced the tearful mother, expressing his sympathy once again. The small crowd dispersed; the torches were extinguished. Once again, night enveloped the River Seine.

The next day was Wednesday, the day of the drama in Parliament. Antoine did not sleep well. He rose early, and went out to walk up and down along the wharf. It was tedious waiting for the sun to come up, but at last it was time for his early Mass with the nuns and those of the sick who could manage to walk to the chapel. He was terribly distracted during the Mass prayers.

After his usual light breakfast he was anxious to be on his way. There was an urgent baptism which delayed him. The depressing scene of a terrified mother hoping for the life of her child who had just come sickly into the world was all too familiar. It was a scene he could not leave quickly because it was not an ordinary occurrence for the helpless mother, weak as she was.

There were two bedside appearances for him before he could get away. One for a feverish man who wanted confession to dispel his fear of death, and another for an old man who was already in a coma.

Finally, Antoine was free. He hurried through the streets with his cassock flying. Surprised pedestrians wondered why he was in such a hurry and why he was walking in a direction away from the Cathedral of Notre Dame. Soon he reached the hall of the Parliament. The main entrance was closed because a guard blocked the way.

"No room in the vestibule, nor any place in the balcony, even for standing," he barked to the large crowd of the curious. Many in the crowd still believed that someone would be burned at the stake. Antoine turned away, deeply disappointed. Then he had an idea. Parliamentarians entered through a side door. He disengaged himself from the crowd and headed for the side entrance. He adjusted his clerical hat on the way, brushed the dust off of his soutane and walked up to the side door with authority.

"I am from Melum, Monsieur," said Antoine, in his formal best. "I am the Abbé Antoine Cartier, friend of the Abbé Giroux, lately of Martinique. I have been delayed."

The guard hesitated, and began to consult his list.

"I am an assistant to the Abbé who has personally authorized me to join him at his desk. Unfortunately, in my haste, I do not have his letter on my person."

The guard hesitated again.

"Monsieur, surely you cannot believe that a priest would not be in good faith!"

The guard's reply was to reach for the large key that hung on his waist.

Antoine, unfamiliar with the parliamentary chamber, was shocked to find that he had been ushered in to the left front of the tiered room, thirty paces from the podium where the Abbé Giroux was reaching the climax of his tirade against the Jesuits. He stopped in mid-sentence and looked directly at Antoine. The parliamentarians as well glared at the intruder. There were gestures and exclamations. Antoine was convinced that he heard his name. The procedure stopped entirely. He tried to be inconspicuous. However, two steps at a time up a staircase was no way to be inconspicuous. Fortunately, the legislators had other things on their mind besides a stray cassock stumbling up the stairs.

"I conclude," roared the Abbé, after Antoine had managed to drop out of sight. "I conclude by reading a declaration which I have personally received from His Holiness, Pope Clement." Ostentatiously, he raised a document and waved it back and forth, as he walked around the rostrum to face his audience. In a louder voice, he proclaimed:

> "It has been a constant source of preoccupation to us that cease-less controversy continues to involve the Society of Jesus within our Catholic realms of Portugal, Spain, France and Naples and Sicily.
>
> "In the country of the eldest daughter of Holy Mother the Church, our beloved France, we have seen bitter rivalry nationwide between Jesuit spokesmen and other theologians for more than a century.
>
> "And recently, the Jesuits, as a group, have signed the Gallican Articles which challenge the authority of the Supreme Pontiff. In addition more than one Jesuit author has been accused of espousing doctrines that threaten the life of his Majesty, Louis XV.

"We heartily endorse any steps by King and Parliament to remonstrate with Superiors of said Society to reach a just and amicable peace.""

The Abbé put much more emphasis on the word *"just"* than he did on the word *"amicable."*

"It is quite clear from the foregoing that His Holiness, Clement XIV, is of one mind with us that certain theories of the Jesuits are a threat to God and country. Our beloved Louis XV has expressed his approval of our contention through his distinguished Minister of State, the Duc de Choiseul here present." The Abbé gestured toward the seat on the aisle where Choiseul quickly stood up to bow profoundly. "I hereby recognize the honored Duc who wishes to address us."

"Honored Gentlemen," began Choiseul, "we have listened respectfully to the Reverend Père Alfonso Bordoni, who earlier today was the spokesman for the bishops of our nation who have expressed their defense of the Jesuit Order in eloquent fashion. However, we have also heard our Speaker, Abbé Giroux, read to us a decree from the Pope in Rome. As Catholics, we owe prior allegiance to His Holiness, not to his bishops. In addition, I have received the approval of his Majesty for the proposal I am about to make. In my judgment and in that of my colleagues, the greater weight of Pope and King is on our side. We, in conscience, offer to you the following as a necessary precaution to protect our people from the pernicious and controversial teaching of the Jesuits."

He unfurled a parchment adorned with the finest calligraphy, "Be it resolved, that in view of the dangerous opinions expressed in the many books written by Jesuits, that we condemn these writings. Pope, King and Parliament are of one mind that these writings should be burned in the presence of the assembled citizens in *La Place de Grève* on this day the 14th of October, 1769.

"In testimony whereof," continued the Duc de Choiseul, "I respectfully request of the Speaker that in my name, and in the name of my colleagues, he present this proposal to this legislative body for an immediate vote as a sign of our disapproval, and as a public manifestation of the pernicious doctrine said Society."

The Abbé had the clerk reread the proposition and declare the voting process open. Antoine, who had succeeded in finding an obscure spot in the vestibule, listened to the roll call with sadness. It rushed along at unseemly speed, never interrupted for a moment by any challenge or request for debate. Finally, the tally! The result was overwhelming. One hundred thirty-four to forty in favor of the Abbé and his contingent.

Once the final count was announced, the victorious majority arose to applaud and cheer. They left their seats to come down to the rostrum and celebrate. But the cheering did not last long. The victors all donned the parliamentary robes used only for special occasions. Then they began to exit by the same door through which Antoine had entered. Once out in the street, they quickly formed a contingent of three to a row which made the one hundred thirty-four members extend into an impressive marching front. The victors waited briefly for the Abbé to take his place in front because he was the official priestly consultant to the body. Next, a contingent of soldiers approached to stand at attention, four abreast. They appeared so quickly that it was quite obvious the whole scene had been long prepared.

Ahead of the soldiers were four trumpeters. With a signal from the Abbé, trumpets began to sound and the march began. Behind the marchers, at least five hundred of the curious followed in somewhat disarray. Black-robed and self-conscious, Antoine tried to hide among the crowd. Soon a squadron of the royal cavalry trotted up to form an outside escort.

The number of citizens began to grow. By the time the crowd reached *La Place de Grève*, the crowd was twice its original size.

The bonfire was already reaching forty feet. A wooden ramp had been built. Alongside the ramp, a platform had been also erected on which the Abbé now stood. At the beginning of the ramp was a stack of folios. Nearby stood a man in the green attire of a court jester with peaked cap. The Abbé waited for stragglers to come as close to the streaking flames as possible. For the most part, the populace was hushed, not really knowing what to expect. Rumors had not ceased. There were still many who expected a live victim.

The trumpets blew. Solemnly, the Abbé began to shout.

"Citizens of France. We, your legislators," he swung his cloak in a wide gesture to formally-garbed colleagues, "are gathered here to defend our nation against the pernicious doctrine of a group of priests who threaten the well-being of our beloved country. We stand before you with the approval of our King Louis, our Pope and your Parliament. By our action we are saying to France and the world that the Society of Jesus-ites is no longer fit to teach in our realm, in token of which we are about to burn those texts which contain pernicious doctrine."

Once again the Abbé paused. He signaled to the chief trumpeter who obediently blew a loud note. Silence reigned. He signaled again to the court figure in green who picked up a manuscript.

"I give you the Jesuit, Robert Bellarmine." He unfurled a scroll from which he read. "Robert Bellarmine teaches that the Pope can overrule the King in temporal affairs. Because of his absolute supremacy in spiritual matters, whenever there is a conflict between the spiritual and the temporal, the Pope's judgment must reign because there is only one society under God in which the temporal power must always be subservient to the spiritual. I hereby mandate that Bellarmine be submitted to the flames."

Obediently, the green clad jester raced up the ramp and threw the manuscript into the flames to the accompaniment of trumpets and a huge roar of approval from the crowd. He then returned to his post at the end of the ramp. The jester picked up another manuscript.

"I give you the Jesuit, Juan Molina," shouted the Abbé, after he had waited for the noise to subside. The jester picked up another manuscript.

"Molina has set off the most acrimonious theological battle in the history of the Church with his teaching on free will which, because of its insidious nature, confuses our citizens in their task of obeying our King and the laws of the land."

Once again the man in green ran up the ramp and tossed the manuscript into the flames.

Next, Juan Mariana was announced. After the blast of the trumpet, the soldiers' bugles blew, followed by a furious drum roll.

"Juan Mariana teaches regicide. He teaches that the King can be removed by force from his imperial office. There is no such thing as the divine right of Kings."

Once again, the toss into the fire, the roar of the crowd and trumpets.

Now I give you the Jesuit, Bernard Busenbaum."

The drums and the bugles preceded this announcement because in addition to teaching that tyrannical Kings could be deposed, he also held that they could be assassinated. Busenbaum had won notoriety after the attempted assassination of Henry IV in the previous century, so his name had become a watchword to the opposition. With the help of some facilitators imbedded in the crowd, the roar that went up when the Busenbaum manuscript landed in the flames was loudest of all.

"I give you Francis Suarez," shouted the Abbé. He was beginning to get hoarse, but he summoned up his mightiest effort.

"The condemnation of Suarez was vital, because he taught:

"1. all power comes from God to the Pope; Kings receive their authority indirectly;

"2. the King's power comes from God through the people;

"3. the King's power comes to him only by the free consent of the people;

"4. because of the free consent of the people, the King's power is not absolute."

The Abbé further strained his voice to make the teaching of Suarez clear to the assembly. He was unable to go on after that. A substitute came to the platform and began reading sixty-five propositions, all chosen to illustrate the lax moral instructions of the Jesuits. He had a deep baritone voice so he was easily heard. He began by accusing the Jesuits of teaching that it was valid to believe that one could spit on the cross if, as happened in China, you were threatened with death for being baptized. You were not denying that Christ died for you on the Cross. You were spitting on a piece of wood.

By now the crowd was used to the rhythm. The blaring of the trumpets, the roll of the drums, followed by the declaration of the Jesuit teaching.

"It was not sinful to receive Holy Communion several times during the month," intoned the speaker, as he held up to ridicule the lax theory that undermined the proper awe and respect for the sacrament of Christ's presence. "Once every two months should be the norm for all good Catholics."

Again the trumpets, the drums and then. . . .

"It was grossly insufficient to approach the sacrament of confession if your motive was merely the fear of hellfire. Your true motive should be deep sorrow for your sins, sorrow motivated by the love of God, not fear of damnation."

The shouts of applause died, and after that the drum roll ceased. The crowd heard the next denunciation.

"Imagine, anyone teaching that a mere headache is a probable cause for excusing you from attending Sunday Mass. That a mere headache is grounds for not fulfilling your sacred Sunday obligation, commanded by God! How can the Catholic Church possibly tolerate such teachers in our midst?"

It did not take long for the lengthy recital to bore the hearers. They had not come to hear theology; they had come from all over in anticipation of a public execution. The bonfire, the trumpets, the drums, but above all, the wild rumors had brought them. Now, they began to disperse while the crier thundered on.

Antoine, trying to be as inconspicuous as possible behind a line of bushes alongside the gendarme's station, stayed to the very end of the recital. By noon the drama was over. Antoine rushed out of his hiding place, stumbled on a root and tore open the collar of his soutane. He also bruised his temple against a branch. He left his clerical hat hanging on an adjacent branch.

He started out in search of Père Bordoni. He remembered seeing a group of blackrobes standing far back in the crowd when he took his place. He raced to catch up to them. Making his way as fast as he could was not easy. He was being jostled by the crowd and assailed verbally. Someone had recognized who he was.

"That's the one; that's the priest that caused all this in the Parliament."

"Hey, priest, hold on, I want to ask you a question!"

"What's a Jesuit, anyway? What's Jesuitical mean?"

Before any others could stop him, Antoine found an opening and hurried on. Try as he might, he could not move quickly. By the time he reached the priests' residence, there were more than a half dozen clerics talking quietly in the yard. More soutaned figures clustered on the porch and in the front hallway of the house. The front door stood open.

"Who's that?" Antoine heard one say, as the group stopped to look at the wild-eyed stranger rushing up the steps into the residence. He was hatless, hair in his eyes. His cassock was mud stained.

Fortunately, Antoine was beyond hearing the remarks.

"That's the famous, or infamous if you will, Lavalette from Martinique. He's the one whose bankruptcy roused the Parliament against us."

"They ought to burn him at the stake and let us alone."

By this time, Antoine was in the house and up the stairs, heading for de Sacy's office. He entered without knocking. Bordoni was there also.

"I am not responsible for that public condemnation. I only had a debt to pay. I didn't bring this on the Jesuits. What is going on here? I don't understand; I simply don't understand."

Both men stood up at once.

"Antoine, I know you are upset. But I think you should calm down. Alonzo here can help you more than I can. Just sit down and relax a bit. I will leave you two together."

With that, de Sacy put his arm on Antoine's shoulder and helped him sit down. The door closed softly behind him.

Bordoni pulled his chair closer to Antoine.

"Père, you remember the other day when I was talking to you about the Reductions and Pombal and the burning of Père Malagrida?"

Antoine nodded.

"I said you had been in the Caribbean too long. Today's burning of the books had nothing to do with you. You were in no way even the remote occasion of what happened. In *L'Hôtel Dieu*, you may have been too occupied to notice that before the Parliament sentenced us to pay your debts, they demanded a copy of Jesuit rules. Already they had something else in mind.

"The key point to keep in mind is that the Bourbon family is linked to all the Catholic monarchs. What happens in Spain and Portugal is quickly communicated to France and Naples. Remember the adage we learned in philosophy: *Nemo gratis Mendax*. So no one lies without some motive of gain. It says something good about us. Namely, that our first tendency is to tell the truth. At the same time it underscores the inner need of justifying any or all departure from the truth.

"I don't know whether I succeeded in making clear what marvelous work was going on in the Reductions of Paraguay. Indigenous people were taught leather making, tanning, carpentry, construction, reading and writing, drama, literature. They were taught basic government, hygiene, cooking, and even self-defense. Soldiers were trained to protect the tribes from the marauding Spaniards and Portuguese. You remember me telling you that.

"I am not trying to go into all that again. The point I am trying to make is that to destroy that marvelous enterprise required some powerful motive, powerful enough to silence the conscience of the statesmen in both Spain and Portugal. After all, they influenced the Kings.

"What we were doing for the indigenous peoples provided the motive for all of this."

Bordoni was exhausted in his effort to calm the traumatized Antoine. But he went on.

"If you add what Suarez is teaching about the origin of authority, not only in our schools, but to the native Guarani in Paraguay, do you still think our good Catholic politicians and the merchant class that they protect have any real concern about what happened in Martinique?"

In his agitated state, Antoine was somewhat puzzled by the question. Bordoni realized that his listener was still in the Caribbean. He tried to be clearer.

"Antoine, what's happening has nothing to do with a faraway French possession. This is Europe. Four Catholic countries, all with ties to the Bourbon family, have their own special agenda implemented by their influence at the Vatican."

"But it seems to me that if I were allowed to return to the islands where I could reduce the debt, start paying off the creditors, I could free us from this entanglement." Antoine's spirit was still far away.

Bordoni eyed him for a few moments. Yes, the strain had been too much. He paused, groping for the gentlest way to continue.

"Look, Antoine, this has been a very trying day for all of us. Sleep is the best remedy. We can talk tomorrow."

Bordoni saw Antoine to the door, then went back to sit down. Antoine would have been traumatized further by the information that several hundred Jesuits were on the high seas, herded together like slaves. The Portuguese had shipped them out of the Paraguay missions to be dumped on the Papal States. In addition, to the Pope's dismay, French troops had quietly marched into Avignon. The bonfire of Catholic books were minor occurrences in a bigger drama which was beyond Antoine's present capacity to comprehend.

Like many, but not all of his confreres, Bordoni spent a restless night.

CHAPTER XIII

A month passed. From Rome came a solemn decree.

"The peace and tranquility of Christendom have long been troubled by a group of religious, known as the Society of Jesus, founded by one Ignatius of Loyola. Our dear sons in Jesus Christ, the Kings of Spain, France and Portugal, and of the Two Sicilys, have seen it necessary to take steps to banish all members of this same Society from their Kingdoms, States and Provinces, convinced that this extreme measure is the only remedy for the theories, volumes, actions and teachings of this group, also known as Jesuits, which have caused untold controversies within their domains. These same Kings, our most dear sons in Jesus Christ, have humbly advised US that the good of Holy Mother Church and the spiritual welfare of Catholic faithful can only be preserved if this Society of Jesus in addition to being expelled from these realms should be wholly suppressed and abolished in God's Holy Church.

After careful prayer and consultation before God and man, it is our decision to regretfully agree to a formal act of suppression,

Sincerely in Christ

Clement XIV, Pope.

Two weeks passed in which the papal decree became known all over France.

It was evening; darkness engulfed the corner of the Rue Saint Remí where it intersected with the Rue Palais. In the Jesuit residence a tiny bell tinkled. It summoned a dozen Jesuits in black robes to a small chapel. One by one they filed into the rows of *prie dieus*. They genuflected and knelt. Two flickering tapers were on the altar that fronted them. A crucifix graced the altar between the candles. When all had assembled, Père de Sacy began the recitation of the Litany of the Saints.

"Lord, have mercy," he intoned.

"Christ, have mercy," echoed the deep chorus of male voices.

"God, the Father of Heaven," continued the leader.

"Have mercy on us," the Jesuits responded.

"Holy Mary, Mother of God,"

"Pray for us."

Solemnly, de Sacy began to go down the roster of saints, calling on them for help and mercy from God. The invocation and response from the masculine voices continued. As it went on, another rhythm became audible to the men as they prayed. It was the rhythm of marching feet. It became louder as the marchers came closer. Soon there was a pounding at the front door. The prayer stopped.

"My dear Fathers and Brothers in Christ. We all know what this means," interrupted Père de Sacy. "Brother Marc, please go to the front door to tell them we are coming."

He then opened up his Bible and began to read as the men stood up and filed past him.

"I, too, am a servant of Christ. I have been in prison more times; I have been whipped much more, and I have been near death more often; five times I was given thirty-nine lashes by the Jews; three times I was whipped by the Romans, and once I was stoned. I have been in three shipwrecks, and once I spent twenty-four hours in the water. I have been in danger from floods and robbers, from my fellow Jews and Gentiles; there have been dangers in the cities, dangers from false friends."

By this time, the soldiers in the vestibule had ushered all into the street. Though they had been shouting before, the soldiers were silent now in the corridor and in the street, as the Jesuits passed by one at a time. They did not interfere with de Sacy as he finished his reading from St. Paul. Obediently, the black robes walked out to where two tumbrils awaited them. One was empty, the other held six priests. Torch bearers lit up the scene. There were no commands. Most of the soldiers, being Catholics, found it awkward to add any harsh orders. No orders were needed since the priests offered no resistance, as they climbed into the tumbrils.

The Captain of the cohort consulted a paper, then shouted, "To *L'Hôtel Dieu*."

The horse drawn wagons loaded with Jesuits began to roll. The entourage made for the Rue Tivoli and on towards the bridge and the Cathedral of Notre Dame. It headed toward the arm of the Seine where *L'Hôtel Dieu* stood. There were few passersby at this hour. Shortly, the tumbrils pulled up in front of the hospital. One of the soldiers hit the door with the butt of his musket, another jangled the big handbell that hung in the archway.

The banging and the jangling went on.

At last, Mère Elisette appeared at the door. She surveyed the scene coldly. She did not seem surprised at the unusual sight. Undoubtedly, she had received some kind of advance warning, but she was not intimidated.

"Sirs, we are busy with our sick. Are you bringing someone who needs our care?"

The Captain doffed his cap, and took out a parchment.

"Sister," he began, "I have orders to pick up a priest by the name of Antoine Lavalette."

"Sir, he is our chaplain. At this moment he is attending a dying woman. How dare you treat these religious men like criminals? Be off with you."

"Sister, I am only following orders. I have orders from my major who has been commissioned by the Parliament of Paris to arrest all Jesuits for deportation. I cannot disobey. I will have to come into the hospital and conduct a search for this priest, Lavalette."

"I find this hard to believe. I will not allow your soldiers to terrify my patients. You stay right here; I will speak with Père Antoine."

The soldiers stood waiting uncomfortably looking at one another. Do we defy a nun? This was the unspoken question.

After a short time, Mère Elisette appeared with Antoine at her side.

"You are Père Antoine Lavalette," the Captain addressed the priest. "You are under arrest, and condemned to banishment with the rest of these Jesuits. Get into the tumbril at once."

"Sir, Captain," said Antoine without moving. "I am no longer a Jesuit. I have papers to prove that."

"Then, why are you here on my list?" demanded the Captain.

"That is easy to explain," said Antoine producing a paper from his cassock pocket.

"This morning I was summoned before the Prefecture of Police. I was presented with a series of questions about the Jesuit Order which I signed." As he said this, he dared not look up at the group of Jesuits in the tumbril, illumined by the torchlight.

"This is proof that I am no longer a member of the Order," he continued. "Mère Elisette will substantiate my statement."

"Let him alone," said Père de Sacy from the tumbril. "He is no longer one of us." He got down from the wagon and approached the three people. "I can assure you, Monsieur le Capitaine, that he is not one of those who are to be expelled from the country."

The Captain called a torchbearer to his side. He looked over the paper that Antoine handed him. After a bit the Captain handed back the paper, satisfied and turned to the cohort.

"All right, men, let's go."

Antoine began to follow the priest and the Captain to the tumbril. Mère Elisette was at his side.

Antoine had difficulty trying to speak.

"Please, forgive me," he pleaded to the religious. "Everything went wrong in the islands. I didn't mean to cause you this; forgive me, forgive me."

Most of the Jesuits in the tumbrils turned their backs.

Only de Sacy looked down on him with kindness.

"It wasn't your fault, Antoine."

The tumbrils started to roll away over the cobblestones with the marching soldiers. Antoine stood there watching them disappear in the wavering torchlight. He tried to wave good-by, struggling to hold back more tears.

"Come, Père Antoine, we need you in the hospital." Mère Elisette took him by the arm.

EPILOGUE

Père Antoine Lavalette was born the 26th of October, 1708 in the city of Dmartin, France, in the ancient Diocese of Valeres, under the jurisdiction of the Bishop of Rodez. Lavalette died on the 13th of December, 1767 buried in the chapel of St. Germier, in the church of de la Dalberde.

Père Lavalette went to the island of Martinique in 1742, at the height of the sugarcane trade. He was recalled to France for the last time by his religious Order in the early 1760's.

William Brennan
April, 2006

Author William Brennan, S.J. is a member of the Wisconsin Province of the Society of Jesus. He is based in Milwaukee, Wisconsin and presently serves as a prison chaplain and advocate for the poor.

For over 19 years, Bill, as he is affectionately known, served as a missionary to Central America. His novel, A Drama of the Caribbean, recalls events from the 18th Century which have nearly been forgotten — namely the suppression of the Jesuit order in France and universal suppression of the Society by Pope Clement XIV in 1773.

In addition to this novel, Brennan has authored an article entitled "A Bridge For Santiago" an informative and historic piece about the building of a bridge for the people of Yoro and the devotion to St. James after which Santiago is named.

Artist Celine Farrell is a member of St. Patrick's Catholic Church, a Jesuit parish in Milwaukee's historic Walker's Point where she is restoring a 123 year old building for home and studio.

She received her BFA degree in advertising design from Milwaukee's Layton School of Art, an MFA degree in painting from Cranbrook Academy of Art in Michigan and, on scholarship, an MA degree in sculpture from Pius XII Institute, Florence, Italy.

Her earlier work was most frequently in copper and bronze. Recently her metal preferences are aluminum and aluminum/bronze combinations The artistic medium chosen for illustrating A Drama of the Caribbean is wood-block printing — prints which depict poignant moments within this historical novel.